She got the feeling staying warm would not be an issue tonight

Besides, the last thing Colin seemed interested in was the ambience of his surroundings. He had eyes only for her, and Emily shivered—not from any chill in the air, but from the intensity of his gaze.

She leaned back on the bed, forcing herself not to cover up her naked body. She felt a delicious rush of anticipation roll through her.

He took off his shirt, and she smiled in appreciation at the pure beauty of his masculine torso. His muscles bunched and flexed as he removed the rest of his clothes. When he stripped off his boxers, she couldn't help but gasp a little. It had been a while, after all, since she'd seen a naked man, much less one in all his erect glory.

He smiled. "Stop it. You'll make me blush."

She wanted to toss back some witty comment, but words seemed lodged in her throat. Instead, she put her arms out, inviting him to her.

Blaze™

Dear Reader,

Everyone loves the holiday season—the parties, the traditions, all the celebrating and fun with family and friends. But on the other hand, this time of year can be very stressful. So, I thought what happens when you take a woman who embodies small-town tradition, and match her with a guy who thinks "home for the holidays" is a sure recipe for disaster? And just like that, I got *Baby, It's Cold Outside*, a story I hope you'll really enjoy!

Best,

Cathy Yardley

CATHY YARDLEY
Baby, It's Cold Outside

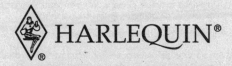

HARLEQUIN®

TORONTO • NEW YORK • LONDON
AMSTERDAM • PARIS • SYDNEY • HAMBURG
STOCKHOLM • ATHENS • TOKYO • MILAN • MADRID
PRAGUE • WARSAW • BUDAPEST • AUCKLAND

ISBN-13: 978-0-373-79370-9
ISBN-10:   0-373-79370-7

BABY, IT'S COLD OUTSIDE

Copyright © 2007 by Cathy Yardley.

www.eHarlequin.com

Printed in U.S.A.

ABOUT THE AUTHOR

Cathy Yardley needs to get out more. When not writing, she is probably either cruising the Internet or watching movies—those featuring pirate captains and those not. Her family is considering performing an intervention for her addiction to pop culture. She lives in California. Please visit her at www.cathyyardley.com.

Books by Cathy Yardley
HARLEQUIN BLAZE

HARLEQUIN SIGNATURE SPOTLIGHT

Don't miss any of our special offers. Write to us at the following address for information on our newest releases.

Harlequin Reader Service
U.S.: 3010 Walden Ave., P.O. Box 1325, Buffalo, NY 14269
Canadian: P.O. Box 609, Fort Erie, Ont. L2A 5X3

To my agents, Annelise Robey and
Christina Hogrebe, for being extraordinarily patient.
Thank you!

Prologue

Sixteen years ago...

"COLIN REESE, YOU disappoint me," Mrs. Norton, the principal of Tall Pines High School, said with an exaggerated sigh.

Colin shrugged. He'd developed shrugging into a highly complex sign language. This shrug said, *I'd love to care, but I really don't.*

"You're a senior, Colin. I would have thought you were old enough—and mature enough—to have moved beyond these juvenile pranks."

Colin sent her a slight grin and shrugged again. *You'd think, wouldn't you?*

"Defacing school property..." Mrs. Norton patted her hair, making sure her bangs were still lacquered in place, a sign that she was really upset. Colin had been in the principal's office enough in the past four years to read her like a comic book. "We could have you arrested, Colin."

"Oh, come on, Mrs. N.," he protested, the statement outrageous enough to prompt more than a shrug from him. "Putting a statue of Eamon Stanfield in a dress isn't defacing school property."

"You made him look like a hooker."

"No, I made him look like Sexy Mrs. Santa," Colin corrected, quoting the mail-order catalog. "It's Christmas. I thought it'd be festive."

"You put makeup on him," Mrs. Norton added. "The janitors are having a hard time getting the lipstick off."

Don't laugh, he warned himself. His latest prank may have gone a bit too far. "I'll wash off the old guy myself," he volunteered.

Mrs. Norton sighed heavily. "You continually pick our town's most honored and cherished traditions to poke fun at, Colin. Last summer, you put pickled herrings in the planters at the Ladies' Auxiliary Orchid Show—"

"That was never proved," Colin said.

"Then there was the incident with the Otter Lodge fountain being filled with Jell-O…"

Colin opened his hands in a gesture of innocence. "Again…"

Mrs. Norton frowned. "And the bronze plaque that had the names of all the town's founding fathers, including Eamon Stanfield, went mysteriously missing last semester."

"Hey," Colin protested, "I had nothing to do with that one. I don't steal."

"What I want to know is—when is all this nonsense going to stop, Colin?"

Colin felt a surge of anger. *"When I get the hell out of this town."*

Mrs. Norton looked surprised, then supremely saddened. Colin immediately felt like a jerk.

"I'm sorry," he said. "I don't mean to hurt anybody. I'm blowing off a little steam, that's all. They're stupid little jokes, meant to be funny, not destructive. I mean, I see the absurdity in a lot of our traditions, and nobody else seems to."

"What you see as absurd," Mrs. Norton said stiffly, standing up, "a lot of us see as sweet and comforting. And every little act of rebellion you commit doesn't make you look sophisticated. It makes you look mean-spirited and petty."

Colin grimaced, roiling in his own unhappiness. "I'm sorry," he apologized—and he meant it.

"I'm suspending you for a week, Colin."

He nodded. He'd been expecting that. "I'll head on home."

"No, you'll wait here," she said. "Your mother's on her way to pick you up."

"My mother?" He winced. "Why? I just live a few blocks away."

"I had to call her, Colin." Now Mrs. Norton seemed smug. "Besides, I wanted to talk about plans for the Spring Fling and then the grad-night party, since she's head of the committee."

Of course she is, Colin thought and wallowed in his misery.

"She was very, very upset to hear what you'd done to the statue," Mrs. Norton added. "I imagine she'll have some words for you when she gets here."

He nodded unhappily. *Some words.* A mild way to put what promised to be a very unpleasant episode.

He sat out in the lobby of the administrative office wearing his best trademark scowl.

"Oh, Colin," Ruthie, the front-office secretary, said with a small shake of her head. "How can such a sweet kid get into so much trouble?"

"Don't tell me you didn't giggle just a little seeing Eamon Stanfield all tarted up," he coaxed.

Ruthie glanced at the principal's office, making sure the door was closed. Then she broke out into a wide grin. "It *was* funny," she admitted. "Especially since, from what I understand, Eamon Stanfield would keel over dead before wearing ladies' clothes."

Colin grinned back. "Exactly."

"Which is why we're in so much trouble." Ruthie sighed.

"What do you mean?" he asked.

Before he could get an answer, the door opened. A young girl, about sixteen years old, walked in. She was wearing a navy-blue plaid pleated skirt with a big safety pin in it and a moss-green sweater set. She was also wearing stylish boots— a nod to the weather. Her pale cheeks were rosy from the cold, and she wore her long auburn hair in a simple ponytail.

"Hi, Ruthie," she said. "Just wanted to drop off the money for the Spring Fling fund-raiser from the booster club. We raised even more this year than we did last year."

"Emily, you are a doll," Ruthie said with approval, taking the envelope. Then she looked pointedly at Colin. "Never in here for any trouble."

"I know," Emily replied. If Colin didn't know better, he'd think she sounded annoyed by the comment.

Ruthie's voice dropped. "Is your father still upset about the…statue incident?"

Colin sank lower in his seat. Emily Stanfield. Of course he knew her. She was only a living, breathing legacy of Tall Pines, Connecticut. Her family had been in the town since the beginning; it was her great-grandfather's statue that he'd dressed up in the red minidress. She was on almost every committee or volunteer organization imaginable. As a sophomore, she'd already been voted onto the homecoming court. She might as well have an entire wardrobe with *I Love Tall Pines* emblazoned on it in big sparkly letters. Like all her forebears, she'd probably live in this little town till she died.

She was the complete opposite of Colin, the angel to his devil. She even looked angelic. Which might explain why he couldn't stop staring at her when he thought she wouldn't notice. He chalked it up to a perverse fascination—as if by studying her he could figure out how she avoided the frustration and rebelliousness that the town of Tall Pines seemed to invoke in him on a daily basis.

Emily nodded. "I told my father it was a senior prank." She shot a quick glance over at Colin, her blue eyes meeting his green ones. "I said it was a tradition. He's still sort of steamed, but he's calming down."

"So…no police?" Ruthie said.

"No police," Emily assured her, and Colin felt his muscles unknot with relief. Then she shot him another glance, only this time the smallest ghost of a smile haunted her lips.

He found himself smiling back with approval. She was awfully cute for a sophomore. Not to mention cute for a Tall Pines poster child.

"*Colin Reese,* are you insane?"

He blinked, wondering the same thing himself, although he was still staring at Emily as he thought it. He turned his attention to the woman yelling at him. "Mom?"

His mother stormed into the lobby, looking like the Angel of Vengeance in a lavender-blue pantsuit. "I have *had* it with you, mister," she said sharply. "I swear, if you weren't so close to graduation, I'd send you off to…to *military school!*"

He sighed. This was going to be a bad one, he could tell.

"You're coming with me." She held the door open. "And you wait till your father gets home!"

Colin sighed, rolling his eyes. Ruthie sent him a look of sympathy. Emily, he noticed, had a mischievous smile. Then, to his shock, she winked at him.

Which was why he was smiling as his mother yanked on his arm and dragged him out the door. He barely heard her as she launched into yet another tirade on the problems with his behavior and why couldn't he be more like his sister and brother and why in the world he had a problem with the small town.

"For God's sake, Colin," she said, exasperated, "can't you think of one thing, just *one thing,* that represents Tall Pines that you don't feel like mocking and making fun of?"

He closed his eyes for a moment, thinking hard.

Emily Stanfield, his mind supplied. Given the chance, he got the feeling he'd take her very, very seriously. But he couldn't admit that, so he stayed silent and let his mother continue her litany. He'd be out of here by June, anyway, and then all of this, including Emily Stanfield, would be a thing of the past.

EMILY WATCHED AS Colin Reese stalked off, his mother lecturing him in a growing crescendo of chastisement.

"That kid." Ruthie let out a long breath. "It's hard to believe he's Ava Reese's son, you know?"

Emily didn't say anything, although she knew what Ruthie meant.

"So have you decided who you're going to the Spring Fling with, Emily?" Ruthie asked.

Emily cleared her throat. "Not yet," she said. "Too busy, and it's not for months yet."

"Still dating that Rothchild boy?"

It was funny, Emily thought. Ruthie knew about everybody in the school. Granted, it wasn't that big a school, but Emily wondered halfheartedly if the kind woman didn't have better things to do with her time than track the little social dramas of teenagers.

"I wasn't really dating him," Emily demurred, her voice almost prim. "Anyway, I'd better get going. Don't want to be late for Biology."

She fled the office, heading up the hallway. She couldn't stop thinking about Colin.

She'd had a crush on him for years, since she'd been in elementary school. It wasn't just that he was good-looking, although he was—devastatingly so. It was that he was so...reckless. Daring. He'd been voted Most Likely to Do Anything two years in a row by the yearbook committee. He was in trouble a lot, but she also knew that he was very sweet—

she'd seen a bunch of bullies picking on a younger girl because of her thick glasses and braces, and Colin had sent the bullies away with the mere threat of physical violence. He'd then made sure the girl was all right, saying a few quick words and sending her a lightning-fast smile. The girl had stared dreamily at Colin, and so had Emily, touched by his thoughtfulness.

It was silly. Everyone knew that Colin was practically building a tunnel to get out of Tall Pines, and Emily doubted she'd ever leave. But it didn't stop her from dreaming.

1

"SO IS HE HERE YET?"

Emily Stanfield smiled coyly at her best friend, Sue. "You're the desk manager. You tell me."

Sue made a face. "I knew I should've stayed at the inn. That way I could've called you when he checked in."

Emily shook her head. "Impossible. First of all, this is Ava Reese's annual Secret Santa party we're at. It's more than a tradition, it's an *institution*. We couldn't miss it." Much as she'd wanted to this year.

Sue sighed. "True, true."

"And secondly—" and Emily let her voice drop to a whisper "—there's no guarantee I'm going to sleep with this guy...this J. P. Webster."

Sue made a sound of protest. "But you said..."

Emily put a hand up, stopping Sue, then glanced around. No one was listening, thankfully—folks were too intent on their gift swapping and drinking from Ava's generous open bar.

"I said I was finally going to do something about my two-year celibacy. And I meant it," Emily declared, her body sending a pleasant zing dancing over her nerve endings at the thought. "But I've never even seen J.P. before. We've only exchanged emails."

"My sister got married to a guy she met on the Internet," Sue countered.

Emily rolled her eyes. "The last thing I need is to get married. I'm just… I just want…" She searched for a noncrude way to put it.

"You're just looking for someone to stuff your stocking." Sue winked.

So much for noncrude. Emily felt her cheeks redden. "Well, that's not how I would've put it. But…well, yes."

"So why shouldn't it be this J.P.?" Sue pressed. "You guys have been e-mailing for almost two years now."

"About business stuff only." J. P. Webster worked for a big hotel chain and taught a class on hotel management online. Emily had taken the class, then asked some questions after it was done. J.P. had been tremendously kind and helpful. They were exchanging e-mails once a month lately, and the correspondence had turned more friendly than academic. "Maybe he's ugly. Maybe he's old. Maybe he's *gay,* for all I know. We've never flirted or anything." Emily frowned, thinking about it. "We get along really well. Like we're old friends."

"Well, maybe he's young, cute and ready to be really, *really* friendly."

Emily smirked. Privately, that's exactly what she was hoping.

For the past few years Emily had lived for one thing and one thing only: the Stanfield Arms, the hotel she'd created from her family's mansion, one of the oldest buildings in Tall Pines, Connecticut. She'd buried herself in work and she hadn't even bothered with a relationship. Part of that was because she'd been far too busy, but part of it was also because of Tall Pines itself. A definite problem with living in such a small town was that with everyone weighing in on your dating decisions, if things didn't work out, not only would you face a postmortem from everyone on why the relationship ended, you were face-to-face with your ex almost every day. She'd experienced it in action. It was nightmarish.

So the hotel filled her days, but lately her nights were leaving her more and more restless. After Thanksgiving, she'd made the decision: she was going to have a physical relationship, something brief and discreet, preferably with an out-of-towner who would then leave. So far, the only prospect was J.P., who'd suggested staying at the hotel over the holidays.

Please, please let him be cute.

"Come on," Emily said. "Let's swap our gifts and get out of here. I want to head back to the inn."

Sue smiled knowingly. "Attagirl."

They walked over to the crystal bowl that held the names of everyone at the party on slips of paper. Sue drew a name first, grimacing as she read it.

"Damn. I got old Reverend Smith," she said. "I don't think he's going to like the Chocolate Orgasm hot chocolate I brought."

Emily laughed, drawing a slip of paper. She opened it, staring at the name and frowning. "Colin. Colin who?"

Sue's eyes widened. "Wait a minute. *Colin Reese?*"

Emily felt heat explode in her chest. "No. It couldn't be," she murmured. "He hasn't been back in town for the holidays since high school."

Sue shrugged. "I'm not surprised. He hated this town." She nudged Emily. "Didn't you have a crush on him? Way back when?"

Only for ten years, Emily thought, her heart rate picking up speed. She shook her head. "Okay, I'm going to give him the gift and get the heck out of here."

"I'm planning on grilling you the minute I get into work tomorrow," Sue said. "I want every detail about J. P. Webster!"

Emily chuckled. "If there's anything to tell." She was trying not to get her hopes up too high. She hugged Sue goodbye, then went in search of Colin.

She found him sitting in the living room, half-hidden by the enormous Christmas tree, drinking eggnog. She paused for a minute, trying to get her bearings.

For a woman who hadn't had sex in two years, the sight of Colin Reese was enough to blow out all her sensual circuits.

He was wearing a gray sweater that molded itself nicely to his broad shoulders, and his dark brown hair was still flecked with streaks of copper, even though it was cut shorter than she remembered…back when she used to stare at him, all those years ago. His eyes were still the same deep, deep green, she noticed, as he gazed absently across the crowded room.

Her palms started to sweat.

Just get it over with, she chided herself. No matter how much she'd fantasized about him, he was *not* a candidate to end her sexual drought. For one thing, he was the town's black sheep—if word leaked out, she'd never hear the end of it.

She gripped her gift bag, took a resolute breath and walked up to him. "Hi, Colin."

He looked at her, obviously distracted. Then he stood and focused on her, gracing her with a slow visual perusal and a lazy smile.

"Well, hi."

She smiled back, ignoring the tingle of excitement his drawled greeting sent shooting through her. "Merry Christmas. I'm your Santa this year."

"I'm in luck." His deep voice sounded sinfully smooth, rich and luscious as a dark chocolate truffle.

She handed him the bag, watching as he opened it. He raised a skeptical eyebrow. "Scented candles," he said with obviously fake enthusiasm. "Thanks."

She couldn't help it. She giggled. "Sorry," she said when he looked at her inquisitively. "Women usually outnumber men two to one at this party. Scented candles are normally a slam dunk."

"Well, maybe I'll enjoy them with a cup of tea and a bubble

bath," he joked. Unfortunately his comment caused her wayward mind to conjure up a picture of him naked and waist deep in hot water, the chiseled planes of his chest lit only by candlelight....

"So, um, what have you been up to?" she asked hastily, trying to dispel the image.

He shrugged. "I'm working on a new building. In Paris. I start after the new year."

"That sounds exciting," she said wistfully. "I've never been to Paris. Never took the time."

They stood there for a second in awkward silence.

Just tell him goodbye, she thought. *Then get back to the hotel and find out if J.P. is as cute as he is nice.*

"So, er, what about you?" Colin asked before she could open her mouth and make her escape.

"Same old, same old," she said noncommittally. "The inn's doing really well. In fact, I have to—"

"The inn?" He frowned. "What inn?"

He'd been gone for a while, she realized. "I turned the Stanfield mansion into a hotel, what, four years ago," she supplied. "It took two years to renovate, and then the past two I've been building up—"

"Stanfield," he said, then his eyes widened. "Wait a second. You're *Emily* Stanfield?"

That's when it hit her. He hadn't remembered her. He hadn't even known who she was until just now.

Glad I made an impression, she thought, her flush of infatuation chilling as though she'd been dropped in a snowbank. "Well, it's been great catching up, but I've got a hotel to run, so..."

"A hotel. Right here in town," he mused, and to her shock, he took her hand before she could turn and walk away. "Emily Stanfield, you're more than my Santa, you're my godsend."

She chuckled nervously, trying to ignore the sexual heat that his warm palm was sending up her arm. "That seems a little excessive for candles."

He smiled slowly, his eyes dark and persuasive, his voice going low. "Please, please tell me you've got room at the inn."

"What?" She blinked, confused by his sudden change of topic. "For who?"

He took a step closer to her, and she could feel the heat coming off his body as if she were standing in front of a fireplace.

"I was hoping," he said, "that you might have room…for me."

"I REALLY APPRECIATE this," Colin said, sitting in the passenger seat of Emily's Volvo, his bags in her trunk.

"Your mom may never forgive me," Emily answered with a rueful sigh, "which is going to make being on the Easter Festival committee with her next year a little unpleasant. Why couldn't you just stay at her house again?"

Colin grimaced. "My brother and sister and their spouses and kids are all staying there. I was sharing a room with my eight-year-old nephew, and with two more days till Christmas…"

"Been driving you crazy, huh?" There was a hint of a smile in her voice.

"You have no idea."

Colin closed his eyes, remembering the scene at the breakfast table that very morning. They'd taken turns subtly—and not-so-subtly—grilling him. Why was he moving so far away? What happened to his last girlfriend? Why was he traveling all over the place and changing jobs so often? When was he going to settle down? And the perennial *why couldn't he find a nice girl and move home to Tall Pines?*

He'd known it was a bad idea to stay at his parents' house

for the week before Christmas, while his apartment in Paris was being readied. He just hadn't known how bad it was going to be until it was too late. The past three days had been hellish. He'd even suggested checking in to a hotel in a nearby town.

"And be so far from the house?" his mother had protested, scandalized. "With bad weather threatening the roads? You might miss Christmas with the kids!"

She'd had a point and he'd conceded. He did want to spend Christmas with his nieces and nephews, who were still small enough to make the whole thing fun.

Of course, his mother had neglected to mention the fact that there was a hotel right here in town.

He glanced over gratefully. Emily was staring intently at the road. Her auburn hair was swept up in a smooth French twist. Her high cheekbones and patrician nose, combined with her flawless skin, made her look cool and perfect, like a marble statue. Only the flash in her violet-blue eyes betrayed an inherent warmth.

No, he corrected himself, remembering. More than warmth. *Heat.* He'd definitely felt heat from her gaze when he'd looked over to find her standing in front of him.

Which called to mind his first look at her—crisp white blouse with a discreetly low neckline, knee-length black skirt, black nylons, black boots. Combined with her tasteful jewelry and her wire-rimmed glasses, she'd looked sophisticated and proper, sort of like a professor.

He'd always had a thing for prim teacher types. They usually hid anything-but-proper desires, and he had a sneaking feeling that Miss Stanfield was no exception.

Who would have thought that Emily Stanfield, daughter of one of the founding families and walking infomercial for all things Tall Pines, would have grown up to such a hottie?

"You're lucky I had a cancelation," Emily said, still not

looking at him. "It's one of my smaller rooms, but I think you'll find it quite comfortable."

Colin cleared his throat, feeling as if she could read his mind and realize the direction his thoughts were heading. "I'm surprised your family was okay with turning the mansion into a hotel," he said, fishing around for a safe topic.

She paused for a second. "My mother moved to Florida with her new husband. She doesn't really care one way or the other. My father probably would've minded, but he died five years ago, so…"

Colin felt guilt wash over him. "Oh, jeez. I'm sorry. I didn't know."

"You haven't been here. I didn't expect you to."

He sighed. "And the town? They were okay with it—you opening a hotel?"

"There are some people who are still getting used to it," she answered. "You know how Tall Pines is."

He clenched his jaw. Everything had to be preserved, as if the smallest mailbox was some kind of historical monument. If there was a town more resistant to change, he never wanted to visit it. "Yeah," he muttered, "I know how Tall Pines is."

"It's been good for the local economy, so that's brought a lot of people around," she said. "And, honestly, being a Stanfield helped."

"I'll bet."

The name *Stanfield* was synonymous with *Tall Pines*. Still, Stanfield or not, he imagined Emily was both organized and driven enough to start her own business if she wanted to. Two years younger than he was, she'd always been visible in school: editor in chief of the school newspaper, on the yearbook committee, in student government. She had been everywhere, it seemed. Her uncle had been the mayor before he'd died, and Colin could even recall Emily handing out campaign flyers, looking like a crisp autumn morning in her plaid skirt and pink sweater.

By high school, his lone goal had been escaping the Norman Rockwell normalcy of Tall Pines, while Emily had seemed to represent everything that the small town stood for. He'd hated the town but had been reluctantly fascinated with the girl, even if she never knew it.

That fascination seemed to be alive and well, he noted with some amusement.

They drove past the town square and up the hill to where the fancier houses stood, legacies of days past, when several tycoons had had hunting lodges here. The Stanfield mansion was one of the most opulent and, decked out with Christmas lights, it looked downright regal. "Wow," he said, taking in the picture-perfect scene.

She parked the car, sending him a quicksilver smile that caused his stomach to tighten unexpectedly. "Thanks. This hotel's my life."

"It shows." She'd obviously lavished a lot of love on the place. For a brief, puzzling second, he envied the brick building.

Okay, you're losing it.

That was why he hated the holidays, he thought as he hefted his bags and headed for the front door. They made a guy maudlin. He lived his life exactly the way he wanted it—full of adventure, with something new happening almost every day. He had no regrets. And right now the last thing he needed was to have some confusing, sentimental thoughts about a girl he hadn't seen in years.

The large foyer had a curving staircase to the second floor "Evening, Phillip," she greeted a guy in a suit who stood behind an oak reception desk. "I'm going to need a key for Mr. Reese, here. For room twelve."

The guy—Phillip—looked ruffled. "That's going to be a

problem," he said. "The Rivers party showed up after all. They decided to brave the weather and have the vacation."

"Oh?" Emily looked nonplussed for a second, then she turned to Colin, her expression apologetic. "I guess there's no room at the inn after all."

He winced. There was no way in hell he was going back to his parents' house. "Considering the season, I don't suppose you've got a manger or something," he joked, feeling a little desperate. "I don't take up much room."

She shook her head. "Even the garage is filled up with cars. Sorry, Colin. I'll drive you back."

"Wait a second," he said, pulling her aside, away from the inquisitive Phillip. "Seriously. Isn't there anyplace you could stick me? Maid's room? Good-size pantry? I'd even be happy with a broom closet."

She sighed. "I'd love to help you out, but…"

"You don't understand," he interrupted. "My six-year-old niece has been waking me up at five-thirty every morning to watch *Sesame Street*. My eight-year-old nephew, who's sharing my room, has been keeping me up until two because he's convinced that there are monsters. I've been crammed onto an army cot." He could see that it wasn't getting through to her…that no matter what his plea, she was the type who could withstand it.

He swallowed hard and played his trump card.

"My mother's been asking me why I haven't gotten married yet," he said. "At every. Single. Meal."

Emily's eyes widened. Then she laughed—a soft, rich sound that made him feel as though he'd just been brushed by mink.

"Knowing Ava, I can only imagine. I love her, but she is…" She grinned mischievously. "Shall we say, *persistent*."

"As a Sherman tank."

She looked up at the ceiling as if mentally debating something. Then she sighed. "Okay, tell you what—I converted the attic to my own private apartment," she said. "You can crash on my couch for tonight. But just for tonight. Tomorrow we'll think of something else."

Gratitude washed over him. "I owe you for this. Big-time."

She nodded absently, then went back to the desk. "I'm going to have Mr. Reese here stay with me," she said, and Colin watched as a look of calculation and a slow smirk crossed the clerk's face.

"On her *couch,*" Colin emphasized.

"Of course," Phillip returned blandly.

"One other thing, Phillip?" Emily asked, her voice going soft. "Did a J. P. Webster check in?"

"At around six," Phillip said. "Room five."

"Perfect. Thank you."

There was an edge of excitement in her voice, Colin noticed. Unexpectedly he felt irritation. Who the hell was J. P. Webster? And why did she suddenly sound so thrilled?

"Colin, why don't you follow me and I'll get you settled in."

Colin followed her to a small private elevator, taking it up to her apartment. It was roomier than he'd expected. There was a small kitchen, a living room, a bathroom and the bedroom. There was even a small fireplace. It was well decorated and obviously expensive, but it still looked cozy and inviting. To his surprise, he felt tension start to ebb out of his body.

"This is it," she said artlessly. "If you'll excuse me, I'm going to change really quickly, then I need to go downstairs for a while. Business."

But that breathless quality in her voice suggested it had nothing to do with business. That irritation that Colin had felt before doubled.

"Mind if I light a fire?" he asked to give himself something to do besides ruminate on what exactly her *business* might be.

"Please do," she said before shutting the bedroom door behind her.

Within minutes he had a small fire going in the hearth. The room smelled like spiced apple cider. He'd probably be asleep in minutes, he realized. He hadn't felt this relaxed since he'd returned to Tall Pines.

He heard the bedroom door open and he turned. "I can't thank you enough…"

His words died on his lips.

She'd changed, all right.

Emily's hair tumbled in loose auburn waves, dancing slightly below her shoulders. She was wearing a rich red velvet robe with Stanfield Arms embroidered on the crest. He wondered absently if she was wearing anything under the robe.

Just like that, his body went hard as steel and all thoughts of sleep fled. He bit back a groan. "That must be some business."

Her ivory cheeks flooded with color, and she avoided his gaze. "It's nine o'clock at night. I just want to make sure that one of my…special guests…is comfortable."

Colin didn't say a word.

"Sheets, blankets and pillows are in the cupboard in the hallway there." She pointed, still not looking at him. "The fridge is stocked if you're hungry, and if you need anything, just dial eight for the front desk."

"When will you be back?" he asked.

Finally she met his gaze.

The heat in her eyes could have set the room on fire.

"I don't know when I'll be back," she said quietly. "So don't wait up."

IT WAS RISKY. Possibly even stupid, Emily thought as she belted her robe tighter around her waist. But she was going to do it anyway.

She was going to J. P. Webster's room wearing only a silk shortie nightgown and one of the hotel robes and—if everything went perfectly—she was going to have sex.

She could only imagine what Colin was thinking of her little announcement. She'd done everything but say, "Make yourself at home, I'm off to get laid." The look he'd given her as she'd shut the door was one of shock mixed with something else she couldn't quite identify. She hoped it wasn't shame on her behalf. Still, Colin was a world-famous hotshot architect now, and if rumors were true, he had romanced women all over the continent. Several continents, actually, if his mother's complaints were to be believed. "Always with a different girl every month," she'd griped loudly at the last Otter Lodge pancake breakfast. "Last month, a lawyer from Hong Kong…the month before, a model from Brazil…." So she'd be damned if she let herself be judged by Mr. Commitmentphobic, especially since this was going to be her first fling ever.

Emily felt heat on her cheeks. She was blushing. She knew it.

Please, please let him be cute and let me go through with this. She couldn't face another restless night. She wanted to feel the delicious release that only a man could provide—even if it was only temporary.

She got to room five and knocked on the door. "J.P.?"

The door opened slowly. She took a deep breath.

A beautiful blond woman, also in a robe, was standing there. "Can I help you?"

Emily goggled momentarily. This she hadn't anticipated.

"I'm sorry." *Of course he would have brought his girlfriend! God, I'm an idiot!* "I was looking for J. P. Webster. I didn't mean for it to be so late…."

"That's quite all right," the woman said genially. "You've found her."

"Her?"

"J.P. stands for Joy Patricia. My friends call me Joy." She held out her hand, and, dumbstruck, Emily shook it. "I'm sorry…what's your name?"

"Oh. Right. I'm Emily Stanfield, the owner of the hotel." *And a moron.* "I just wanted to stop by and make sure that you had everything you needed."

Unfortunately J.P. did not have anything *Emily* needed.

"Emily! It's so nice to finally meet you in person. And thank you again for suggesting I stay at your inn instead of spending the holiday alone while my family was in Bermuda. I got in and fell in love with this place," Joy enthused, seeming not to notice Emily's discomfort. "It's everything you said it was and more."

"Well, that is high praise," Emily said. "And I'm glad it's made such a good impression. I'm sure you're exhausted. I'll just say good night and let you sleep…."

"Are you sure you didn't want to hang out, talk shop?" Joy asked.

Emily shook her head. Considering the real reason she'd come down, she doubted she could spend the evening discussing linen-use rates and remodel tips. "Just wanted to make sure you're comfortable."

"I love these robes, by the way," Joy said, rubbing her hand over the sleeve. "I see you do, too."

Emily was blushing again. "Normally I don't meet business associates dressed this casually," she said, hugging her arms and making sure her robe was still tight around her. "But I was, er, about to go to bed."

"I see." Emily could have sworn she saw a glimmer of humor in the woman's eyes. "Well, good night, then."

"Good night," Emily echoed, then turned and made her escape.

She got in the elevator, turning the key for the top floor…and then froze.

Oh, great. Bad enough that she'd just had one of the most humiliating mistakes of her life. Now, she had Colin Reese to deal with.

When the door opened, he was making up a makeshift bed on the sofa in pajama bottoms and nothing else.

He looked good enough to eat.

All the frustration that had been building up and threatening to explode, especially in the past few months, seemed to bubble to the surface at the look of his half-naked body. Her hands itched to stroke over all that chiseled chest.

Thankfully she had the fiasco with Joy/J.P. still stinging her ego or she'd probably do something she'd regret. Like jump him.

He glanced at her, puzzled. "Forget something?"

"No," she responded coolly. "I got finished sooner than I thought. Now I'm tired and I'm going to bed."

Colin smirked at her. "How'd business go?"

"Fine." Damn him for bringing it up.

He studied her as she stepped in front of him. Then he put a hand out, surprising her by touching her shoulder gently.

"You look sort of upset."

"I'm fine," she repeated. She ran her fingers through her hair, a gesture of frustration. "That is, I *will be* fine."

"Listen, I've been really stressed this week," he said. "I noticed you had a bottle of wine, but I didn't want to open it, especially just for me. Care to join me?"

She hesitated. "I really shouldn't," she murmured as she breathed in some of his woodsy-smelling cologne.

"Just to unwind a bit," he coaxed. "It'll help you sleep."

Emily laughed at that. Sit next to this unbelievably sexy half-dressed man, drinking wine in front of a crackling fire…and he thought that was going to make her *drowsy?*

He had to be joking.

He stroked her arm, distracting her. "Come on. One glass."

"Just one," she heard herself say and then found herself sitting on the couch.

Oh, this is such a very stupid idea.

Colin went into the kitchen, opened the fridge and got out the light pinot grigio that she'd been chilling. He poured two glasses and handed her one, sitting next to her.

"Aren't you, uh, cold?" she said, nodding at his bare chest. If this kept up, she'd be blushing a permanent pink.

"Huh? Oh. I got sort of hot building the fire up." He glanced at her. "Does it make you uncomfortable?"

Uncomfortable *is one word for it,* she thought. "I wouldn't want you to get a chill."

He let loose one of those slow, sexy smiles. "Don't worry," he reassured her. "I did an eighteen-month build in Iceland once. I don't think I'll ever feel cold again."

She let her gaze dip down to his washboard stomach…and then lower still, to the dark blue flannel pajama pants.

No doubt about it. The man was definitely hot.

Emily took a sip of wine so hastily she choked on it. "So will the couch be comfortable enough?" she asked when her throat cleared. "You look pretty big." His eyes widened, and she realized he'd caught exactly where she'd been looking a moment ago. "I mean broad. That is, tall. Well-proportioned!"

He chuckled.

"Oh, hell," she said and drained the glass, barely noticing when he poured her some more. "I am not usually this stupid. I've just had a rough night."

"Do tell," he invited, taking a swallow of wine and then putting the glass down on the coffee table.

She surveyed him over the rim of her glass. "I barely even know you."

"And yet you're letting me sleep with you—in a manner of speaking," he said, causing her to laugh. "So what happened?"

She took a deep breath. What the hell. It wasn't as if he was *really* a citizen of Tall Pines, anyway. "Promise to keep it a secret?"

He made a gesture of crossing his heart, then held up his fingers in the Boy Scout salute.

"Okay. I was planning on having an affair tonight." She said it quickly, all in one breath.

He let out a low whistle. "That explains the robe." he said. She felt the heat of his gaze trace over its contours. It felt wonderful—and after the Joy incident, was a gratifying balm to her injured ego. "With whom, if I might ask?"

"An out-of-towner, someone I've been in correspondence with," she said, shaking her head. The wine was warming her, she thought, letting herself sink back into the plush cushions of her sofa. Or was it the company? "Anyway, it was a disaster."

"What, was he ugly or something?"

"Worse," she replied, finishing her wine and putting her empty glass down. "He was a woman."

Colin choked, then burst into laughter. Reluctantly Emily joined in.

"Serves me right for building up a fantasy around someone I haven't even met. It seemed like a good idea in theory. Unfortunately the theory got shot to hell."

"Why did you decide to sleep with someone you didn't even know?"

"Let's just say it's been a while." She sighed, feeling embarrassment start to swell up again. "And I thought an out-of-towner would be less, you know, complicated."

He nodded. "This town. A fling with a resident would be like having a fling in the gazebo in the square, complete with the high school band playing accompaniment."

"Exactly," she agreed, grateful that he understood.

"So now what are you going to do?" He leaned back, as well, resting his chin on one arm. He looked devastatingly handsome with his hair falling rakishly over one eye. Like some kind of mischievous sex god.

She swallowed, trying to moisten her suddenly dry mouth. "I have no idea, honestly." Emily closed her eyes, smiling ruefully. "If some gorgeous out-of-town hunk decides to stay and seduce me, maybe I'll let him. We'll both have a great weekend or whatever and then he'll go on his merry way and I'll go on mine. But I think I'm done attempting to plan for it. If it happens, it happens."

"Very philosophical."

She stood up, noticing that her robe had come a little undone. She tightened the belt again. "Thanks, Colin," she said. "It's funny, but I really do feel a lot better. I appreciate that."

He stood, too. "No problem."

"Good night." Emily had started to turn and walk away when he stopped her again with a hand on her shoulder. She turned back.

Without warning, he leaned forward, kissing her with slow, deliberate, almost overwhelming intensity. His mouth was firm and hot and amazingly mobile. He didn't assault her. Rather, he coaxed her. And before she realized what was going on, she was kissing him back with equal desire.

Her passion leaped to life. She clutched his shoulders, reveling in the feel of the muscles bunching beneath her fingertips. His tongue swept through her mouth, tracing the outline of her lips before tangling with her tongue. She moaned softly.

He pulled away, almost as out of breath as she was.

"Just thought you should know," he rasped. "Technically *I'm* from out of town."

The sentence was like a slap, bringing her temporarily dormant conscience to life. *What are you doing? This is Ava Reese's son! This is the guy who couldn't even remember who you were a few hours ago!*

"Sorry," she breathed, taking a careful step back. "*Technically* isn't going to cut it. And I've made enough of a fool of myself for one night."

With that, Emily beat a hasty retreat to her bedroom, locking the door—not for her sexual safety but for his.

2

"MERRY CHRISTMAS, Uncle Colin!" his nieces and nephews chirped.

"Merry Christmas," he answered, taking a long swallow of his coffee and trying desperately to jump-start his sluggish system. It was nine o'clock Christmas morning, and he was dragging.

He'd spent the past two nights on Emily Stanfield's couch and had managed to get perhaps one hour's worth of sleep total, it seemed. While comfortable, it was still a couch—and worse, a couch that put him approximately seven feet away from Emily Stanfield.

Ever since his first night they'd been the picture of civility, and the only words they'd exchanged were pleasantries and logistics: "Good morning," "Do you need a key?" or "Please help yourself to breakfast in the dining room."

It was torture.

"What is *wrong* with you?" his mother asked as she put a plate of her famous Denver omelet and hash browns in front of him. "You're acting like a zombie. You're not sleeping well at that hotel, are you?"

"No, it's fine," he lied. "I've just been preoccupied."

"I knew she shouldn't have opened that inn," Ava fretted. "That lovely home, opened up to God-knows-who. Really a shame."

"She's done a great job with the place," Colin said. "I've stayed in a lot of hotels, and hers is top-of-the-line."

"Humph." His mother sounded unconvinced. "Well, her father's probably turning in his grave. You know how much Tall Pines and its traditions meant to him."

"Yeah." Then, without looking up from his French toast, Colin added, "Seems to me Emily is something of a traditionalist, too."

His mother didn't notice his sudden curiosity, thankfully. "Oh, she's still a Stanfield," she said, as if that explained everything. "She knows her duty. She's on the Garden Club Committee, the Easter Committee, she helps plan the Otter Lodge festivals and parties." She smirked, nudging his father. "She's dating the mayor, you know."

Colin's eyes widened. "Actually, no, I didn't know that." And it was something of an unpleasant surprise, he realized as he felt temper start to simmer in his bloodstream. Was she hiding it from him? And what about that whole sob story about not being intimate for a long time? "How long have they been together?"

"Well, now, I wouldn't exactly say they're *together,*" his father corrected.

"Perhaps not technically. But they're perfect for each other," his mother continued, frowning at his father. "It's only a matter of time."

Colin instantly felt at ease. It was matchmaking, not an actual relationship.

Which meant Emily was still available.

And why exactly does that matter to you? She's already shot you down once, and you're only in town till tomorrow, anyway.

It was dumb. But for whatever reason, Emily's availability *did* matter to him.

"Enough about that," his mother said, sitting down next to him at the kitchen table. "So. You're single again."

He sighed, finishing a last forkful of the savory breakfast like a man enjoying his last meal. "Alas, yes."

"You're not thinking of marrying a French girl, are you? That's an awfully long way to travel for a wedding." She brightened. "Unless she'd like to live here."

His father chuckled. "In which case, you have our blessings, sight unseen."

Colin rolled his eyes. His father understood his mother's relentless nature and obviously sympathized with his son, but he also knew enough to stay out of it. After all, the man had to live here. "I'm still a bit young to worry about marriage, Mom."

"You're thirty-four," she corrected. "Before you blink, you'll be forty, and that's going to be hell on your system when you get to 2:00 a.m. feedings."

"Let me worry about the wife first," he grumbled, "before stressing about our kids."

"You need someone who can give you the stability and comfort of small-town living," she said. "I know that you haven't always enjoyed living in Tall Pines...."

Understatement of the year, he thought, taking another jolt of coffee.

"But I can't help but think you're not giving it a chance. Just like you're not giving marriage a chance." She crossed her arms.

This was more than her usual pestering, he noted. She was genuinely upset.

He sighed again. "Mom, we've had this conversation before," he said quietly. "I love you, and I'm glad you and the rest of the family want me to be settled and happy. But I need to travel. I need adventure. I can't explain it," he finished miserably. "It's not that I don't want to be happy. I seem to need...I don't know...something I can't find."

"Well, maybe you haven't been looking in the right places," she pointed out.

He rubbed his eyes with the heels of his palms. On top of very little sleep, this conversation was more than he could handle. "Let's watch the kids play with their toys, okay? I'm only in town till tomorrow morning—I'd like to enjoy it."

"Maybe," his mother continued with her trademark determination, "you could even look right here. Locally, I mean."

"Oh, I'm sure," he snapped. "I'll just go and marry Emily Stanfield tomorrow and give you a dozen more grandbabies, how about that?"

"Colin, don't be ridiculous," she chided. "There's no need to be snide."

"Sorry," he said. "I'm a little tired."

"Besides, Emily's not right for you," she said in a tactful tone.

Colin blinked. That wasn't the response he was expecting.

"She means Emily wouldn't have you in a million years." His brother Ted entered the conversation. "Mom, where are the batteries? Kasey's remote-control pony needs them."

"Well, that's insulting," Colin said. "What's wrong with me?"

"She's small-town right down to her marrow," his father pointed out. "And as is painfully evident to everyone including yourself, you're nothing of the sort. Beyond that, she's known for being somewhat discriminating when it comes to beaus."

Even his father thought Emily would have nothing to do with him?

Well, if their kiss was any indication, she might not want to marry him, but she certainly approved of some aspects of him.

Of course, she did *turn you down.*

He grimaced.

"She wouldn't be your type, anyway," his mother continued, her tone obviously meant to soothe the affront. "And like I said, she's dating the mayor."

"She isn't dating him," Colin growled.

His mother's eyebrow went up quizzically. He could just imagine her maternal-matrimonial radar beeping to life.

Damn it. "Listen, all this talk about marriage and stuff is giving me the heebie-jeebies," he said. "I don't mean to be cranky. I'll be on my best behavior. I just want to play with the kids and enjoy my family on the holiday, before I have to go. Okay?"

She sighed, finally relenting. "All right," she agreed, hugging his shoulders. "But I wouldn't pester you so much if you didn't worry me, kiddo."

"I know," he told her, hugging her back as they went over to the living room.

They watched the kids enjoy their presents all morning, and by lunch Colin was feeling more like himself. However, he had a new problem to deal with.

"It's been ages since I've been over to the hotel," his mother said. "You never mentioned—how's your room?"

"Great." Which was true. "Very comfortable."

"Queen-size bed or king?"

He had no idea. "Er…queen."

"She's a good manager, from what I've heard. A very hard worker. She's been obsessed with the place ever since…" His mother paused, frowning. "I'm sorry. You're probably bored with Tall Pines gossip."

But when it came to Emily, Colin was hanging on every word. "Ever since what?" he asked.

She smiled the satisfied smile of a storyteller who knows she's got her audience hooked. "Ever since her father died and her mother remarried shortly afterward," she said dramatically. "Her mother told her that she'd sell the place because she was tired of upholding the Stanfield family traditions. There was no way Emily could manage a building that size by herself, but she knew her father would have hated to lose it. So she came up with a plan to use her trust fund and turn it into a hotel."

Colin was riveted. "That's a lot of work."

"I didn't agree with it," his mother said. "It's not the same, having the Stanfield house open to strangers. Paying customers."

"What was she supposed to do?" Colin defended. "Give up and get rid of it?"

His mother wrinkled her nose. "Well, if she'd gotten married to someone rich, she could've kept the house."

Of course marriage would be the solution his mother came up with.

"She was engaged, you know," she added. "Years ago. To Richard Gaines."

"That jackass?"

She glared at him. "Language, please."

Colin fell silent, but he was still shocked. Ricky Gaines was a jerk. A rich jerk, granted, but still a complete waste of space.

"They were engaged as soon as she graduated from Amherst," she said. "But they never did get married. The town was pretty divided on who was at fault."

"So what was your vote?" It was unheard of for Ava Reese not to have an opinion.

"I say he was." She sniffed. "Since he got married and had his first baby a few short months after. Some rich blond girl from Boston. Of course, if Emily had been a bit more attentive when they were dating, he might not have strayed, but that's neither here nor there. Richard and his new family lived here for a year, and it was *very* awkward for Emily."

Poor Emily, Colin thought. No wonder she didn't want to get involved with anybody from town.

His mother put her hand over his. "She's a lovely girl, and I've always felt like the right person might help make her happier. She always seems sad to me, for some reason."

He'd noticed that, as well. "Poor kid."

His mother sighed. "She could use a good husband."

Colin had to change the topic away from marriage—and Emily—in a hurry. "You know," he finally said, "I thought maybe I'd stay here. One last night with you guys." Even though the cot was even less comfortable than the couch, it would probably do wonders for his peace of mind. He'd been fixated on Emily for long enough.

"Oh, we'll miss you, but I think you had the best idea," his mother said breezily. "It's far too crowded here with your brother and your sister and the grandkids. As long as you have the room at the inn, you might as well stay, right?"

"I suppose."

"You know," she added speculatively, "you're right."

Colin's eyes narrowed suspiciously. He knew that look on his mother's face. "I'm right how?"

"Emily *isn't* dating the mayor yet," she said, smiling mischievously.

He saw the light of hope in her eyes…and calculation.

Oh crap.

Good thing he was leaving in the morning, because one more day in Tall Pines could mean real trouble if his mother decided she'd found him a wife.

"EMILY, YOU LOOK great this evening," Mayor Tim Ryfield said, sitting at the head of the dinner table at his house. "I'm so glad you could make it…especially since we've never had dinner together before."

Emily forced a smile of her own. "A Stanfield has been a guest at the mayor's Christmas party for the past fifty years, Tim," she said. "I'm glad to attend."

There. That showed that she still wasn't really having dinner with him. The last thing she wanted was to date the mayor of Tall Pines, even though she was continually tossed together with him. She wouldn't be surprised if there was some Getting Emily and Mayor Tim Married committee meeting on a monthly basis.

Ava Reese was probably the chairperson. She chaired nearly everything else.

Emily caught herself grinning at the traitorous thought. She blamed Colin's influence. Not that they'd had much interaction in the two days he'd been staying with her. Still, the mere knowledge of his presence had been severely disquieting to her state of mind.

"Stanfields always do their duty," Mayor Tim agreed. "You know, if you'd run against me for mayor, you probably would've won."

"Why would I want to be mayor?" she asked, bewildered.

"I'm not saying that," he corrected. "I'm saying you're a big part of this town. People like you and trust you. They know they can count on you."

She stared at him. "Tim, did you want me to be your campaign manager next year or something?"

He laughed. "That's the other thing I like about you, Em. You're honest and straightforward."

"Honest, straightforward, trustworthy," she muttered. "You're making me sound like a Boy Scout. So spit it out. Why are you buttering me up?"

He looked thoughtfully at his roomful of guests. There were a lot of other people sitting around the large table—the mayor's Christmas party was a long-standing tradition—but everyone else was involved in their own conversations, thankfully. Tim's voice lowered.

"You know how everyone's been matchmaking between us for the past year or so?"

She nodded heavily, feeling pained.

"I've been fighting it, too," he pointed out. "But I've been thinking about it. And maybe, just maybe, they're on to something."

Her eyes widened. "I know you've asked me to dinner, but I've never really thought you've been serious about it."

"I wasn't," he admitted. "But I'm not getting any younger. I've been focused on politics since I was in high school, Em."

"I remember," she said, shaking her head. "You were the only junior I knew who had a press kit."

"It got me this far. And I'd like to go further. To do that, I'm going to need a wife."

Now her eyes bugged out. "Holy crap, you're not asking me to *marry* you, are you?"

As it happened, her statement popped out when there was a lull in all the other conversations. You could have heard a spoon drop. The entire table was riveted on the two of them.

"I'm not asking you to marry me—*yet*," Tim said, eliciting a suggestive chuckle from the other partygoers. "I'm saying maybe we should try going out."

"Oh, Tim," Emily protested, shaking her head. "That's not such a great idea."

"Why not?" He managed to sound reasonable, even logical about it. "I'm not seeing anybody. And you're not involved with anyone." For a fraction of a second he looked tentative. "That is, you aren't seeing anyone, are you?"

She closed her eyes. Unbidden, the image of Colin wearing just pajama pants sprang into her mind. The scent of him, the feel of his hands, his mouth…the wine-edged taste of his kiss.

"No," she admitted, her voice ragged. "I'm not involved." *And whose fault is that?*

Not that a one-night stand really equaled involvement. That was the point of it, being one night, after all.

"So there you have it," Tim said as if that was the only barrier to their relationship.

"You're sweet, and we've known each other for a long time," she said gently. "But—"

"You haven't given this a fair shake," he said implacably. "I know I've fallen into nice-guy syndrome with you, but if you give me a chance, I think you'll discover we're quite compatible."

"Come on, Emily," Mrs. Rutledge said from across the table. "You have to admit, you've been pretty chilly about the whole thing."

"No harm in trying," Mr. Rutledge added.

"One simple date is not going to kill you," Mrs. Macnamara said, contributing her two cents.

Emily was appalled. Apparently they'd all ganged up on her tonight. "Let me think about it." She saw that they were ready to ply her with a second assault, so she quickly said, "Oh, and by the way, I hear that there's a big supermarket chain that's trying to buy the Henderson lot."

With that, she set off a tidal wave of debate—which was the point.

Under the cover of the heated rhetoric, she turned to Tim. "Don't ever, *ever* put me on the spot like that again."

"It wasn't entirely my idea," he said mildly. "You're the one who yelped about a marriage proposal."

"Well, I hate feeling cornered. And you're a great guy, Tim, but I just don't feel that way about you."

"What way is that?"

She took a deep breath. "I don't… that is, I'm not… Oh, hell. There's no fire between us. No *passion.*"

"Yeah, I know," he said, grinning and taking a forkful of turkey from his plate.

Emily blinked. "I'm not head over heels in love with you is what I'm saying."

"Good God." He sounded horrified. "I'd hope not!"

She finally shook her head. "Okay, apparently somebody

slipped acid in my Christmas punch, because I'm having a hard time tracking here. Weren't you trying to date me a second ago?"

"I do think we should date. And if everything works out, I think we should get married," he said as easily as if he were picking an item off a lunch menu. "This is political, Em, not personal. I'm not looking for somebody I'm madly in love with—assuming I could fall madly in love. Which I seriously doubt I'm capable of, by the way."

She tilted her head, surveying him. She'd always seen him as a good guy, maybe a little too ambitious and nose-to-the-grindstone but still overall decent. Now she realized that there was something sort of melancholy about him…something he kept carefully hidden.

"You've never been in love?"

"Thankfully, no," he said. "But you have. And you've been hurt." He smiled, and it was genuinely kind. "I wouldn't hurt you, Em. I'm just saying let's be partners. Give it a try. What have you got to lose?"

She thought about it. What *did* she have to lose?

Again Colin blazed through her mind, almost overwhelming her senses even in the comparative dimness of memory.

I need passion, she thought.

But did she really want to fall madly in love again?

Emily started fidgeting with her linen napkin, crushing it into a wad on her lap.

It was so much easier when all I wanted was sex. She got the feeling that sex with Tim would be…

She wrinkled her forehead, trying to visualize it. Actually, she couldn't even *imagine* sex with Tim. Whereas she could imagine weeklong scenarios of sex with someone far more inappropriate. Like, say, Colin.

Oh, give it a rest, you idiot.

"Trust me. It's a cliché, but passion fades," Tim said quietly. "Good friendships, a relationship based on partnership and mutual goals—now that's got staying power."

"Hmm."

"Man, you're stubborn," he said, leaning back. "You're going to the New Year's Eve ball, right?"

She nodded.

"Flying solo, I'll bet. Well, why don't you go with me? Dinner here beforehand, and then the limo will drive us there and back." He winked. "Don't look at it as a date. Look at it as a ride share with a free meal thrown in."

She laughed. "You're charming, I'll give you that."

"Got me elected two terms in a row," he replied smugly.

She focused back on her meal, but she was still thinking about passion. And Colin.

He's leaving, anyway.

The thought came unbidden. He'd said he was leaving the morning after Christmas, which meant tomorrow morning. She'd only have one more night with him. Then it'd probably be years before she ever saw him again.

Technically he really is *an out-of-towner,* her subconscious suggested conspiratorially.

So where did that leave her?

"Merry Christmas, everybody!" Tim called out, raising his glass.

"Merry Christmas," she echoed. If she married Tim, this would be her future—formal dinners, companionable friendship, a partnership made with the town in mind. Comfortable, idyllic, picture-perfect. It wouldn't be all that bad, considering.

If you slept with Colin, even if you never felt passion again, at least you'd have an incredible memory to live with.

Emily blinked. Sleep with Colin? Ava Reese's son? The guy Tall Pines loved to gossip about?

Who would ever know besides the two of you?

The thought caused a wave of heat to curl through her. He wasn't even going to see his family afterward if they did spend the night together. He'd just go straight to the airport and that'd be the end of it.

No one would find out.

"There. Now you look happy," Tim said.

She nodded. She *was* happy.

Or at least she would be happy…as soon as she got home.

IT WAS AROUND ten o'clock when Colin got back to Emily's place. He entered quietly, wondering if maybe she was asleep. He wished he were. He was exhausted. He loved visiting with his family, but still, he'd be glad when his cab came and took him to the airport in the morning.

All he needed to do was avoid any contact with Emily, leave her a nice thank-you note and he'd be home free.

The fire was lit, he noticed, and there was a bottle of champagne in an ice bucket. His scented candles were lit, as well, making the room smell like autumn, with subtle hints of pine, nutmeg and cloves.

He glanced around, puzzled. "Emily?"

She stepped out of the bedroom wearing the robe he'd seen her in his first night at her apartment. Her feet were bare, her hair was loose and tumbled wildly around her shoulders. She smiled. "Colin," she said, and her violet-blue eyes were dark with promise. "Merry Christmas."

"Merry Christmas." She looked like a present—waiting to be unwrapped.

"I thought since you'd be missing New Year's, maybe you'd like some champagne." She nodded to the bottle. "If you'd do the honors?"

His gaze went from the champagne to her loosely belted robe, then back to the champagne. Then, furtively, back to her robe, which opened up into a tantalizing V of creamy, exposed skin.

Things were not going to plan.

In fact, things were going to hell in a hurry, and he'd be in too deep in a matter of moments if he didn't take action.

Ah, but what a way to go.

He shook his head, trying to clear it of his prurient thoughts. "Um, Emily…this may not be all that swift a decision."

"What do you mean?" She sat down on the couch, and the hem of her robe shifted to reveal a very shapely leg. Her feet were small with high arches, and her toenails were painted crimson, like ripe cherries.

It took him a second to remember her question. "We've been through this once already, remember?" he said, referencing his very spontaneous—and very rejected—kiss.

She smiled, a slow, deliciously wicked smile. "I'm simply asking for champagne," she purred, leaning back. The motion caused her breasts to press against the robe, forcing the neckline open a few fractions farther. "At least, that's all for right now."

Colin almost knocked the bottle over in his haste to turn away from her tempting display. He opened it and slowly poured two glasses, keeping his back to her.

She's hot, no question. But she's trouble. Remember?

No matter how tempting Emily Stanfield might be, sleeping with her would open a can of worms.

"So," he said slowly, handing her a champagne flute and carefully sitting as far from her as the couch would allow. "I take it you've reconsidered my out-of-town status, then?"

He closed his eyes. He shouldn't have asked, but he was curious as to her change of heart. She laughed, and the sound warmed his bloodstream like brandy.

"The more I thought about it, the more I realized—you *are* an out-of-towner."

He shifted uncomfortably, remembering his early exchange with his family. Emily Stanfield was small-town to her bones. Wholesome values, dedication to her community. Tall Pines to the core.

And you're not.

Her seductive smile slipped, revealing an expression of concern. "You're worried because I turned you down before, aren't you?" she said softly. "I hurt you. I'm sorry."

"No, no," he reassured her, unconsciously moving closer. "It's not that. In fact, I think you were right. We probably *shouldn't* sleep together."

Her eyes snapped, a luminescent blue, fierce as a welding arc. "Why don't you think we should?"

Now she was the one who sounded hurt. He stroked her hair, trying to take the sting out of his statement. "The same reasons you had. I'm not quite out-of-town enough…and the good people of Tall Pines would have a field day if they found out."

"Who were you planning on telling?"

"What?" he asked, startled. "I wouldn't tell anybody."

"Neither would I," she said, and he watched, hypnotized, as her hand trailed down and untied her robe. It fell open to reveal a deep-cherry-red silk teddy edged in white lace. "It's nobody's business but ours, Colin. Nobody else needs to know."

His body went hard in a rush. No Christmas morning had ever held more promise than this moment, with this beautiful woman offering herself up as if she were every toy that he'd ever wanted in his entire life.

But she's not a toy. And he couldn't treat her like one.

"I'm leaving in the morning, Emily," Colin said carefully, even though his voice was rough with desire.

"I know," she answered. Was he imagining it or was there a thread of regret in her voice? "But we still have tonight."

His body was clamoring for her, his heart beating double

time, his cock harder than a steel girder. Were it any other woman, he'd have bridged the distance between them five minutes ago. If she were any other woman, they'd be well on their way to making it a very memorable night indeed.

Of course, if it were any other woman, he'd wake up in the morning and leave without a second thought. But it was Emily—and for whatever reason, he sensed that leaving her would cause a lot more repercussions than that. She deserved better than to be a one-night stand, one on a list of fond memories.

On the other hand, he had the sinking feeling that Emily Stanfield was not the type of woman he'd forget easily. And that caused a whole different kind of problem.

He sat on the couch, frozen in indecision.

She made a small sigh of irritation and then scooted closer, shrugging out of the robe. Emily had freckles on her shoulders, he noticed—a pale sprinkling. She leaned forward. "What time do you have to leave?" she whispered, her breath tickling the sensitive spot just below his ear.

"N-nine," he stammered, struggling against another tidal wave of lust.

"That gives us hours," she breathed, brushing a tiny kiss against his collarbone. He groaned. "Let's not waste any more time."

Colin couldn't help himself. His hands moved forward, his fingertips caressing her long, swanlike neck, then smoothing down the petal-soft skin of her shoulders. His mouth consumed hers in a sensual assault, teasing her for only the briefest of moments before simply devouring her. He could hear her muffled cries of longing, feel the way her hands bunched in the fabric of his shirt, clutching him as if she couldn't bear to let him go.

Did he position himself on top of her or did she pull him? He felt drunk on the taste of her, dizzy with it. He hazily registered the length of her body beneath his…the way her breasts crushed against his chest, the heat from between her thighs warming his jean-clad erection. Her quick fingers tugged his shirt out of his waistband, then found the naked skin beneath. With a low, unbelievably sexy growl, her hands rubbed up against his bare back, then with gentle insistence she drew her oval nails down his bare skin, causing him to shudder with need. He tore his mouth from hers for a second, gasping for air, fighting for control.

"Oh, Colin," she panted. "No matter what happens after this, *I want you*."

In that second, her statement pierced his desire-soaked consciousness long enough to force him to pause. With superhuman effort he rolled off her, practically falling to the rug. "Damn it," he said, rubbing his hand over his face. "Damn it!"

"What?" she asked, her eyes wide, her voice breathless. "What's wrong?"

"This. Us." He closed his eyes, and a litany of curses rolled through his mind. "You said no matter what happens after this. You *know* this is going to be complicated."

She huffed. "Maybe. But if anything did happen, I'd deal with it." She sent him a shaky grin. "So far, you're more than worth any consequences."

While the compliment only threw more fuel on the fire of lust snaking through his system, he grimaced. "In other words, you don't care what the fallout winds up being if this leaks out."

"Basically."

He frowned. "Wouldn't you resent me for just leaving you holding the bag?"

"Colin, not to be callous," she said, rolling her eyes, "but even if I hated you for it…honestly, what difference would it make? You wouldn't be here to see it. And what are the odds we're going to see each other again so you'd have to deal with them *or* me?"

Now, of all the things she'd said, that stopped him cold. She was offering every man's dream—no-strings-attached, smokin'-hot sex without the need for so much as a phone call after. And he wouldn't make it back to Tall Pines until next Thanksgiving at the earliest, so he would miss any repercussions.

So why did it feel so damned *wrong?*

"I know you think you mean this, Emily," he said as neutrally as possible. "But you've admitted you haven't had sex in a while. And I'll bet you haven't had sex with all that many people in your life, period. Am I right?"

She didn't say anything, just drew her full, pouty lips into a tight line.

He was right. He *knew* he was right.

"I just think," he continued reluctantly, "that when this is all over, you're going to regret saying yes. Maybe for a long, long time."

There. He'd done it. He was listening to his conscience rather than his body, for once in his life.

Emily stared at him, studying him. She seemed to almost crackle with an aura of frustration and need. Then she stood up, stalking back to her bedroom and shutting the door.

He swallowed the rest of his champagne without tasting it. Despite his various love affairs, sex wasn't something he took lightly—and anything related to Tall Pines was a time bomb. He still felt guilty over the stupid stuff he'd done when he was a kid. He wasn't about to compound it by doing stupid stuff as an adult.

He'd probably done the wise thing, although he couldn't help but…

Suddenly the door swung open.

Emily stepped out, totally, gloriously naked.

He stared at her in wonder. Her lithe limbs stretched gracefully from her perfectly proportioned torso. Her waist nipped in before curving out into gently flared hips, and her full breasts were tipped by luscious raspberry-hued nipples that puckered appetizingly with arousal. She stroked one hand over the flat planes of her stomach, stopping just short of the thatch of auburn curls at the juncture of her thighs.

"I *do* want you," she said quietly. "I *do* know what I want. And I *can* make my own decisions, thanks very much."

He was taut as a bowstring, barely registering her words. She looked like an avenging goddess—one that, even if it cost him his life, he couldn't bring himself to look away from.

"Now I'm going to my bed," she said. "I'm waiting for you there. And I can guarantee the only thing you'd regret would be saying no."

She turned, her saucy teardrop-shaped derriere making him groan out loud. Then she glanced over her shoulder.

"And, trust me, you'd regret it for the rest of *your* life." Neatly tossing his words back at him, she disappeared into her bedroom but left the door wide-open.

Colin wasn't made of stone—though it felt like it. And he sure as hell wasn't a saint.

He paused for all of a second before following her soft foot-steps. It might not be the wisest move, but as far as his body was concerned, there was no way he was leaving this place without giving one last, thorough, phenomenal Christmas present to Emily Stanfield.

3

EMILY WAS SHAKING by the time she'd made it to her bed. It had taken all her courage to make that dramatic speech. She'd never acted so cavalier about sex before, especially considering Colin had called it right on the money—she'd only had sex with two other people in her entire life. She wanted him, though, and she knew that if she didn't act as if she could coolly handle a one-night stand, he was principled enough and compassionate enough to never touch her. So she'd put on a very convincing act.

Obviously sexual frustration was making her brave, not to mention revealing talents she didn't even know she had. On the other hand, it might also be making her stupid.

Colin stepped into her room and she held her breath.

But this is going to be worth it.

He closed the door behind him. The bedroom was lit with candles, a multitude of votives washing the pale green walls with a warm glow. She had no silk sheets to trot out—her thick comforter and flannel sheets were meant to keep her toasty during the bitter winter nights.

She got the feeling staying warm would not be an issue tonight.

Besides, the last thing he seemed interested in was his surroundings. He only had eyes for her, and she shivered—not from any chill in the air but from the intensity of his gaze.

Emily leaned back on the bed, forcing herself not to cover up her body with her arms. She felt a delicious rush of anticipation roll through her and she rubbed her legs together, the friction lessening as her body began to get wet at the mere thought of him.

He took off his shirt, and she smiled in appreciation of the purely masculine beauty of his torso. His muscles bunched and flexed as he removed the rest of his clothes. When he stripped out of his boxers, she couldn't help but goggle a little. It had been a while, after all, since she'd seen a naked man, much less one in all his erect glory.

He smiled. "Stop it. You'll make me blush."

She wanted to toss back some witty comment, but words seemed lodged in her throat. Instead she put her arms out, inviting him.

Colin spread out next to her on the flannel sheets, kicking the covers out of the way. He felt like a furnace, and she warmed herself against him, shuddering at the slide of skin over skin. He kissed her neck, her collarbone, her shoulder. His hand stroked gently over her hip before sliding up and cupping her breast.

She gasped softly as sensation seeped through her like a hot bath. When he started to pull away, she grabbed his hand, keeping it on her breast. Moaning, she closed her eyes, enjoying the sensation as his mouth increased its pressure on her neck and his thumb gently circled her nipple. She stroked her leg against his, her breathing coming in soft, sweet exhalations.

"Emily," he murmured, then his mouth found hers and claimed it with a slow thoroughness. His tongue teased hers, and she teased back, the back-and-forth a precursor to the joining she really wanted. His other hand found her other breast, and he stroked expertly. Her fingers dug into his firm shoulders in response.

After what seemed like a pleasurable eternity, he released one breast. She whimpered in protest, only to stop when his hand moved lower, reaching between her thighs and dipping into her moist heat. She bit her lip as the sensation overwhelmed her. He gently parted the folds of skin until he found her sleek clit and rubbed it with firm precision. She felt pressure building up in her and she arched her back, trying to bring herself in closer contact with the man who was causing her to react so strongly. He kept working at it, insistently, delicately, until she thought she would explode.

Then he pressed a finger into her, and she couldn't help it. She came, and it was more than an explosion…it was a supernova. She threw her head back, letting the experience rock her.

When she came back to Earth, she looked at him and saw he had a beatific smile on his face. "That was…" She struggled to find a word that covered it and couldn't.

"You're welcome," he said, winking at her. "I wouldn't have pegged you as a screamer."

The blush washed over her entire body. She was sure he noticed, but she didn't care. "I didn't know I was," she admitted. "I don't think I was before."

"You don't say." He moved his head down, sucking first on one nipple, then the other.

Emily still felt desire, but the raw, slicing edge of it had been dulled by her orgasm. Now she was hungry for him, but she wasn't starving the way she'd been before. She could take her time, and enjoy the interplay of their bodies much more intently.

I don't know when I'll have this sort of chance again, she thought. *I'm going to make every moment count.*

She nudged his head up, and he sent her a puzzled look. "Your turn," she said, smiling wickedly.

"Oh?"

She pushed him down against the mattress, enjoying the way his erect cock stood, large and prominent, demanding attention. She pressed a few slow kisses against his chest, then his

stomach, her tongue tracing the defined muscles. She was grati-
fied to see his breathing go shallow. Slowly she stroked her
hands on his thighs, drawing her nails down the sensitive skin.
He drew in a sharp, hissing breath, releasing it in a slow, ragged
sigh as she finally encircled his erection with her fingers.

"Your hands are so soft," he marveled, his eyes closing. His
hips arched up to meet her as her hands traveled up and down
the length of his shaft.

"Think so? Try this," she answered playfully, then took the
head of his penis into her mouth.

He groaned loudly. She traced the head with her tongue
before sucking ever so softly, caressing the velvety skin with
her lips. His breathing increased in pace.

"Emily," he rasped.

His cock was like iron wrapped in satin. She reveled in the
clean, masculine taste of his skin, taking him in a few more
inches, her fingers stroking the round globes of his balls.

After a few moments, he reached down, pulling her up
roughly. "I have to be inside you," he said, his voice coarse with
need. "*Now.*"

She smiled, feeling triumphant. He sounded just the way
she'd felt when he'd given her that first orgasm. She liked that
she might be able to make this man tremble, mindless with
need. "Condom," she breathed, reaching over on her nightstand
and getting one of the newly purchased foil packets. She tore
it open, rolling it onto him slowly, taunting him with it. He was
shaking by the time she was done.

He rolled her onto her back, and she felt the glorious weight
of him pressing her into her mattress. He kissed her fiercely,
and she responded with equal ferocity, parting her legs so he
could fit himself at her snug opening. She felt the head of his
cock slide slightly between her wet folds. He reached down,
teasing her clit with his hardness until she was gasping with

desire, her legs twining around his as she struggled to bring him closer.

"I want you inside me," she said.

Without a word, he finally relented and thrust into her, filling her completely. It felt so incredibly good she could have cried. She circled her hips, instinctively tightened her muscles as she enveloped him in her warmth.

He groaned, withdrawing slowly, and she moaned in return. "Deeper," she breathed, and he returned, with maddening patience, going farther into her. Her legs tightened around his hips, cradling him inside her.

"Colin." She shivered as the first luscious tremors of passion inched through her. "I'm almost there...."

Taking her cue, he increased his speed, his hips moving more quickly as his cock moved in and out of her willing wetness. Emily felt her body start to tighten and she ran her nails down his back as her hips bucked to meet his every thrust.

"Baby, I'm going to..." he groaned, and she cried out in approval. The two of them were frenzied in their joining, as if they couldn't get close enough to each other. He let out a guttural shout as he emptied himself into her with a hard, definitive motion, triggering an orgasm that eclipsed her first. She cried out again, a sound of pure pleasure, as her body clutched around him. To her surprise, he shuddered again as their hips melded together, rocking in the aftershocks of climax.

After long moments, he rolled off her, leaving them both sweaty and breathless. He stared at her, his green eyes like beacons.

"You were right," he said. "I would have regretted saying no to you for my entire life."

She basked in the compliment of his words, even as a small part of her conscious brain registered what he was saying.

This is a one-night stand. She'd just had her world spun on its axis by a man she'd fantasized about for years…but this was it. This was all she was going to get.

Is this going to be worth it?

She glanced at him. In the aftermath of sex, he still looked sinfully tempting. There was no sense of regret, no lingering return of reason that asked her, *What were you thinking?* She knew exactly what she'd been thinking when she decided to seduce Colin Reese. She knew because she was still thinking it.

But what are you going to do when you can't have him again?

He'd made it clear that there was no future. He was leaving, crossing an ocean to get away from Tall Pines. He was certainly not about to return to the small town that he had caused so much grief—and which wanted to return the favor by prying into every minute detail of his now almost famous local-rebel-makes-good life.

So where does that leave you?

She sighed. It left her here, in Tall Pines. Alone.

He leaned over, kissing where her heart beat. "You are going to haunt me," he said softly.

He was going to haunt her, too. But then again, it never could have lasted. She'd been well aware of that going into this little arrangement.

She might settle for the comfort of friendship and a passion-less relationship, she thought as his fingers brushed over the surface of her skin, bringing the nerve endings to life. She was a realist. Would she ever find a man she reacted to as strongly as she did to Colin? She could either agonize over the question or simply enjoy the moment.

Tonight was all they had, and she would make the most of it.

"You have to leave at nine tomorrow, you said?" Emily asked.

"Uh-huh."

"We've still got hours," she reminded him, just as she had before, in the living room.

"Really," he drawled. "What shall we do with ourselves?"

She smiled, licking her lips. "As it happens," she said, her voice husky with sexual promise, "I've got a few ideas I'd love to try."

"I SAID, WHERE TO, mister?" the cab driver asked, slowly and carefully, as if Colin were hard of hearing.

Colin guessed that the man must have repeated the question several times. "Sorry," he said. "I need to get to the airport in Hartford."

The cabbie snorted. "I'll give it a shot." The taxi began slowly creeping out of the Stanfield Arms's circular driveway.

Colin stared out the window in a daze. The entire town of Tall Pines was smothered in mountainous drifts of snow, making the whole scene seem oddly muted. It only added to Colin's feeling of surreal displacement.

Did last night really happen?

Yes, it had happened—and in a way was still happening for him, since he'd gotten no more than a catnap or two the entire night. Once he'd given in to his urge and slept with Emily, it was as if he couldn't get enough of her. Fortunately, she'd seemed to feel the same way, because the two of them had feasted on each other for hours, and even now weariness hadn't quite settled in.

They'd made love twice in the bed, once in front of the fireplace, once in the shower and once on the countertop of her bathroom. He hadn't had sex like that for years. His body felt well used, just this side of sore. His mind, on the other hand, kept replaying the more vivid highlights of the previous night— and suggesting new and exciting variations that they might try in a second round.

Pity there isn't going to be a second round.

That was why they called them one-night stands, he reminded himself. One night. He wasn't quite sure where the "stand" part fit in. Although now that he thought about it, the shower…

"You all right, mister?"

Colin refocused on the cab driver. "What?"

"You look sorta out of it," the guy said, peering at Colin from his rearview mirror. "Don't tell me. You had yourself a merry little Christmas, huh? Really tied one on?"

"You could say that," Colin said ruefully, obviously not willing to divulge secrets.

"Hard to believe you could party that hard in a town like this. Tiny little mom-and-pop stores, all those wrought-iron lamp-posts with holly around 'em. It looks like an old movie or something."

Colin looked out the window as if seeing the place with a stranger's eyes. It was picturesque, he had to admit. The windows were decorated with paint and candles, and the streets were clear of the litter and debris that he was so used to in the sprawling cities he normally worked in. Most of the stores were brick or stone, not concrete. The houses had nice land-scaping and everywhere were Christmas decorations, tasteful and old-fashioned.

"I'll have to tell my wife about it," the cabbie continued cheerfully. "She loves this kind of crap. You live here?"

"No," Colin said.

"Just passin' through, then?"

"Yup. Just passing through." The thought brought a pang. *How long is this sensation going to last?*

He'd known that sleeping with Emily was going to be trouble even before he'd set foot into her bedroom. Apparently it was going to be more trouble than he'd bargained for…and he hadn't even been away from her for an hour.

"Well, it's cute and all, but it's a pure pain in the ass to get to," the cabbie stated. "Especially with the blizzard."

"Wait a minute," Colin interrupted. "Especially with the *what?*"

"Blizzard. Man, it's been on the news all over the place," the cabbie said. "They've had travel advisories. It's been on the radio and the television and the newspapers. Where have you been?" He shook his head. "That must've been one hell of a party."

"It was," Colin said. "I've got a flight to New York, then a connection to Paris. Any word on airports shutting down?"

"I think there are delays but nothing too bad," the driver reassured him.

"Oh," Colin said. "That's…good."

"Don't sound so enthusiastic," the cabbie joked. "Paris, huh? Ooh la la. Vacation or something?"

"No, I'm moving there."

Without warning, his body suddenly felt exhausted. He wished the cab driver weren't quite so chatty. Maybe it was the thought of a transatlantic flight or maybe it was the thought of leaving, he wasn't sure. Nevertheless, his body abruptly decided to remind him that he hadn't gotten a premium on sleep last night and he wasn't a teenager anymore. Suddenly he was having a hard enough time staying conscious, much less carrying on a conversation.

He wondered absently whether Emily was sleeping. She'd been naked and bundled up in her bedding when he'd said goodbye. She'd smiled, kissed him and turned over so she didn't have to see him leave.

It had been harder than he'd ever imagined to walk out that door.

"Moving to Paris? Wow. The wife would love it, but me, I can't see leaving the States," the cabdriver continued relentlessly.

Colin listened halfheartedly to the cabdriver's cheerful patter. He watched as the town's landmarks moved slowly past them, enveloped in fluffy flakes that almost turned the air white with their abundant barrage. The gazebo in the town square looked like an igloo, piled high with a dome of snow. The statue of the town's founder waded waist deep in a drift, while the Otter Lodge sign was almost completely covered up, revealing only the "Otter."

The cab skidded abruptly, and Colin realized he'd been drifting off. "Whoa!"

"Sorry about that," the cabdriver said. "I've got chains on, but this is nuts. I haven't seen a storm this bad in years."

Colin wondered if Emily was going to be okay. She was up in the attic, after all, and as luxurious as the small apartment suite was, it was awfully close to the roof, which was probably piled up with tons of snow.

He suddenly had a horrible vision of the roof caving in and fought the absolutely irrational desire to have the cab turn around and return him to the inn.

Even if the roof's not strong enough, what were you planning on doing to stop it? Hold the thing up with your arms?

He wasn't sure what he would do. He just knew that he hated the idea of Emily in any kind of trouble. And, if he were being completely honest with himself, some part of him was searching desperately for an excuse to get back to the inn. To *her*.

He knew that it was stupid, but there it was.

Chalk it up to lack of sleep.

"So what kind of business are you in?" the cabdriver asked.

"I'm an architect," Colin said.

"Houses and stuff?"

"Not exactly. My next project is a hotel on the Left Bank, about a stone's throw from the Eiffel Tower."

"Must be nice," the cabdriver said with a low, appreciative whistle. "So, what, they aren't building any hotels on this side of the ocean?"

"Now you sound like my mother," Colin said, and the cabdriver snorted.

"Well, to each his own," he said affably. "You like what you do?"

"Love it," Colin told him, feeling better. "Love the challenges, the new places, the clients. All of it."

"Now you're sounding better," the cabbie pointed out. "That hangover wearing off?"

Colin smiled tightly. "Seems like it."

"I hate hangovers," the cabdriver continued. "Still, every now and then you've got to indulge, you know?"

Colin thought about it. *Indulgence.* That seemed like an inadequate word to cover what had taken place last night. But still, wasn't that basically how Emily was looking at it?

Ten bucks says she isn't mooning about you this morning, pal. She's probably sleeping it off, or getting back to work. The way she'd talked about it, it was the experience she wanted, and the fact that it was with him was incidental. As though he was a stamp in her passport or something.

He didn't believe it at the time, but now, after seeing her in action—honestly, he wasn't sure what to believe anymore.

"So your wife and family going with you or what?"

"What's with the twenty questions?" Colin snapped.

The cabdriver paused. "Sorry, man. Didn't mean to bug you. Some people like to talk, you know?"

Colin sighed. "I'm sorry, too," he said. "I guess that hangover's stronger than I thought. I didn't mean to bite your head off." He paused. "And no. No wife, no kids."

"Huh. Not surprised, actually. You don't really seem like a family man."

Colin sat up straighter, as if someone had smacked him on the back of the head. "Why do you say that?"

"Sharp dresser, goin' off to Paris the day after Christmas, hungover." The cabdriver barked out a laugh. "But, hey, I've seen weirder from married guys, so I wasn't absolutely sure. I remember driving this guy to two of his mistresses' apartments on Thanksgiving, if you can believe it...."

Colin settled back against the cold vinyl seat of the taxi, feeling disgruntled. It all circled back to his family's comments. He wasn't the small-town type. He knew that, had known it since before high school. He'd be the first to say so in most cases. So why should the observation bother him now? Why was he getting so ticked off every time someone pointed out that he wasn't small-town and family-oriented?

You're getting a little tired of being alone.

The thought was so alien Colin actually blinked in disbelief for a second. He'd had lots of relationships, sure. Brief, exciting relationships. But it hadn't occurred to him that he might be lonely.

While he did love his job, there was more to life than work.

Unbidden, the picture of Emily riding him with abandon in the early hours of the morning sprang to mind...causing other things to spring, as well. Embarrassed, he tried to force his unruly body to relax.

Even if you want a relationship, it can't be Emily. For reasons they both understood.

Still, damned if he didn't feel disappointed.

"What's this now?" the cabdriver said, causing Colin to look through the windshield. There was a heavily dressed police officer waving them down with a flashlight. "Is there a problem, Officer?"

The cop nodded. "You can't get to the interstate," he said, his breath coming out in clouds of steam. "The blizzard's gotten too bad."

"But I have to get this guy to the airport," the cabbie protested, "then I have to get home!"

"Not today, you don't," the police officer said grimly. "You'd better find someplace in town to stay, because nobody's leaving Tall Pines. For a few days, if this storm front keeps up. Get off the roads as soon as you can."

The cabdriver grumbled but carefully turned around. "Guess I'd better find a motel," he said. "Where should I drop you?"

Colin paused for a second. He should probably go to his parents' house. They'd be worried about him and they'd love to see him.

But when he opened his mouth, he heard himself saying, "If you could take me back to the hotel, that'd be great."

"The hotel it is," the cabdriver agreed.

Colin sat, silent. He wondered what Emily was up to at that moment. He wondered what he should do when he saw her.

He also wondered what she'd do when he unexpectedly showed up.

"WE'RE STRANDED HERE!" one of the guests was yelling to be heard over the general clamor. "What are we supposed to do now?"

"I only booked the reservation for four days," another guest protested. "You can't expect me to pay for a day that I'm forced to stay here."

"And I have work to do," yet another protested.

"Emily," Sue whispered. "We've got some concerns about the roof, we're running low on towels…"

Emily smiled easily. "Don't worry. Everything's going to be fine."

Sue's eyes narrowed. "How do you figure? It's turning into a disaster!"

Emily didn't stop smiling as she turned to the mob of angry guests. "I'm so sorry for the inconvenience," she said, and although her voice was raised enough to carry over the chaos of multiple complaints, it stayed sweet and pleasant-sounding. That was enough to quiet most of the people milling around the foyer. "The blizzard has caught us all unawares. I can assure you that we are going to do everything we can to make this temporary setback easy and even pleasant for you. I can't offer you the rooms for free," she apologized, ignoring the one customer's irate glare, "but I can offer you a blizzard discount since, as you said, you're being forced to stay here. I'd also like to offer you our breakfast—complimentary, of course—and I can send it to your rooms if you'd prefer." Emily smiled broadly. "If you have to take another vacation day, you might as well take advantage of it, and it's never too late to have breakfast in bed, I always say."

That drew an appreciative chuckle from several of the guests.

"Light up a fire in your rooms' fireplaces, have some cider or wine and enjoy yourself. If there's anything we can do to make your stay more comfortable, please let us know. And if you must work, our business center is open twenty-four hours a day."

The guests wandered away, mollified. Emily turned to Sue. "I've got a call in to Dale Albee to look at the roof, and we'll get some loads of towels going in the basement since the linen service can't get here. And I've already got the French toast in the oven for complimentary breakfasts, so we're set."

Sue stared at her, eyes wide. "Okay, what are you on and where can I get some?"

Emily laughed. "Don't know what you're talking about, but thanks. I think."

"You must have had a great time at Mayor Tim's last night," Sue noted.

"Come on, Sue." Emily sighed. "I thought you of all people would leave me alone about him."

Sue grinned. "Hey, you're single. He's single. And lord knows it's high time you stopped sleeping alone."

Emily quickly turned back to the front reception desk, pretending to look over some bills. She prayed that her cheeks weren't stained with the usual telltale blush.

"Tim's not exactly the type to get a girl hot and bothered. I mean, he's sweet and all, but..."

"I know. But still, those quiet types can surprise you," Sue pointed out.

Colin was a quiet type—the deep, intense, loner type. That had always been a huge draw for her, back when she'd doodled his name on notepaper in high school. He'd seemed like a cross between James Dean and Johnny Depp, with his dark good looks and quirky, iconoclastic behavior. And, yes, he had surprised her.

Heck, she thought with a private smile. She'd surprised *herself* last night.

"I agreed to go with Tim to the New Year's ball," Emily said. "So we'll see how it goes."

"Good," Sue said, and Emily was grateful that her friend wasn't paying that much attention, being so frazzled by the blizzard situation, since she felt as though she might as well be wearing a T-shirt that said *I had fantastic sex with Colin Reese!* Fortunately, keeping busy was helping her stay grounded. "Anyway, I'm really impressed with how you handled all those guests this morning. Honestly, you're a rock. I don't know what we would do if you weren't so unflappable."

Emily shrugged, embarrassed. "You'd manage, I'm sure."

"If you say so," Sue said dubiously. "All I know is you managed to get that raving mob to back down and go to their rooms, and they've been chewing me out since eight o'clock this morning. I know you were going to take today off, but..."

"Hey, there are no days off for a business owner," Emily said. "Don't worry about..."

Suddenly Sue's statement sunk in.

"Wait a minute. Since eight?"

"Yeah. I know—it was only two hours ago. I shouldn't sound so dramatic...." Sue saw that her friend was genuinely upset. "Why? Is that a problem?"

Emily did the math. "So the road to the interstate has been closed since…"

"Since about seven this morning," Sue answered. "Some vehicles got in, but they're not letting anybody back out. The roads are too dangerous, they're saying."

Emily felt the blood rush from her face. She sat down.

"Whoa. Are you okay?" Sue was at her side in a flash. "You look terrible all of a sudden. What's wrong?"

"I drank a little champagne last night," Emily said, "and I didn't get much sleep. It must be catching up with me."

All of which was true, as far as it went. But there was one thing she'd left out.

If they weren't letting anyone leave, then Colin was headed back for town.

Emily felt as though her limbs were floating. She felt numb and yet tingly, as if her entire body had gone to sleep but she was still awake.

What were they going to do now?

Her mind instantly supplied a few details of what they *could* be doing…things that sheer physical exhaustion had prevented them from doing the night before. But she'd had her one-night stand. As much as she'd love to spend more time with—and energy on—Colin Reese, she knew that it was a bad idea. There would be talk. His family hadn't realized he'd been staying in her apartment, but they'd probably figure it out if he came back. While the logical, mature side of her argued that she and Colin were adults and what they did was nobody's business but their own, the idea of dealing with Ava Reese, not to mention the whole town just-dropping-in to pump her for information, was enough to make her cringe.

On the other hand, what makes you think he'll come back here at all?

That thought made her feel as though she'd been dropped headfirst in a frozen lake. She was so worried about how to handle seeing him that it hadn't occurred to her—he might not come back. He might not want to see her again.

That was the point of one-night stands, after all.

Emily quickly went downstairs and loaded their industrial washer/dryer with towels, grateful for the physical activity. She probably should sneak in a nap at some point, just to clear her head. But she got the feeling sleep would elude her, especially knowing that Colin was maybe somewhere in town that very minute.

Somewhere, trying desperately to avoid her.

She set her jaw. Well, it had been her idea to have a one-night stand, after all. She didn't need him to hang around. She knew how the game was played. If he couldn't take more than one night, then maybe she'd wrung him out. Maybe he simply couldn't handle another night with her, she thought with a smug internal grin. She'd gotten everything she wanted out of it—a completely memorable night. Even if she never got anything else, she'd cherish the memory. That was enough. It'd have to be.

Emily was so intent on running that mental pep talk through her brain in an endless loop that she ran right into Colin before she registered who he was.

"Hey, there," he said, smiling sheepishly...although his eyes sparkled warmly. "Long time no see."

She couldn't help it. Her heart leaped happily and she felt like an idiot. Her body, in the meantime, was so attuned to him that the mere scent of his cologne was already starting to kick her libido into overdrive—even with her sleep deprivation.

This was one hell of a man.

"I heard about the interstate closing," she said apologetically, trying not to stare at him and failing miserably.

"Got room for one more?" he asked.

His question was completely innocuous, but the tone suggested a lot more. Was he asking for more than one night of what they'd done the night before? Or just for a place to sleep? Should she assume?

He leaned in. "I can sleep wherever you want me to sleep." Now his tone left no question as to his intent.

Her breasts tightened, and she felt the now-familiar dampness rush between her legs. She smiled at him with invitation.

"I'm sure we can…"

"Sorry to interrupt, Emily," Mr. Albee, the roofer, said, clearing his throat.

"Oh. Yes," she said, and damned if the blush didn't settle into her cheeks. "How can I help you?"

"Your roof's holding up okay. The reinforcements I did over the summer are doing their job, just like I told you they would." He looked from her to Colin, his expression appraising.

"Hello, Mr. Albee." Colin sounded like a schoolboy who had been caught smoking in the bathroom.

"Colin Reese, right?" Mr. Albee smiled slowly. "Didn't know you were staying in town."

"I don't think anybody was planning on staying quite this long," Colin replied. "What with the blizzard and all."

"Well, you'll have to give my regards to your mother and father," Mr. Albee said. "If you get over that way. You're staying here, are you?"

"Just because it's so crowded…" Colin stammered. "What with my nieces and nephews and everything…"

"I was just doing him a favor," Emily supplied.

"Of course you were," Mr. Albee said. "Well, I won't keep

you. There's an emergency town meeting tonight, and I'm sure I'll see you there, Emily." He shook Colin's hand. "Nice seeing you again, son."

He left and Emily groaned.

"What's wrong?" Colin asked.

"He's married to Evelyn Albee, remember?"

Colin frowned. "So?"

"So she runs the beauty salon. Which everyone knows is like the CIA and the blogosphere combined," Emily pointed out. "By the time most of the women in this town get their usual manicure and cut-and-color, everyone's going to know we're an item."

"We're not an item, though," Colin said.

She felt a little sting at that. Well, she'd asked for it. "I know. But they're not going to care. And it'll only get worse if you bunk here at the hotel. In my apartment."

"I thought," he said suggestively, "that you weren't going to care about the consequences."

"That was last night," she muttered. "I would have walked over hot coals to have you last night."

He grinned. "Oh?"

"Now I'm about to face the gauntlet at tonight's town meeting," she said. "So it'd be better if you *weren't* staying here."

"You're not telling me to stay at my parents' house, are you?"

She nodded. "That's exactly what I'm telling you."

"So…" His voice was barely audible. "You *don't* want anything else to do with me? It really was just a one-night stand?"

She stared into his eyes and read the hurt there. Emily held her breath for a second, staring at him.

"It ought to be," she said softly. It was going to be trouble, she just knew it. Evelyn Albee, Ava Reese, all the busy women of Tall Pines and their gossip circles…

With a slow, subtle motion, he reached forward and stroked the delicate skin on the inside of her wrist.

She almost melted into a puddle right there in the lobby. "Okay. Put your bags in my room. We'll figure it out."

Houston, she thought, watching him disappear down the hallway, *we have a problem.*

4

COLIN SUPPOSED HE ought to feel at least a little ashamed of himself for pushing the issue with Emily, knowing that the seeds of gossip were being sown. But as he sat down in the main dining room, helping himself to some pecan French toast, scrambled eggs and bacon, he was having a hard time feeling anything but satisfied.

I get another night with her, he thought. *And maybe more.*

And, as she herself had said, it wasn't anybody's business but Emily's and his. The town might talk, but that's all it would be. Talking never killed anyone.

Sexual frustration probably never killed anyone, either—but he wasn't taking any chances.

"There you are!"

He glanced over and promptly choked on a bite of bacon. "Mom?"

His mother and father and the rest of his family quickly overtook the dining room, helping themselves to the buffet. "We decided to try the breakfast here at the hotel," his mother said innocently. "Especially when you called and told us you were staying here."

"Your mother wants to find out what the inn has that we don't seem to have at our house," his father added, then winced at his mother's responding glare. "Well, that's what you said in the car."

There were only a few other guests enjoying the buffet—most of the rest were taking breakfast in their rooms, apparently—so his family was able to surround him at the large oak table. "Can we get a look at your room?" his mother asked.

"Uh…" Colin felt his mind go blank. He was hardly going to show them Emily's apartment. "I haven't got a room."

"You don't? Why not?"

"There are a lot of people stranded," he improvised hastily. "And they weren't expecting me to stay, so I think they gave it away."

"Then you can come home," his mother said as if the matter were settled.

Now what? He couldn't offer a logical explanation without revealing his new arrangement with Emily, and that was the last thing he wanted. "I think they'll find a place for me," he said. It sounded lame to his own mind.

His mother's mouth set in a tight line. "All right, son. What's going on?"

"What do you mean?"

"Don't play coy with me. I've been on to you since you took my car the week before homecoming your junior year and went parking with Mary Sue Reynolds—didn't think I knew about that, did you?"

Colin gaped. "Mom!"

"It would've been better if she hadn't left her bra in the backseat." His father snorted. "That was dumb, Colin."

"Why was there a bra in the backseat?" his niece Elizabeth asked.

"Never mind," his mother quickly replied. "Colin, the bottom line is, I know that there's something going on. So either you can tell me or I'll find out on my own."

Colin's mind raced for an explanation. Before he could come up with something plausible, Emily walked in.

For someone who hadn't gotten a lot of sleep, she looked luminescent. Her pale skin glowed in the lights of the dining room's chandelier. She was wearing a plum-colored V-neck cashmere sweater and a pair of black slacks. Her auburn hair was tied back with a matching plum-colored velvet ribbon. Combined with her glasses, she looked about eighteen years old—like a student, maybe headed off to the library.

He definitely had a thing for girls with glasses.

He smiled at her before he could stop himself and he caught his mother noticing his smile. He quickly schooled his expression, trying to redeem the situation.

"Ava," Emily said, smiling genially as she poured coffee into their cups. "It's so nice to see you and your family here."

"I hope you don't mind," Ava said. "We thought we'd enjoy the hotel's restaurant. I've heard good things about your brunch spread."

If Emily were suspicious, she didn't act like it. She looked cool, refined—the perfect hostess. Colin was in awe of her reserve. "We're happy to serve anytime," she answered with grace. "You'll have to try us in the spring. The cook does these fresh strawberry pancakes that are to die for."

"I've also heard good things about the hotel," his mother said, and Colin braced himself. "Obviously it's so incredible my son is hoping you'll find room for him here."

Emily's smile faltered slightly, but so imperceptibly that Colin felt as if only he would notice. "That's flattering. We're certainly trying to accommodate everyone who's been stranded by the storm." She paused. "It might mean some doubling up, I think...."

Before she could continue, a blond woman walked into the dining room. She was obviously *not* a Tall Pines resident. She had all the look of a big city about her, like New York or Los Angeles. Hell, maybe even Milan. The bright red suit she was wearing, replete with tight skirt and matching heels, looked razor sharp and ready for business. Her makeup was flawless. He would have pegged her as a big executive—he'd run into the type before when he'd started to get some acclaim as an architect. When he'd designed and built a big new art gallery in London, the opening party had been almost entirely populated with women who'd looked like this. This polished, cosmopolitan blonde would've blended right in.

"Good morning, everyone," she said, her voice friendly. "Hey, Emily! This is a great spread. I can't believe you pulled all this together on such short notice. Have I mentioned lately just how impressed I am with this hotel?"

"Hi, Joy." Emily was obviously grateful for the interruption. "These are a few of our Tall Pines townsfolk, the Reese family. Everyone, this is Joy Webster, a friend of mine from out of town."

"Well, *hello,*" Joy said when she saw Colin. Her eyes went low-lidded and she smiled. "Always nice to meet the locals."

"I'm not local," Colin was quick to point out.

"Are you staying here in the hotel?" she asked after nodding her hellos to the rest of his family.

"Um…that remains to be seen." He forced himself not to glance at Emily. He was trying to quell gossip here.

"Well, if you need a place to crash, I've got a huge room." The expression on her face was obviously extending a slightly more intimate invitation.

"Uh, thanks," he said before feeling a sharp kick under the table. "Ow!"

His mother was studiously cutting her bacon and eggs with a fork and knife, pretending she hadn't done a thing. "So how are you enjoying our town, Joy?" she asked, her voice as mild as milk.

"I'm loving it," Joy replied, sounding genuinely enthused. "It's perfect. And have I mentioned how much I adore this hotel?"

"Always nice to be admired," Emily said.

Colin finally looked at Emily. She looked…well, *peeved* wasn't quite the right word, and it was hard to tell behind the smooth facade she seemed to habitually wear. But he could sense there was some kind of irritation hovering just below the surface.

"Seems like the table's pretty full. I'll just take this up to my room, if that's okay," Joy said. "Nice meeting you all. And don't forget—" she smiled privately at Colin "—if you need a place, I'm your girl."

Colin didn't say anything, just smiled back weakly as she left the room. When she disappeared, he felt angry glares aimed in his direction from not one but two women.

"So that's why you're waiting to stay in the hotel," his mother said, with a note of disgust. "Good grief. I might have known that even here in Tall Pines you'd find one of your…your *women*."

"What do you mean, one of my women?"

"Please. I could have picked her out of a lineup," his mother scoffed. "You always like those high-society, high-fashion, high-maintenance types. She fits the description of your usual dates down to a T."

"Hey, I resent that," Colin protested. "I don't have a type."

Emily's eyes had widened at his mother's very thorough diatribe. "I ought to get going," she now said hastily. "Nice to see you again, Ava, Harry. Bring your family by anytime."

With that, she disappeared into the hallway.

Great, Colin thought, glaring at his mother. "I am *not* staying here just to score with Joy," he said, his tone curt.

"What's 'score with' mean?" his nephew asked.

"Language, Colin," his mother warned. "You don't want the kids picking up that sort of thing."

"You're the one that started it!"

"She is pretty," his father noted. "You'll have to give our son that, Ava—he's got good taste."

"Oh, Colin, when are you ever going to settle down?" She sighed melodramatically.

"Okay, *this* is why I'm not staying at the house," Colin declared. "Everything is always about why I won't settle down, why I'm not married, who I'm dating and why I won't move back to Tall Pines!"

The rest of his family fell silent, staring at him. He felt like an ogre.

"I love you guys," he added. "Very, very much. But…I'm doing the best I can, okay? I know you worry about me and you want me to be happy, and I love you for it. But I have to do things my own way."

His mother bit her lip, looking uncomfortable. "I know I can be a tiny bit pushy.…"

His father's eyes popped at that statement.

"Harry, not one word," she interrupted, frowning at him before winking. "Okay, I can be *very* pushy. But I really do want what's best for you. If you'd rather stay here at the hotel, I'll understand."

"Thank you," he said gratefully.

They all fell into more comfortable conversation, and he had to admit it was nice to spend more time together as a family, over a delicious meal. When they were done, they all hugged him goodbye.

"I don't suppose you'll be at the town meeting tonight?" his mother asked, hugging him. "It's a special one to deal with the storm."

Colin groaned. "You know I hate those things."

"Okay," she said. "Well, we'll do something before you leave. Good luck in finding a room."

"Thanks." They all left, and feeling a wave of relief, he went to the front desk.

"Excuse me," he said to Sue, the woman running the reception desk. He seemed to remember her from high school. "Is Emily around?"

"No," the woman replied, looking at him suspiciously. "She had to run some errands. Is there anything I can help you with?"

"Uh, no," he answered quickly. "I'll, er, catch up with her later. Thanks." She was still staring at him strangely as he walked away.

He sneaked back up to Emily's apartment, hoping he'd find her there. But for the rest of the day she remained conspicuously absent. It got darker, and by dinner he still hadn't seen her. The cook told him she would be gone until later—she was going to the town meeting.

She was avoiding him, he knew it. He wouldn't put it past her to find someplace else to stay that night just to miss dealing with him. All that talk about Joy, and her blatant invitation, had obviously upset Emily.

Well, he'd have to set Emily straight. They might not have a relationship, but whatever weird thing they did have was pretty special.

And if that meant going to the damned town meeting to tell her… He cringed.

He'd just have to go there and face the fire.

"THANKS FOR HAVING me to dinner, Sue," Emily said, finishing the last of her coffee.

"We love having you," Sue said graciously. "Are you okay leaving Phillip to hold down the fort by himself?"

Emily put her hand in her pocket, pulling out her cell phone. "The apron string he's attached to is now cellular," she answered, knowing Phillip's penchant for panicking. "Besides, he's handled us both being gone for a town meeting before. A little stress won't kill him."

"I'm still surprised you didn't stay at the inn. Especially after you convinced some of those people to double up with the strays."

Emily grinned at the term. "Well, since the highway patrol wouldn't let the poor people leave, the least we could do was put them up."

"Sometimes, I swear, you could sweet-talk the Devil into buying thermal underwear." Sue shook her head. "You're charming, you're persuasive—and yet you're a bulldozer."

"Thanks?" Emily questioned, laughing.

"I meant that in the good way," Sue assured her.

Sue's husband, Vernon, stuck his head into the kitchen. "Honey, if we're going to the town meeting, we'd better get a move on."

Emily swallowed hard. She'd been steeling herself to ask Sue her question since she got to the house, but somehow she couldn't quite come up with a way of making it sound casual. Now it was make-or-break time. "Say, Sue, could I ask you a favor?"

"Anything. What do you need?"

"I was wondering if I could stay here tonight."

Sue looked at her, surprised. "Of course, sweetie. But what's wrong with your apartment?" She rolled her eyes. "Don't tell me. You gave it up to some of the strays, right?"

"One of them," Emily answered, feeling relieved. "I figured it'd be less awkward if I could camp out on your couch."

"We've got the guest bedroom, silly. Don't even worry about it," Sue replied.

Emily felt relief wash through her. Sue was her best friend and had been since grade school. As a result of all those years together, she tended to be frighteningly adept at reading her like a book. Emily had never kept a secret from her about even the smallest thing, much less something of this magnitude.

"Who wound up in your place, anyway?" Sue asked,

clearing away the dinner dishes. "The cabdriver? That lost delivery guy?"

Emily briefly considered lying. Instead she decided to try and brazen it out, quickly loading the dishwasher. "Colin Reese, actually."

There was a long pause. Emily deliberately avoided eye contact as she made quick work of helping Sue clean up. When all the dishes were stowed away and she had nothing else to do, she finally met Sue's gaze.

Her eyes had the piercing quality of an Interpol interrogator. "Colin Reese?"

"Yeah." Emily glanced around. "You don't have any cookies left over, do you? I feel like something sweet."

"Colin Reese," Sue repeated, refusing to be sidetracked. "Colin I'm-too-sexy-for-Tall-Pines, guy-you've-crushed-on-since-high-school Reese."

Emily sighed. She should have known she wouldn't get away with this. "That's the one."

Sue let out a frustrated huff. "Weren't you the one that was telling me you want to break your celibacy streak?"

"Colin isn't a candidate," Emily countered. *At least he shouldn't have been.* "Besides, he's just staying in my apartment, that's all."

Sue rolled her eyes. "Don't kid a kidder, Em. You've got a sexy guy in your apartment. Even out of practice, you can't tell me you haven't considered simply seducing the guy."

Emily bit her lip. *I've done more than consider it.* That was the problem. "It's complicated."

"Doesn't have to be."

She frowned. "Remember J. P. Webster? The hotelier that I've been e-mailing?"

"The woman?"

"Yes," Emily said, grimacing. "Well, she offered to share her room with Colin already." She put obvious emphasis on the word *share*. "And apparently she's completely his type, so he's probably going to take her up on it."

"Oh," Sue said. Then her eyes narrowed. "So if he's probably not going to use your place…why are you asking to stay here?"

Emily froze. "Uh…"

"Oh. My. God." Sue let out a squeal of excitement. "You guys *already did it!*"

There was a problem with having a hair-trigger blush reflex, Emily realized. It was like walking around attached to a lie detector. Her cheeks heated, and she braced herself for the onslaught.

"Details!" Sue crowed, tugging Emily toward the kitchen table and nudging her into a chair. "I want details!"

Her husband stuck his head in again. "Honey…"

"Not now!" Sue said. "Emily has dirt to dish!"

Smirking, he retreated.

"I wasn't supposed to tell anyone," Emily said. "And you'd better not say anything to anybody, got that?"

"Of course," Sue reassured her. "So spill. How was it?"

Emily sighed…then smiled. "There are no words."

"So *that's* why you looked so floaty and happy this morning," Sue marveled. "I should've guessed you'd gotten laid."

"I wouldn't quite put it that way," Emily said. Then grinned. "But, yeah."

"How many times?"

Emily's blush intensified. "Er…four." She mentally counted again—her body tingling with each memory. "Wait—five. I forgot the shower."

"In the shower!" Sue clapped her hands girlishly. "And *five* times? What, were you guys popping vitamin E every hour or what?"

"I've been saving up for two years, you know," Emily said

wryly. "I don't know what his excuse was, but he certainly didn't seem tired." If anything, he'd been as good the last time as he was the first.

She wondered how he'd hold up a second night.

Not that you're going to find out.

"So what's the deal?" Sue said. "Why aren't you going back there and trying to break your record with six in one night?"

Emily fidgeted. "It was supposed to be the one night, nothing more."

"So what? Tell me that's not the only thing that's stopping you."

"And there was the Joy thing—her inviting him up to her room."

"Did he say yes?" Sue asked, eyes narrowed to slits.

"Well…no." Emily sighed. "But he wouldn't say yes right in front of me, would he?"

"Not if he knows what's good for him," Sue muttered darkly. "So why don't you ask him what he's going to do?"

"I don't want to put him on the spot," Emily said.

"Did he say he wanted to stay with you?"

Emily remembered that morning when she'd tried to turn him away—the look in his eyes, the subtle, sensual brush of his fingertips. "Well, yes."

"So there you are," Sue stated matter-of-factly. "He wants you."

"But Mr. Albee saw us and I think he made some assumptions."

"Evelyn's husband?" Sue let out a low whistle. "Oh. I guess you'll be hearing about that one."

"And Colin's family was at breakfast—and then they jumped all over the Joy thing."

"Oh." Sue sat quiet for a minute.

"So what do you think?" Emily asked, chewing on her lip. "Is it okay if I stay here? I just don't want to deal with him."

"I love you like a sister, you know that," Sue said warmly.

"Thanks," Emily said, feeling grateful.

"That's why I'm not letting you stay here."

"Wait!" Emily said, the grateful feeling evaporating. "What?"

"You're copping out. The guy asked to stay with you, you said yes. Somebody else hit on him, but he didn't take her up on it. So that means he still wants you," Sue pointed out. "And I'm guessing you still want him. Am I wrong?"

Emily slowly shook her head.

"So after the town meeting, go home, find the guy and enjoy yourself," Sue ordered in a tone that brooked no discussion.

"But what about the gossip?"

"*Screw* the gossip," she said. "There's always gossip. You should be flattered to be considered a hot topic for a change."

Emily paused a moment, stunned. Then giggled.

"I didn't think about it that way," she said, feeling tickled.

"I know. Emily Stanfield, town pillar, yada yada."

The feeling of amusement ebbed. A dim echo of her father's voice reverberated in her mind.

A Stanfield never does anything to cause unflattering discussion.

"Yeah," Emily agreed, feeling bitter. "Town pillar. That's me."

Sue could obviously tell she was still worried. She squeezed her shoulders. "Really—don't worry about it. They might speculate a little, but you've done nothing to give them anything to really talk about."

"And I'm trying to keep it that way," Emily pointed out.

"Em, it's going to be cold damned comfort to have on your tombstone 'She never gave anybody anything to gossip about.' Now head home and boink Colin's brains out."

Emily laughed ruefully. "I have to go to the town meeting. Then I'll decide what to do about Colin."

Sue rolled her eyes. "Okay. It's your life. You've gotta do what you've gotta do."

Emily hugged her. "Still think I should date Tim?"

"Why not?" Sue asked, surprising her. "Colin's a fling. Tim's a keeper."

"Right," Emily said, feeling her stomach drop.

"Hey, there's nothing wrong with a fling, though," Sue said. "It spices things up before you settle down. In fact, in your case, I strongly recommend a fling."

"Right," Emily repeated, and got her coat to head out to the town meeting.

Colin wasn't a keeper. He was a fling. And she could get one more night out of him, so she might as well enjoy herself.

But she'd already mooned about him all day, and then she was genuinely upset by the idea that she wasn't his type. So what was she going to do if she saw him again? She felt as if she were starting to get addicted. Maybe it'd be better to quit cold turkey.

Emily set her jaw resolutely, driving to the town hall. That was it. He'd probably leave in the next day or two. She'd just avoid him and things would work out fine. She'd barricade herself in the bathroom if she had to, but she wasn't going to get back into bed with Colin Reese, even if they did wind up sharing a room.

It was, as Sue said, cold comfort. But it was probably the smart way to go.

MAYOR TIM STOOD behind the dark cherrywood podium that had been in the town hall almost as long as the town itself had been in existence. He pounded the gavel, bringing the unruly crowd to order.

"It's nice to see so many of you here for this emergency meeting, especially considering the fact that snow is still falling," he said solemnly, the microphone crackling only slightly. "We've got a lot to discuss, but I promise I won't keep you here long."

Emily heard Sue snicker softly. There were perhaps sixty people in the auditorium, a small house by normal town meeting standards, but seeing that the "usual suspects" were present, there was no way that the meeting would be less than two hours, impromptu or not. The people who'd braved the weather were die-hard Tall Pines citizens.

Herself included, she realized with a frown.

"Why don't I start off with concerns from the floor?" Tim said, shuffling a few papers and readying a pen.

There was a cacophony of volunteers. Emily glanced at her watch. Make that three hours.

Suddenly the chaos fell silent as the door to the auditorium opened with a loud, ominous creak. Like everyone else, she glanced over, curious to see who the latecomer was.

Her eyes almost popped out of her head when she recognized Colin Reese, looking cold, irritated and obviously on a mission. He scanned the crowd, who were all staring at him.

"Evening." He spoke casually, as if he'd attended these meetings all his life. "Sorry I'm late."

"No problem," Tim said graciously. "Have a seat anywhere."

Ignoring Ava and Harry Reese's waving hands, he continued looking, his eyes finally lighting on Emily. Her heart caught in her throat.

"Look who's here," Sue whispered in a low singsong.

"Hush," Emily said, snapping her eyes forward. Still, she couldn't help but feel the rush of blood in her veins.

He hated Tall Pines events, especially the free-for-all discussion and endless opining of the theatrical town meetings. He'd probably rather be tossed into a snowbank naked than show up here tonight. But he was here—and he was, from the looks of it, searching for her.

Since Emily had sat toward the back of the auditorium, it didn't look odd for him to sit just behind them. Sue shot him a quick, mischievous smile before snuggling up against her husband in the adjoining chair. Emily tried hard not to turn and look at Colin.

He leaned forward, his voice only barely audible. "I wanted to talk to you," he said.

She shook her head. "This isn't a good place," she murmured back, still not turning.

"I know," he said. "But you kept hiding out. I figured you'd be here and I thought I'd come to you."

She felt the telltale blush heat her cheeks. She *had* been hiding. But the way he put it made her seem so cowardly.

Damn it. It wasn't as if she had sex all the time so she could be cavalier about these things—no matter how she'd made it sound before she'd slept with him.

You're being silly.

"So you tell me when and where," he whispered, "and we'll…talk."

With that, he fell silent.

She felt the burning intensity of his gaze on the back of her head throughout the next hour as the town discussed the state of the roads, the blizzard, the people stranded here in town, the possible repercussions for the Otter Lodge gift exchange and, most importantly, the annual Holiday Ball. They pondered the problems as seriously as if the world's fate hung on each decision.

As far as Emily was concerned, the conversations sounded like a buzzing monotone. She found it impossible to focus on anything but the presence of the man sitting behind her.

After an hour and a half, Mayor Tim suggested a break for coffee and the delicious snacks provided by Mrs. Albee, which everyone dived for gratefully. Emily looked at Sue. "I'm going to the ladies' room," she said, more to escape than anything. She exchanged pleasantries without thinking as she threaded through the crowd, making her way to the door that led to the hallway.

She didn't have to look behind her to know that Colin was here, following her, just far enough away not to draw attention.

Once she got out in the hallway, the chill of the air was a welcome relief compared to the heat of all the bodies in the auditorium. The sound of her heels clacking against the old wood floors echoed in the empty air. She headed down the hallway, away from the restrooms, toward the offices.

Within minutes, Colin emerged, looking up and down the hallway. She motioned to him silently and he followed.

She'd been coming to the town hall since she was five years old, when her uncle was mayor. She knew every room in the place. Glancing around to ensure they weren't seen, Emily opened a door marked Boiler Room and took him down a narrow flight of stairs. The door shut behind them.

"This is new," he said when they reached the bottom of the stairs. The room was warm, thanks to the furnace, and was strewn with various cleaning equipment, old cast-off furniture and bric-a-brac. "Do you come here often?"

She shrugged. "I wanted to talk to you and I didn't want anyone else to hear," she explained. "First off, you're right. I *was* hiding today."

"I know."

She rubbed her arms as if cold. This was so hard. "I don't sleep with people often," she said. "And this has gotten a little more complicated than I expected."

He sighed, leaning against the cinder block wall. "I tried to warn you," he said. "Before we did anything. I wasn't sure if you knew what you were getting into."

"I knew what I was getting into…if it was only the one night," Emily countered. "Then you showed up again, and suddenly it wasn't quite so simple."

"Are you sorry we did it?"

His voice was casual, deceptively so. But his green eyes blazed like emeralds in firelight.

She couldn't help it. She touched his face with her hand, stroking the harsh planes of his cheek. "Of course not," she said, and her sincerity rang in her voice.

He let out a breath, and she watched his body relax almost imperceptibly.

"But I wasn't expecting to feel this much," she admitted, and her voice sounded small.

He smiled then, and this time Colin was the one offering comfort. He took her into his arms, wrapping her in his embrace. She felt herself ease against him, enjoying the way his hands stroked down her back.

It felt wonderful. Beyond wonderful.

Soon, though, her body started remembering the night before, and the gentle, reassuring feel of him started to turn to something beyond mere comfort. He leaned his head down, tilting her head with a gentle nudge of his fingertips. Then he kissed her, softly at first, then with growing insistence.

She moaned against his mouth, feeling heat explode through her that had nothing to do with the furnace. Hunger tore at her, surprising her. Her hands slipped beneath his jacket, rubbing against his sweater impatiently. Then, without thinking, she sneaked beneath the waistband of his sweater and felt the hot flesh of his chest beneath her fingertips. He acknowledged her action with a sharp, pleased intake of breath.

He slipped off her jacket, letting it fall to the floor, and he opened the buttons of her blouse, just a few, until her lacy bra was revealed.

Emily knew it was foolish—there was a town meeting going on mere feet away, right up the stairs.

But nobody knows you're here, some wicked part of her

mind reassured her, and then all thoughts ceased when Colin leaned down and took her nipple in his mouth, licking it through the lace. She gasped, arching her back to allow him better access. She felt as if she were on fire.

"I've been thinking of you all day," he said, his words burning against her skin. "I can't stop thinking about you."

"I can't stop thinking about you, either," she murmured, forcing his jacket off and rubbing the broad expanse of his shoulders. "You're amazing."

He grinned wolfishly. "I'm staying with you tonight," he said, pausing to see if she'd say no.

She thought about it. This was an opportunity she'd never get again... and one she'd dreamed of. Still, one thing needed to be clear.

"So you're not staying with Joy?" she heard herself ask and winced.

Colin looked puzzled for a second, then chuckled. "You weren't jealous of that lady, were you?"

She bit her lip. "I don't know. This is all new to me." She frowned at his obvious amusement. "And apparently she *is* your type."

He pressed a kiss against her neck, causing her heartbeat to race. "You're my type. You're perfect. Believe me—all I want is you."

She thrilled at the sound of his longing, and she held him tight, rubbing her body against his shamelessly.

"Why, Miss Stanfield," he said, easing off her blouse. "I never would have guessed you'd be necking with that Reese boy in the town hall."

She felt wicked...and powerful. "That's not all I'm going to be doing," she said, producing a condom from her purse.

He blinked at her, and she laughed to find he was finally shocked. "Here?" he croaked.

She didn't say anything. Instead she unbuttoned her pants, inching the waistband down. "Unless you don't want me."

His eyes gleamed. Then he kissed her, hard, and she felt herself go damp between her legs. She'd never done anything so wanton, or reckless. And, honestly, she'd never done anything that felt so deliriously decadent.

He slipped a hand down her panties, his fingers sliding into her already slick opening, and she whimpered with pleasure.

"I want you," he whispered roughly, unbuttoning his pants and tugging them down. "Seems like I've always wanted you."

Emily knew how he felt. She let her pants and panties drop to the floor, standing there naked in front of him. "Then have me."

Colin groaned as she rolled the condom on his rock-hard erection and then leaned against the wall. He pressed against her, picking her up with his strong arms and hooking her legs around his waist. He entered her quickly, and she leaned her head against his shoulder, reveling in the feel of him filling her. *Fulfilling* her.

"Emily," he moaned, drawing back, then returning, slowly drawing the hard line of his shaft against her clit with deliberate motions.

She made soft sounds of excitement, surprising herself. This was crazy, she thought briefly.

This was *incredible*.

She locked her legs around his waist, pushing him in deeper, and he started to increase in tempo. She felt the climax roar through her, shocking her with its swiftness and intensity. Emily cried out, and he quickly covered her mouth with his, swallowing her sounds of ecstasy. Shortly thereafter, she did the same as he groaned his pleasure against her, shuddering into her.

Long moments later, he was breathing hard against her neck. Clarity hit her in a wave.

"I can't believe this. We had sex in the town hall," she marveled, feeling a mix of embarrassment and abandon.

"And just think," he said, kissing her, "nobody up there will know."

She closed her eyes. "You bring out the strangest things in me," she admitted softly.

"Run along to the meeting," he told her. "I'm going back to the inn. I'll be waiting for you."

That sentence was a promise. They straightened out their clothes and crept upstairs. Emily could hear Tim trying futilely to get the group back to order. No one saw them leave the boiler room, and Colin shot her one last heated glance before leaving the building. She headed for the auditorium, checked her clothes one more time and went in, wondering if the truth of what had just happened would somehow be stamped on her like an invisible beacon.

To her surprise, some part of her did not care.

"All right, back to business," Tim said forcefully, and the crowd sat down, going quiet.

Sue stared at her quizzically. "Where were you?"

Emily didn't say anything, smiling silently. Through the rest of the town meeting she drifted in a dreamy state, letting the sensual anticipation build…knowing that, whatever else happened, she had at least one more unforgettable night ahead of her.

5

COLIN STOOD nervously in the middle of Emily's living room. He wasn't sure why he was nervous—after all, he'd already had sex with Emily multiple times in the past twenty-four hours. Once in a public place, he thought with a surprised grin. He ought to be relaxed about all of it.

Hell, he ought to be exhausted. But somehow his body kept springing to attention at the mere thought of her.

What is going on here?

It was a question his conscience was raising more and more steadily during his extended stay in Tall Pines in general, and around Emily specifically. He still had a bizarre love-hate relationship with the town: it was adorable, picturesque and still managed to push every one of his buttons. Beyond that, despite the relative brevity of his relationships, he really wasn't all that fond of one-night flings, either.

So why her? And why here?

Colin shook his head. He didn't have any answers, and that worried him.

Instead of brooding, he busied himself readying the apartment for her. They'd left the place a mess after their romp last night—the sheets tangled in a sweaty knot on the bed, the thick down comforter on the floor, food left out on the countertop, empty champagne glasses on the coffee table. He laid a fire in the fireplace, warming the place and giving it the cozy, homey atmosphere he'd soaked up his first night there. He tidied up the kitchen and bedroom, washing the dishes, changing the sheets and turning down the bed. As a joke, he even put small foil-wrapped chocolates on the pillows. It *was* a hotel, after all. Then he considered how he should get himself ready.

Should he be waiting naked? That seemed crass—and even though it was obvious they were going to have sex, for whatever reason he didn't want her to think that was the *only* thing he wanted from her. He genuinely liked her as a person, though what he knew of her was limited to what he'd gleaned from a distance—they had lived separate lives growing up here. She'd always seemed unapproachable: the heiress apparent, the mayor's niece, the golden girl of Tall Pines. He couldn't understand her fascination with the small town. Or how she could manage to please so many people by doing everything so damned perfectly.

But he was starting to discover just how pleasing that perfection could be, Colin thought with a grin. Because last night and this morning—and this evening in the boiler room—she'd been, indeed, perfect. The thing that delighted him was that it had been so unexpected. He'd been reluctantly attracted to her for years, but now that he'd had her, the constant surprise of her, the hidden depths, kept intriguing him.

When she walked in, he was still grinning. "Hi, dear," he joked. "How was the rest of the—humph."

His sentence was cut off as Emily launched herself into his arms, pressing her heated, mobile mouth to his. Her tongue quickly darted out, tracing his lips before coaxing his own into some serious sensual fencing. His cock went from semihard to rock hard in a nanosecond. He pulled back, staring at her in amazement.

Her violet-blue eyes were like crushed wet velvet, deep and dark. She smiled at him. "I'm glad to be home," she said around a sigh.

"I'm glad you're home myself," he said, forgetting for a second that this wasn't actually *his* home.

Her responding look of happiness was like staring into the sun, and for a second he was blinded by her radiance. Then, without hesitation, she took off her glasses and started to strip, letting clothes drop to the floor.

"Whoa," he said, halting her as she had her blouse unbuttoned and was hastily moving to her jeans. "No rush here."

"I know," she murmured, "but the boiler room…well, let's just say it got my appetite going."

He knew how she felt. It had been quick and furtive and intense…and it made him want to do it again, only more slowly and thoroughly. Still, he hadn't thought that she'd simply walk in and they'd pick up where they left off. Not that he ought to be protesting. Maybe he was too tired. Hell, maybe he was getting too old.

Maybe you want to try talking to her. Figure out why she's different.

Colin ignored his conscience's low, insistent promptings. "Maybe I need a little breather." He then cursed himself mentally when her face fell. "Not from you. I'm working on about an hour's sleep and I want to make sure that I do a good job."

Her face eased into a comfortable smile. "Trust me, you're doing absolutely fine."

His muscles bunched eagerly, and he forced himself to sit and calm down. He patted the sofa cushion next to him. "Come on. Why don't we talk for a bit? Ease into it."

Emily looked surprised but sat as he requested. She did leave her blouse open, though, revealing the delicate white lace bra he'd snacked on a mere hour ago. Her cleavage hung temptingly just a touch below eye level. She leaned against his shoulder, presenting her breasts like a display as her eyes gleamed innocently. "What did you want to talk about?"

Now? His mind went blank. "Uh…what have you been doing since I've been out of town?" he asked finally. "I mean, besides the hotel."

"I went to college," she murmured, moving sinuously so her body pressed against his. She placed a slow, delicate kiss in the hollow of his collarbone. "Got my degree in English Lit."

That schoolgirl thing again. He could picture her in the library, her hair pulled back, glasses low on her nose as she pored over a book…legs crossed in a short plaid skirt. His cock throbbed at the mere thought of it.

Easy, he chastised himself. "Couldn't wait to get back to Tall Pines, huh?" he asked, closing his eyes and reveling in the feel of her hand creeping under his sweater, her mouth brushing a lazy line of kisses along his jaw. He couldn't help it. His arm went around her shoulders, holding him to her, his hand smoothing down the tangled silk of her hair.

She paused in her sensual exploration, and he leaned down, nuzzling her neck in return. "Actually, I really liked college," she said slowly. "I even thought about going to grad school in England."

That stopped him. "Really?" The Tall Pines poster girl going off to Europe? "Why didn't you?"

Her eyes grew clouded. "My father got sick. Mom needed help. I knew where my responsibility was."

She sounded so sad. He cursed himself for bringing up the subject out of sheer ignorance. Still, it brought up another issue, and as long as the mood was already serious… "Then your father died," he said. "I'm sorry."

"So was I," she said, and with that Emily pulled away, closing her blouse with one hand, obviously not realizing what she was doing. Now he really felt like a heel. "Before he died, he reminded me that I was the last Stanfield in the line. I was with him in the hospital when he passed. My mother remarried two months later to a man named Ray, a longtime family friend. They moved to Florida. I'm sure your mother probably told you all about that."

His eyes rounded and he shook his head.

"It was a big scandal at the time," she explained, pulling her knees up to her chest and hugging them to her. "She wanted to sell the house and get the hell out of Tall Pines. Dad loved Tall Pines, and it meant so much to him for the mansion to stay in the family.... Anyway, I kept the house, made it a hotel and, well, here we are."

She shrugged, the sentence succinct and deliberately casual—and obviously covering a world of pain. She smiled, but it didn't reach her eyes.

"Suddenly I don't feel like talking." She put her head against his shoulder.

They sat that way, silent, for a moment. For all their sexual interplay, he'd never felt anything as disturbingly intimate as this moment, with a woman in his arms, quietly embracing him in front of a cheerful crackling fire on a snowy night. It was as if they were the only two people in the world.

Colin didn't know what it was about this woman—and suddenly he didn't care. All he knew was she was special and he was going to stop analyzing and start enjoying.

He tilted her head back, kissing her sweetly. "We were far too rushed there in the town hall," he pointed out.

She giggled, then looked at him solemnly. "Definitely."

"I don't think I can go five times again tonight," he said, "but I think I can make one time really, really memorable."

She pursed her lips, teasing. "I suppose the least I could do is let you try."

He tugged her blouse the rest of the way off, then opened the front clasp of her bra, freeing her lovely breasts. Despite the warmth of the fire, her nipples were puckered and pointed.

Topless, she undid the button of his fly, unzipping it and moving her nimble fingers through the gap in his boxers, releasing his cock. Her fingers circled him, and he groaned, pressing forward lightly as a drop of moisture escaped the tip in anticipation.

She leaned down, licking around the head in a tantalizing gesture, then stroked the shaft with steady, gliding pressure. His hips arched again against her palm. "Damn, woman," he breathed. "What are you doing to me?"

"If you don't know, maybe I'm not doing it right."

"Oh, you're doing it fine," he said. "Let's see if I can't catch you up."

He eased off the rest of her clothes, leaving them on a heap on the floor, then rested her against the smooth suedelike fabric of her sofa. "We've already done the floor," he explained, and she laughed. Colin stripped off his clothes and stood naked in front of her, as she parted her legs and waited expectantly.

He shook his head. "Not so fast, remember?" He positioned himself between her thighs but didn't move to enter her. Instead he teased her breasts with his tongue, tracing a wet, winding path around her rib cage and belly button, stroking her nipples with his fingertips. He felt Emily's fingers wind through his hair, heard the way her breathing grew short and choppy. He moved lower, heading for her moist heat, and she tightened her thighs against him.

Slowly he used his fingertips to gently coax her legs apart. She was already wet and ready for him, but her eyes looked nervous. Obviously this wasn't something she'd done very often, and he felt anger on her behalf. She deserved to be lavished over.

He was going to rectify that situation.

He dipped his tongue in, licking at her clit, gently at first, then with growing insistence. Her breathing went ragged and hoarse, her hands bunching into fists against the sofa. She moved against him in jerky, reflexive motions, as if the sheer sensation of what he was doing was more than she could control. Keeping his tongue in motion, he deliberately pressed one finger inside her, then another, searching for the corresponding spot inside.

He knew when he found it. She cried out, a sound of joyous surprise, and she lifted her body to meet his seeking mouth.

He kept up the pace, feeling her pressing against him, tasting the honeyed wash of her response. She was panting, short gasps of sexual exertion. She smoothed her hands over her breasts, exciting him as he watched her obvious enjoyment of her own flesh as well as his tender ministrations.

"Colin," she breathed. *"Colin!"*

He felt her body clench against his fingers, and he almost came on the spot.

When the shudders finished, he clumsily put on a condom, intent on entering her, but before he could, she pressed against his shoulders, surprising him enough to push him on his back. Slick and smooth from her release, she impaled herself on him, and he felt the taut snugness of her envelop him, creating an almost unbearable friction.

Then she started to move, rocking against him with the slightest twist to her hips. Caressing him and carrying him to a frenzy of sensation.

He lost control, plunging into her as she rode him with abandon. He clutched at her hips, drawing her to him, and she pushed back with answering intensity. Before he knew it, the climax roared through him like a wildfire. He sat up, holding her to him even as he buried himself in her welcoming warmth, and she wrapped her legs and arms around him in response.

In the aftermath, they were both breathing hard, clinging to each other like the survivors of a storm…and it was a sort of storm, he realized.

"You do the strangest things to me," he said when he could at last find his voice.

"This is a week I'll certainly never forget." She laughed unsteadily.

And that's when it hit him.

He'd stopped thinking of it as simply a few nights. He was thinking forever. Colin didn't know why or how, but there it was.

I'm supposed to go to Paris, he thought. *I've got a career I love, a building project that's starting, people counting on me. I've got a life that suits me perfectly.*

The last thing he needed was a relationship with a woman who had dedicated her life to a town that he'd spent years trying to escape. Especially when he had no idea how his life and her life could possibly fit together…

THE OTTER LODGE annual gift exchange was a running joke and one of Emily's favorite town traditions—and considering the buffet of traditions the town of Tall Pines had to choose from, that was saying something. It had all started about twenty years ago—which was recent for a tradition, by Tall Pines standards—when the men of the Otter Lodge had complained to each other about several of the gifts they'd received for Christmas. Seeing that "one man's trash was another man's treasure," they'd devised a "gift exchange" where people could swap, steal, and otherwise have a great deal of fun with small gift items. It was a way of prolonging the holiday and also of celebrating Christmas with friends rather than the small family gatherings that typically prevailed. It was also usually rowdy, liberally doused with the infamous and heavily alcohol-laced Otter punch and, all in all, a rousing good time.

Emily's father hadn't approved of the gift exchange initially, thinking it lacked decorum. It was the one tradition above all others that her mother had refused to attend—even though she'd made a point of bowing to Emily's father's wishes and was a central figure of all the other town functions. But from the first time she was allowed to go, at sixteen years old, Emily had reveled wide-eyed in the spectacle.

She was wearing a pair of black jeans, a burgundy turtleneck sweater and a large paper top hat festooned with a flower.

"What are you exchanging?" the head of the Otter Lodge, John Lambert, asked with a wink.

Emily held up her gift, grinning broadly. Actually, it hadn't been a gift—at this point, people tended to buy the most outrageous "gifts" and concoct stories about them, and that, too, was part of the tradition.

"What have we here?" Phil crowed into the microphone, causing people to pause momentarily in their carousing. "An adult-size set of full-body pajamas with feet!"

There was a resounding drunken cheer at this. He opened the package, holding it up. Much like an infant's "footie" pajamas, it buttoned up from the crotch to the neck and had slip-resistant rubber soles on the feet. It was baby-blue and looked as if it could fit a six-foot man easily.

"It's even got a back door, folks!" Phil pointed out, unbuttoning the flap that covered the backside. This brought an even louder round of applause. "Now who's going to want *this* beauty?"

Emily grinned as several venerable members of the Otter Lodge quickly went to work bargaining for the pajamas, offering her their awful gifts: a battery-powered egg sheller, chocolate-covered ants and, finally, edible boxers.

"I'll go with the boxers," she said, tucking her exchanged gift under her arm as the seventy-year-old man promptly started to try the pajamas on over his regular clothes, to much hilarity.

People started catcalling about her choice, and she made comments back. "Hey! You never know. I might need them!"

"Woo-hoo! Better watch it, Tim!" Phil said. "That Emily Stanfield's a live one!"

Emily blushed, as usual, but more because he'd mentioned Tim than because of the gift. This was why her parents had hated the gift exchange. It was classless, tasteless and often a bit risqué.

In short, it was everything a Stanfield *wasn't* supposed to be.

I wonder if that's why I like it so much?

Emily frowned. Strange, she'd never really thought about it in that light before.

She blamed this latest epiphany on Colin. She felt as though she'd been living on autopilot for the past few years, going through the motions of being a Tall Pines Stanfield without ever really looking at why she was doing what she was doing. She was discomfited now to discover that, even after studying it carefully, she *still* didn't know why she was doing some of the things she was doing. Other than Stanfield duty, of course.

Ordinarily that was enough.

You're just feeling restless.

She smiled. She blamed that sensation on Colin, as well. And thanked him for it.

Her ex-fiancé, Rick, a man of exceptional breeding if not much imagination, had been a nice enough guy but, comparatively speaking, a lousy lover. And her high school boyfriend, Billy Rothchild, had been a virgin, just as she had. What they'd lacked in finesse they'd made up for in sheer enthusiasm…and now that she knew the difference, Emily realized enthusiasm didn't count for a whole lot.

She wasn't in high school anymore. While she liked sex a great deal, she'd managed to go without for two whole years.

I'm glad I waited. It made her experience with Colin that much sweeter.

Of course, he might be leaving any day. The roads were cleared, the blizzard was over. He could be gone by tonight.

Don't think about it. She focused instead on the edible underwear, made out of what looked like pressed dried fruit leather. She would have a great time trying it out on Colin when she got home.

"Emily!"

She looked up to see Mayor Tim flagging her down, with the Reeses in tow. "Hi, Tim," she replied, then hugged Ava and Harry Reese, feeling guilty.

Hi, I've been sleeping with your son.

"Thank you so much for taking care of our son," Ava said without preamble.

Emily blinked. "Sorry?"

"In your hotel," Ava clarified, and Emily felt her heart start beating again. For a brief second she'd thought that Ava had found out about exactly where Colin was staying in the hotel—specifically their sleeping arrangements. "Especially when you had to put up so many other people. I hate to admit it, but the hotel really has been a success."

Emily laughed. Ava went red-faced.

"That sounded awful, didn't it?" she fussed. "I didn't mean that I wanted you to fail. I just… I mean…"

"It's hard to see things change, I know," Emily said gently. Despite Ava's relentless tenacity, she really was a sweet woman.

"You live in a town like this because it doesn't change. Not really," Ava said, holding her husband's hand and giving it a squeeze. He kissed her temple. For a second Emily was struck by their tenderness toward each other. They seemed like polar opposites—she was talkative and outgoing, he was retiring and wry—but somehow they made a perfect match. "We love it here. We always thought we'd settle down, raise our kids here, watch our grandkids grow around us."

It did sound nice, Emily thought.

"If only Colin saw things the same way," Ava finished with a frustrated gesture. "He didn't stay with that blond woman, did he? That friend of yours?"

"No," Emily reassured her. "I know for a fact that he didn't."

"Has she gone home?"

"No, she's here through the New Year at least," Emily said. Joy had extended her reservation, she was having such a good time.

"Did Colin tell you he's moving to Paris?"

"It did come up," Emily demurred.

"Why so far away, is what I want to know," Ava carped. "When he's got family and comfort and…and home right here."

Emily bit her lip. "Maybe he's looking for something else," she ventured, wondering herself why he hated Tall Pines so much. Sure, it was a little town. And quirky. And it had a lot of traditions. And, yeah, it really was pretty knee-jerk about any sort of change.

Okay. Maybe she *could* see why someone who loved living larger than life might not be so keen on Tall Pines. And he definitely lived on a larger scale, no doubt about it. Even as a teen, the town hadn't been big enough to contain him. The sheer artistry of his elaborate pranks alone had bordered on creative genius. When he'd won a full scholarship to architectural school, the townsfolk had been shocked.

Not Emily. Colin had been destined for great things and had planned to leave Tall Pines if he'd had to shoot himself out on a rocket.

"Something better than this?" Ava asked, astounded. "What else is there?"

Before Emily could answer, Colin walked up, a glass of

punch in one hand and a scowl on his face. "I got a Chia Pet." He held up a small clay figurine that looked like a sheep.

"Nice," Emily observed, tongue-in-cheek.

He ran his tongue along his teeth, amused. "It was this or some kind of Super Orgasm hot chocolate. From the *reverend,* if you can believe it."

Emily giggled. "Imagine going to Paris and leaving all this behind."

He grinned reluctantly. Ava pounced on the expression. "See? I told you this would be fun!"

Instantly the grin slid from his face like a blackboard being erased. "Mom…"

"I know, I know," she grumbled. But she didn't look deterred.

"Your mother was thanking Emily for putting you up over at the hotel," Harry Reese said quickly, eager to patch over the awkward break.

Emily blushed. "It's my job."

"Well, you do your job well," Harry said. It might have been the longest conversation she'd ever had with the man with Ava present. "Everyone knows that the hotel is one of the best things to happen to Tall Pines. We don't know what we'd do without you."

Emily had been trying hard not to stare at Colin—and equally hard not to look as if she were trying hard not to stare. Harry's comment surprised her. "Well, I doubt you'll ever have to find out. I imagine I won't be going anywhere."

"Naturally you wouldn't, dear," Ava clucked. "You're the last Stanfield. Where would you go?"

Emily sneaked a look at Colin. The scowl was back in full force. "So, Colin…"

"I'm getting some more punch," he said, sounding truculent. "Then I think I'll walk over to the hotel."

"Are you all right, dear?"

"I have a headache." He turned and walked toward the re-
freshment table.

Ava huffed impatiently. "He really needs to loosen up more,"
she observed to her husband. The two of them went off to
dance.

Emily waited, then followed Colin to the table. Sidling up
next to him, careful not to stand too close, she whispered,
"Wait till you see what I got from the gift exchange. It's a lot
better than a Chia Pet."

"Listen, I have to get out of here."

She'd been expecting some playful banter, and his serious
tone gave her pause. "You okay?"

"Holiday hangover," he said bitterly. "I'm leaving."

Emily frowned. His tone sounded…final. "Are you going
to be in my apartment when I get back?" she asked in a soft
voice.

He finally looked at her, and his eyes seemed haunted.
"Honestly," he replied in an equally soft voice, "I don't know."

With that, he walked away. All she could do was watch him,
wondering what had caused the abrupt change…and feeling
bereft. Of all the ways for their brief affair to end, this was one
she had not anticipated.

WALKING IN THE CRISP, snow-covered landscape, Colin felt like
ten kinds of an idiot. There was something about the very air
in Tall Pines that seemed to bring out the prime jackass in him,
and this vacation was obviously no exception. He had no
excuse—and really no idea why he kept succumbing to the bad
humors that plagued him whenever he set foot in the city limits,
but there it was.

The gift exchange had been sort of fun, and he'd spent
some more time with his family without getting into the

vicious downward cycle of "Why won't you move home?" He'd been holding up rather well. But when his mother pointed out that Emily would never leave Tall Pines, and Emily had readily and without any thought agreed, he'd suddenly felt a sharp and unbelievable sense of loss—all the sharper because it was so unexpected.

Apparently his subconscious had been working overtime, subversively contemplating a future with Emily Stanfield, even though everything between them had been sexual and deliberately temporary. Even though he'd warned himself not to get involved because to even begin to consider it was the ultimate foolishness.

He lifted his face to the slate-colored sky. It wasn't snowing right at the moment, but the wind was chill and biting, scraping at his cheeks over the edges of his scarf.

"What are you doing out here?"

He looked over his shoulder and saw Emily walking after him. She'd removed the silly paper hat she'd been wearing at the Otter Lodge and now was bundled up in a black leather jacket, a thick black wool hat and matching scarf. Her black leather gloves completed the ensemble.

She looked less like a schoolteacher and more like a hit woman, and he watched her approach with equal dread.

"You can't honestly expect to drop a bomb like that on me and walk away," she said, her voice colder than the wind whipping through the town square.

"You shouldn't be out here," he dodged, stuffing his hands into his coat pockets. "People might see us together, make some assumptions."

"I don't give a damn," she retorted cavalierly, but all the same, he noticed her glancing around. Almost everyone was either still in the Otter Lodge partying or in their houses, safely tucked away from the cold. "We need to talk."

He let out an annoyed huff that came out as a puff of steam. "I shouldn't have stalked off like that," he conceded.

"You think?" Her eyes pierced him like arrows. "I know we're just having a little fling here, but I do think I expected more than a sudden and inexplicable mood swing, starting with you getting pissy and ending with you telling me that I might not ever see you again."

He winced. He *had* done that, hadn't he?

"What is your *problem*, Reese?" she said sharply. "I swear, you act like Tall Pines is Alcatraz and you're building a tunnel. I know you've been all over the world and love your glamorous women, your traveling, your parties and your high life, but what exactly is so damned wrong with living in a small town?"

"Nothing, okay?" Colin barked back, feeling cornered. "There is *nothing* wrong with living in Tall Pines. It's beautiful. The people are nice. They're concerned about each other. When something happens to one person, everyone knows about it."

"So that's the big deal?" she pressed. "You don't like the fact that we've got nosy neighbors? That they can be invasive?"

He rubbed at his eyes, the chill of his own leather gloves dulled by the numbness of his face. "It's not that."

"So what is it?" She crossed her arms like an impatient and demanding goddess.

"It's not Tall Pines. It's *me*."

She stared at him, looking confused.

"It's perfect here," he said. "It's beautiful. It's what everybody always wanted—ideal, pristine. People care. It's home."

Emily still stared, silent.

"And I never wanted it," he said. "I never, ever fit in here. And I felt like an outcast and a loser for not wanting it."

Her expression softened slightly. "Colin…"

"No, let me finish." He gritted his teeth. "When I was in high school, I didn't have many friends. But the few friends

I did have formed a sort of club. We called it the Escape Committee."

She smiled.

"We were so eager to get out of Tall Pines it was almost stupid," he continued. "And we all did get out. I got in trouble a lot, sure, but I always got good grades. Not because I necessarily loved school, but every day I was here I felt more miserable and I knew college was a ticket out."

Colin couldn't look at her, couldn't stand seeing the sympathy shining on her face when he knew there really wasn't any way she could understand. Cold seeped into his bones that had nothing to do with the weather.

"This probably all sounds ridiculous and melodramatic," he said, kicking at a snowdrift with his foot. "But every time I'm home and someone points out to me how wonderful it is here and asks why I don't want to live here, I suddenly seem to revert to being eighteen years old and feeling like a complete and utter freak."

"Colin." She reached out, putting a gloved hand on his shoulder.

He didn't shrug the comforting touch off, but he didn't step closer to her, either. "So that's my story," he said bitterly. "Stupid, huh?"

"Small-town life is not for everybody," she said. "Just because people here think it's perfect doesn't mean it is."

He shrugged, feeling juvenile—and yet still hurting. "Don't *you* think it's perfect?" he couldn't help asking.

She laughed. "Hardly. Everybody here lives in each other's pockets. If I sneeze when I get out of bed in the morning, Hank Salvatore over at the post office usually sends over some vitamin C with my mail, you know?"

He smiled reluctantly.

"And there's always the petty bickering. It's more like being part of a really big family." She shrugged. "It's not perfect, but it's home."

"That's the thing," he said. "I don't feel like it's home."

She stood next to him, silent, for a moment. Then she said, "That's what you're looking for, isn't it? That's why you move around so much." Emily paused. "You're looking for home."

He didn't say anything. He was surprised by her observation—the fact that she'd figured it out and the fact that he never had.

Without glancing around to see if they were being observed, she reached forward and hugged him. Even though her mere proximity tended to bring out a sexual zing, this felt warm…comforting.

Cozy.

He took her proffered warmth, holding her tightly to him.

"I hope you find what you're looking for," she whispered against his ear.

He held tighter for a moment before letting her go. "Let's head back to the hotel. I'm freezing off various parts of my anatomy that I know you've expressed an appreciation for."

She chuckled softly, falling into step next to him, tromping through the thick snow.

As they walked, Colin found himself still drifting in contemplation. "I have to ask," he finally said. "What makes this home for you? How do you feel living here?"

She blinked. "I don't know. I've never really thought about it."

"You love the traditions," he prompted, feeling a weight start to bear down on his chest. "You love the community."

"Some of the traditions, most of the people," she said with a wry smile. "It's a nice town."

But there was something there—some hesitation. He didn't want to pry. Oh, hell, yes, he *did*. He wanted to understand what bound her there.

He didn't want to think about why he wanted to understand.

"I guess the more I lived here, the harder it seemed to picture living anywhere else," she admitted.

That wasn't enthusiasm, he thought, with a creeping feeling of triumph, that was simply *inertia*.

"So," he asked casually, "maybe you'd be happy living somewhere else?"

"I don't know." Now she sounded troubled around the edges of her voice. "Still, what are the odds of my moving?"

They got to the hotel, and Phillip the night manager was there, shoveling the steps. He saw the two of them and smirked knowingly.

"Hey, Phillip," Emily said, either not noticing or ignoring his smugness. "How are things going?"

"The roads are clear," he informed them. "The sheriff dropped by with the latest news. Most of the strays have already gotten into their cars and left." He glared pointedly at Colin, as if to say, *So what are you waiting for?*

Emily and Colin walked into the hotel, going to the elevator and heading for her apartment on the top floor. Emily didn't say a word, but Colin knew what she was thinking.

"I don't have to be in Paris until after the new year," he said carefully. "That's a whole two days away. If you don't mind putting me up until then?"

She smiled. "No," she said quietly. "Two more days would suit me just fine."

With that, she finally kissed him, the heat of her mouth a jarring counterpoint to the cold of his skin. His blood pumped hot and fierce.

Two more days. Two more nights.

How am I going to leave her when the new year's over?

6

IT WAS THE LAST night of the year and the last night she'd be able to spend with Colin. And yet here she was dressing up to go out on a date with Mayor Tim.

Emily suspected that might be ironic somehow. It certainly felt like irony—going out on a date with the man whom it made the most sense to marry before indulging in one last night of ecstasy with the man least likely to be a husband.

She slipped on diamond earrings, checking her makeup in the mirror. Her black long-sleeved dress had a plunging back, looking both elegant and sexy, depending on where you stood. She'd bought it months ago, long before she'd even seen Colin. Or agreed to a date with Tim, for that matter.

She walked out into the living room. Colin was sitting on her couch, looking irritated.

"I suppose it would be selfish of me to ask you to cancel," he said, his voice detached.

"I have to go," she said. "Stanfields always go to the Holiday Ball. It's tradition."

It felt like an excuse. Probably because it was.

"But do they always go with the single, eligible mayor that everyone is trying to marry off?"

The sourness of his tone made her survey him with a quirked eyebrow. "That didn't sound selfish. That sounded jealous."

He grimaced. "You're right. I guess I am jealous."

Even as part of her heart thrilled at that admission, she crossed her arms, mentally schooling herself not to read into the statement. *What's he going to do? Stay here forever?*

Still, the hungry, sad look in his eye melted her heart, and she went over to him, putting her arms around him.

"I can promise you it'll be an early night. This isn't a real date, it doesn't mean anything. He won't even get to first base."

His hand tickled down her bare back, sending a shiver skittering over her nerve endings. "With a dress like this, I'm sure he'll try."

"It's not like that between Tim and me," she said, forcing herself not to curl like a cat against his palm. If she did, she might never get out of here. "It's…I don't know…like we're brother and sister."

"I never wanted to ask my sister out on a date."

She leaned back, feeling irritation warring with desire. "I want you, you know that."

He smiled, warming up. "And I want you."

"But after tonight you're going," she said quietly. "Remember?"

He fell silent.

"I have to live here. More importantly, I'm going to have a life here—without you. I don't know what it is we've got going between us, but whatever it is ends tomorrow. I can promise you I don't sleep around easily and I would never sleep with anyone else while I'm sleeping with you. But I do have to plan for life after you leave."

"And Tim is part of this plan, is he?"

"I don't know," she answered honestly.

"You said he was like your brother." Colin sounded puzzled. "How could you be happy with a life like that? Without passion?"

She stared into his eyes, willing him to understand. "I don't know if I can be. But if the alternative is living alone, waiting for some grand love affair that never shows up—or one who lives thousands of miles away," she said pointedly, "then maybe I can settle for a good lifelong friendship that might shift into something more comfortable."

He looked at her, shaking his head. "That's the other thing I can't stand about this town," he muttered. "You're all against taking risks."

Emily didn't like the way he was suddenly lumping her in with all the things he didn't like about Tall Pines. She stood up, slipping on her high heels with sharp, jerky motions.

"I took a risk with you," she finally retorted.

"Not enough to let anybody know about us."

"Know what about us?" Her voice had raised, and she clamped down on her anger before their disagreement could explode into a full-blown fight. Which, considering she rarely fought with anyone and they weren't even in a relationship, was sort of shocking in and of itself. "Know that I've slept with you without even a date? Know that I was desperate enough to have a fling with a man who can't seem to leave this place fast enough and wouldn't move back with a gun to his head?"

She tossed a lipstick and her keys into a small clutch purse. "You tell me, Colin. Exactly how should I have advertised whatever 'we' seem to have?"

He walked up behind her, tugging her into his arms. She resisted, anger still burning through her, underscored by humiliation.

My father would be so ashamed of me.

She closed her eyes against the pain of that observation.

Colin was insistent, though, finally holding her in a careful embrace. "I'm sorry," he said softly. "I'm sorry. You're absolutely right. I've got no reason whatsoever to be jealous or to take it out on you. I'm sorry."

She didn't say anything. Instead she leaned her head against his shoulder.

"I might not like the town. But I like you. More than I realized, until tonight. More than I thought I could, especially in such a short period of time."

At that, she laughed weakly. "Well, technically, we've known each other for years."

"Not like this." He tipped her chin up, pressing a slow, gentle kiss against her pliant lips. "It's more than physical. I feel like I've gotten to know you better in the past week than in the past ten years."

"I know," she marveled.

"I don't want you to feel like what we're doing is something you should be embarrassed about," he said, looking deep into her eyes.

She couldn't help it. She looked away.

She heard him growl softly with frustration, and he rubbed his chin over the top of her head as he held her tight. "This is more than just a fling," he said. "You've got to know that."

Emily wanted to believe it. But wasn't that the characteristic of a good fling? Feeling as though it would go on forever—and at the same time that intensity of knowing that it was going to end abruptly?

She'd never had one before, but that was what she'd always assumed—and whatever she had with Colin seemed to be no exception.

"I know it's selfish—and jealous," he said. "But I don't want you to go out tonight. Not out with some other man."

She shook her head, pulling herself gently away. "How many times do I have to tell you? It's not like that. It's not anything."

"It's enough," he argued.

Her phone rang and she answered it gratefully. "Hello?"

"Hi, Em," Tim said cheerfully. "I'm downstairs, ready for our date."

She winced at the term. "Okay. Let me get my coat on. I'll be down in a minute." She hung up, then looked up at Colin.

"I'll be back soon," she said. "And if you still want to enjoy our last night together, then we will. But I'm not putting my life on hold for you, Colin. Not when I know this can't go anywhere."

With that, Emily walked out the door, feeling a lot less sure than she sounded…especially when she had to turn her back on the gorgeous man staring at her each step of the way.

"THIS OUGHT TO BE fun," Joy enthused. "Thanks so much for asking me. I've been dying to check out the town's festivals—and I hear the Holiday Ball is one of their favorite occasions."

"No problem," Colin said, adjusting his tie.

This was probably a bad idea, but he was trying to prove a point. Seeing Emily walk out the door tonight felt wrong. Even though she'd assured him that nothing would happen—and correctly pointed out that it wasn't his business if anything did happen—it still felt wrong.

He wanted a relationship with her. He had no idea how that was going to work, but he knew damned well that it wasn't going to work at all if she insisted on dating other guys. Call him funny, but he felt pretty strongly about that.

"Am I dressed okay?"

He looked at Joy. She was dressed to kill in a midnight-blue velvet cocktail dress that left little to the imagination. Her blond hair was pulled up in a sexy chignon.

"You're stunning," he said. "You'll be the talk of the party."

More to the point, *they* would be the talk of the party, he thought as they walked into the mayor's mansion, where the Holiday Ball was held. The beautiful out-of-towner with the town's notoriously commitment-shy black sheep. It would probably be Tall Pines's juiciest gossip of the night. There was no way Emily wouldn't hear about it.

If she couldn't understand how he felt, then he'd have to give her a taste of her own medicine. She'd see how it felt to watch someone you cared about in the arms of someone else, platonic or not.

"Well, Colin!" Evelyn Albee was working the door, signing people in. "Of all the people I expected to see here, I certainly wasn't expecting you. And who's your lovely companion?"

"This is Joy Webster. She's a guest over at the hotel," he said, paying the entrance fee. "She had nothing to do tonight, so we figured we'd enjoy the party."

"They've outdone themselves this year," she said as she checked in their coats—and took a long, scrutinizing look at Joy's dress—or lack thereof. "You two have a good time."

"We plan to," he replied with a wink.

If that didn't get tongues wagging, nothing would.

He led Joy into the room, and for a split second the sound was reduced to a murmur as they walked in. He felt uncomfortably conspicuous and remembered abruptly why he particularly disliked these town functions. He was a bit of an introvert by nature, and while business had toughened him up, he still didn't love being in a loud and noisy crowd.

Especially now. After the initial surprise, people descended on the two of them like hawks on baby chickens.

"Colin!" This from Mr. Rutledge, one of the oldest and most venerable of the town's citizens. "It's been years! What have you been doing with yourself? And more importantly, who's this pretty lady?"

Colin introduced Joy around, and she was winning, charming and very, very outgoing—something of a relief, since it took the pressure off him. He endured several winks and nudges. Automatically, it seemed, they'd paired the two off. The place was probably ripe with conjecture: Were they having an affair? Had Colin Reese finally fallen in love?

The damned thing being he was pretty sure he *had* fallen in love. Just not with Joy Webster.

"I wasn't expecting to see you here."

He turned at the masculine comment, only to find that the mayor himself had made the comment…and Emily was right there by his side.

"I'm getting that a lot tonight," Colin said, his voice wry. "We didn't have anything else to do and thought we'd drop by."

"Emily, this is fantastic," Joy gushed. "And your town does stuff like this all the time? It's like being transported into a Norman Rockwell painting!"

"So glad we're entertaining," Emily said.

Joy looked taken aback by Emily's chilly demeanor. "I'm not being condescending. I mean it. I love it here."

Her sincerity must have made Emily feel guilty. "I'm sorry," she said. "Sometimes people get the mistaken impression that because we're quaint, we're also hicks, and they write Tall Pines off as a lame small town."

Colin was the one who felt guilty, even though Emily hadn't glanced his way once as she'd made the comment.

"Beautiful, sure. But lame?" Joy shook her head. "What idiot would think this gorgeous little place was lame?"

Now Emily looked at Colin. He cleared his throat, uncomfortable.

"I could live here," Joy enthused, smiling brightly. Colin stared at her, surprised. He knew that she was bubbly by nature, but he hadn't realized just how much she really loved the small town. "This has been just the change of pace I've been looking for…and I didn't know how badly I needed it until I got here." She gave Colin's arm a squeeze.

"Well, I'm glad *you're* having a good time," Emily replied.

There it was again—that tone. This time Joy didn't pick up on it, but Colin felt it like an ice pick in his chest.

"Could you direct me to the ladies' room? I want to make sure my hair's okay," Joy asked Emily, and Emily excused herself, leaving Colin with Tim.

"It's good to see you here tonight," Tim said, taking a sip of his drink. "Your parents are such huge supporters of the town, and I know they miss seeing you."

Colin felt like a world-class jerk. "It's good to be here," he responded, trying hard not to sound like a sham.

"And that's some date," Tim said, letting out a low, appreciative whistle. "Your mom always said you dated supermodels."

"She's an acquaintance," Colin pointed out quickly. "Someone I met at the inn. She didn't have anything to do, so I thought I'd take her out for a bit. Nothing more than that."

Tim's face showed he wasn't buying it. "Must be nice. Living the dream, huh?"

"What about you?" Colin said. "Here you are, mayor for two terms and you're just, what, thirty-six?" He paused. "And now dating Emily."

"Yeah," Tim said, taking another sip. "It's all falling into place. The thing is, she's like royalty around here. Not to mention she'd be a perfect politician's wife."

Colin stared at him, aghast. "You're going to *marry* her?"

The crowd went quiet at that statement. Tim rubbed at his temples with his fingertips.

"Why does everyone feel compelled to yell that particular observation?" he asked, sounding embarrassed yet amused. "I don't know if I'm going to marry her. All I know is we're good friends, I haven't met anybody who fits the bill better and she'd be a great politician's wife. That doesn't necessarily mean she'd be *my* great politician's wife."

"But you're trying it on," Colin supplied, feeling ire bubble through his bloodstream. He strongly repressed the urge to clock good old Tim with a strong right hook.

"No. *She's* trying it on," Tim corrected, and Colin didn't feel any better. "Despite what town gossip spreads, we're just friends."

Colin felt his heart rate slowly calm back down. Until Tim's next statement.

"For now, anyway," he amended. "By Valentine's Day, I imagine, we'll know if it's more than that."

Colin saw red, and it had nothing to do with Valentine's.

Joy returned to them, but Emily was nowhere to be seen. "Where's Emily?" he asked.

Joy looked at them, puzzled. "She said she needed to get some fresh air. I think she headed out for the balcony."

"Fresh air?" Tim sounded aghast. "It's twenty degrees out!"

"Will you excuse me?" Colin said. "I, er, need to…use the restroom."

With that lame exit, he left Joy happily chatting with Mayor Tim, who looked flustered at the beautiful blonde's attentions. Colin quickly went in search of Emily, who no doubt didn't feel the cold. She had fury to keep her warm.

EMILY WANDERED THE upstairs hallway. She'd gone out on the balcony, but without a coat, the below-freezing weather had turned her back. Still, for a second the cold air had been a welcome balm on her burning skin. She wasn't burning with embarrassment, she was red-hot with indignation.

How dare he!

She'd been miserable most of the night, despite Tim's obvious efforts at being a good host and fun date. The problem was she'd felt *guilty* at leaving Colin alone. At treating him like a booty call, some kind of convenient sex toy. She tried to soothe her bruised conscience by telling herself that the arrangement was one they'd both agreed to, the sex was phenomenal, but he was leaving and there was no way they could have anything more permanent.

Nonetheless, she'd still felt lousy.

Then, all of a sudden, she'd heard the buzzing of people around her at the ball, at around the same time she'd been about to plead a headache and head back to the hotel and Colin's supposed waiting arms. Only to find that he had gone and asked Joy Webster, her guest and his "type," to come to the Holiday Ball instead.

Apparently waiting wasn't really his thing.

Jealousy reared its ugly head, but it was dwarfed by the magnitude of her anger at his attempts to manipulate her. The statement he was trying to make was patently obvious: what was good for the goose, aka Emily, was good for the gander. Otherwise known as Colin. And Joy was giving Colin and the rest of the guests a real gander with that dress.

That wasn't nice, especially since she actually *liked* Joy. But she still felt the fires of competition, which was stupid, since it wasn't as if she could keep Colin anyway—he was leaving. Tomorrow, in fact. Therefore, he wasn't even hers to fight for.

She gritted her teeth, rubbing the back of her neck, the base of her skull. At this rate, she wasn't going to have to fake that headache.

"Emily?"

"Oh, great. Just the person I needed to see," she said sarcastically, turning her back on Colin as he hurried toward her. "You didn't abandon Joy, did you?"

"I had to find you," he said. "I needed to explain."

Her eyes widened. "You've got an *explanation* for this?"

"Yeah." He stroked her shoulder. "I'm an idiot."

"I knew that!" She jerked away from him.

"I only asked her because I wanted you to know how I felt," he confessed. "That's small, I know. But I hated seeing you go off with another guy."

She bit her lip. "I didn't like seeing you with Joy," she admitted.

"Thank God for that." He tentatively put an arm around her shoulders, and she didn't move away. He pressed a quick kiss on her temple, and she felt her headache recede. "I ran into Joy in the dining room, and she said that she wished she was doing something tonight, and I thought I'd ask her here. That way, she'd have something to do, and you'd finally realize why I was so upset when you left with Tim."

Put that way, it didn't sound half as selfish and petty as she wanted to believe it was.

Colin paused, irritation crossing his handsome face. "Did you know the mayor's thinking about marrying you?"

She rubbed at her eyes. "Actually, yeah."

"And you're *okay* with that?" Colin sounded outraged.

"It's only come up the once," Emily said lamely.

Colin stared at her intently. "I want you, Emily."

Her body reacted like a furnace kicking on. "I want you, too," she whispered.

"But more than that," he said, holding her in a loose embrace. "I care about you. I can't believe how much or how quickly…but I do."

Now the heat in her body settled into a strong, steady warmth in her chest. "I care about you, too. It's weird, isn't it?"

He laughed, hugging her. "Yeah. It's pretty strange."

They stood like that, hugging casually. She rested her head against his chest, hearing his strong, steady heartbeat pulsing beneath her ear.

"You did all this just to get even with me," she said, and she heard his low chuckle reverberate through his rib cage.

"I never said I was the sharpest knife in the drawer."

She laughed, too. "Well, it worked. When you walked in with her, I was furious. I've never been so jealous in my life."

He leaned down, expertly pressing a kiss on the nape of her neck and causing her to gasp at the sensation. "Now you know how I felt. The idea of anybody else touching you…"

She hated the thought of it. Of him touching Joy. Or anybody.

For that matter, of anybody else touching her.

You're getting in way too deep.

"You're still leaving tomorrow," she said softly as his kisses grew more insistent, tracing down the exposed flesh of her back. His hands followed the path his mouth took, as if smoothing his kisses into her skin.

"I know." He sighed, pulling away.

"So we've only got tonight."

"I know," he repeated.

She paused. "I was going to tell Tim I wanted to go home."

"I told Joy that I wouldn't stay long," he said. "She said she'd go back to the hotel later without me."

Emily felt a fever of anticipation start to bloom through her, starting with her stomach and radiating outward, pulsing between her legs. One last night. One last, memorable night.

"Let's go, then." Turning to him and getting on tiptoe, she kissed him softly…then with growing urgency.

He growled against her lips, his hands roaming her back. She pressed herself fully against him, her hands jetting inside his jacket and wrapping around his waist, holding him to her. The kiss got out of control quickly, like a match held to dry kindling. It was all Emily could do not to undo some of his buttons then and there.

She'd never responded this way to anyone. It was as if he were a walking, breathing aphrodisiac, and she simply couldn't get enough.

"I don't suppose the mayor's got a convenient boiler room

nearby," Colin finally said shakily, resting his forehead against hers. "I'd settle for a broom closet."

"We need to get back to the hotel." Her own voice was unsettled. "In the next few minutes. If not sooner."

"Maybe the cab…" he teased.

She had an image of the two of them in the darkened back of a taxi, their hands roaming under cover of the night. His fingers dipping into her through the slit in her dress. He'd find out soon enough that she was wearing garters instead of stockings, and she'd picked out the underwear with him in mind.…

She moaned softly, biting her lip. As if reading her mind, he grabbed her for one last, long, lingering kiss. She rubbed her pelvis against his, just a suggestion of what she really wanted to do. He groaned, and she felt the hardness of his cock jutting against the fabric of his pants, pressing into her stomach.

"Now," she insisted. "We've got to leave *now.*"

They turned…and promptly bumped into Evelyn Albee.

"I hope I'm not interrupting anything," she said, and from her tone, it was obvious that she'd already witnessed more than they'd intended.

"No," Emily lied, fighting to keep her voice calm and her cheeks pale. If she blushed now, it would probably be the rosy blossom of desire, not embarrassment…but it'd be a close call as to which was stronger. "We were just, er, leaving."

"What were you two doing off by yourselves?"

Colin cleared his throat. "We were catching up," he said, and his voice was casual…although he stood a little behind Emily to try and hide his raging erection. Emily fought a wave of nervous chuckles. "It's hard to hear yourself think downstairs. We thought it'd be easier if we found someplace quiet."

"Really?" Evelyn looked unconvinced.

"Sure. Emily and I go way back."

"I see." And that clearly wasn't all she saw.

"We really were leaving," Emily repeated forcefully. "Come on, Colin."

"I was going to ask," Evelyn interrupted, "how is it that a pretty woman like Joy snagged such a totally devoted bachelor. But I guess that was the wrong question, hmm?" She paused. "And the wrong *person*."

Emily grimaced. She liked many people, but Evelyn Albee got on her nerves. "You're asking if Colin and I are an item."

Eveyln's eyes popped. "Are you?"

"Colin's leaving tomorrow," Emily said.

"And?" Evelyn sounded indecently curious, at the edge of her metaphoric seat.

"And that's it." Emily took Colin's arm, leading him away. Let her chew on that.

"You okay?" Colin said softly.

"I will be," Emily assured him. Assured herself. "Just take me home."

7

COLIN NOTICED THAT Emily was quiet during the short drive from the mayor's house to the inn. He felt somewhat subdued himself.

This was going to be their last night together—for real this time. Technically, they'd covered this territory before, but this time the ticking clock didn't seem to fan the flames of passion as it had before. It didn't feel like an interlude or an adventure.

It felt like a mistake.

Not being with Emily. As far as he was concerned, it was as if Emily had been made with him in mind, both in bed and out. No, it felt like a mistake to approach the night as though it was going to be their last.

They stepped into her apartment, and a strange awkwardness descended. Emily laughed nervously.

"I wonder if this is so weird because the cat's finally out of the bag?" she mused. "The whole Holiday Ball is probably talking about us right now."

He waited until she'd stripped off her heavy winter coat, then he wrapped her in his arms. It wasn't meant to be sexual. It was supposed to be comforting. Yet, as always with this woman, the heat *and* the comfort were inseparable.

All those years we lived in the same little city, he thought as he stroked her hair and held her tight. *Why didn't I find her before now, when I'm leaving for another continent?*

"Don't think about them," he said, his voice thick. "Just think about us."

"I can't stop thinking about us," she murmured, rubbing her hands up and down his back. "That ought to make this easier, but somehow it's not."

"Don't think about the time frame, either. It's not important. The only important thing is right now. How we feel about each other."

He wondered if she understood what he was saying—how much he felt for her. But he was too nervous to actually try putting his emotions into words. She was the one who seemed to think that the short-term nature of their affair, a "fling" by her own words, was a foregone conclusion.

What if she doesn't feel the same way I feel?

Better to listen to his own advice. Right now was all that mattered. He had to focus on the present and nothing else.

They were slower than they ever had been, even though desire still licked at him with tongues of flame. It was as if he were trying to memorize everything about her with slow precision. He held his breath as she took off his coat and jacket, tugged loose his tie, undid each button with fingers that trembled slightly. He shrugged the shirt off his shoulders, feeling his erection stiffen after simply seeing the admiration in her eyes as her gaze traced over his torso and her catlike tongue wet her lips in a quick motion. He tugged at the hem of her dress, pulling it over her head in a slow, smooth movement.

When he saw what she had beneath, he held his breath, then let it out in a sigh of gratitude.

Emily was wearing a strapless black bra, smooth satin, with a matching thong and garter belt holding up black nylon stockings. Still in her black stiletto heels, she reached up, taking her barrette out of her hair and letting the auburn waves cascade around her shoulders. Her full lips were crimson, her violet eyes even larger and smokier than usual.

She looked like a sexual fantasy brought vividly to life. She looked like the type of woman men would sell their souls to be able to possess.

Hell, if there were a dotted line in front of him, he'd sign in blood for the chance to keep her.

She unbuckled his pants, her full lips curving into a slow, inviting smile. Colin groaned as she slipped the pants down to the floor, leaving him only in boxers. He kicked off his shoes and socks, leaving them both in their underwear, there in the living room.

"Nice," he said, pointing to her ensemble.

She stroked her hand over the front of his boxers, where his erection was emerging. "I thought you'd like them." Her lips quirked in that quicksilver smile that never failed to pump adrenaline through his system. "And I must say, they seem to be doing their job nicely."

She reached into his boxers, drawing out his cock and rubbing her fingers gently up and down the shaft. They also fell to the floor. He groaned again, leaning forward against her soft, warm palm.

"Still, I think we can do better," she said, her voice teasing. With that, she knelt down, taking him into her mouth.

All rational thought fled in the face of the overwhelming sensation of her wet, warm mouth caressing him. His fingers tangled gently in her hair, his body twitching slightly as the rough silk of it brushed cool against the heat of his cock. She suckled softly but insistently, and he went harder than he'd even thought possible.

"Emily," he moaned, closing his eyes. Colin felt himself losing control and he tugged her up to her feet. "I need you," he said, his voice thick with desire. "Now."

"You can have me," she responded, her eyes gleaming. "Whenever you want."

Then I want forever.

He didn't say it. Instead he kissed her roughly, feeling the satin of her panties rub the length of his shaft before his cock rested against the smooth plane of her stomach. He lifted her into his arms, carrying her with haste into the bedroom and placing her carefully on the bed. She looked at him, eyes bright with invitation and desire.

For a moment he paused. He didn't want to simply take her. It was more than just sex, no matter how brief their relationship had been up to this point.

He stretched out next to her, taking off her bra, panties, garter and nylons. She looked at him, curious.

"Don't you like it?" Her voice sounded unsure. "I wore them for you."

"They're great," he said, stroking a wayward lock of hair out of her face. "But I don't need them. I don't need anything else to make me want you. And tonight I want it to be just us."

He hoped she understood.

She still looked slightly puzzled, but she nodded. Then she seemed to melt against him, her skin feeling even softer and more sensuous than the satin had felt.

He murmured incoherent words of passion against her skin, touching her like a blind man, tracing every curve and hollow. She kissed his shoulders, his chest, his abdomen. He slid over her, capturing first one nipple, then the other with delicate intensity, laving each until they were rosy and erect. He cupped her breasts carefully, kissing her cleavage, delighting in the way the tempo of her breathing increased.

He saved the best for last. When his fingers finally dipped inside her entrance, stroking her thighs intently, he found she was already wet and slick, ready for him. Slowly he rolled on a condom, then went back to kissing her as if they had all the time in the world to consummate what they'd aroused in each other.

She sighed against his lips. "Colin," Emily breathed, and the word was filled with emotion.

Smiling, he finally positioned himself between her legs, sliding into her like a key into the perfect lock.

For a second he stayed still, relishing the snugness of her, the way she accommodated him so incredibly. But the tightness of her, the way her passage enveloped him and clenched against him, soon made staying still impossible. Nevertheless, he took his time, retreating carefully, maximizing each stroke for the most pleasure possible. Their breathing quickened, and despite his efforts, they moved faster, cycling into the inevitable build of passion. They clung to each other, so close that they seemed to be one person as he filled her and she rose to meet each thrust.

"Colin!"

He felt the clutching tremors of her climax, and they triggered his own orgasm. Oblivious to everything but the sensation of her, he shuddered against her, feeling her thighs tighten around him as his cock pressed deeper and deeper into her welcoming flesh.

When it was over, and his consciousness returned, he couldn't help it. He smoothed his fingertips over the light sheen of sweat on her long-limbed body and pressed kisses against her temples, her high cheekbones...even the bridge of her nose. She smiled at him.

"I..." Her eyes held the faintest trace of tears. "I don't know what to say to you."

Tell me you love me.

He blinked. Was that what he wanted?

Yes. He wanted her. He wanted love. He wanted the whole package.

He rolled next to her, stunned by the revelation.

"You mean a lot to me," he finally said, his tone cautious. "More than I thought."

That didn't sound right. He frowned.

"You mean a lot to me, too," she said.

The silence that fell was a huge chasm, so much that despite the fact they were skin against skin, it felt as if the Grand Canyon lay between them.

"I…" He cleared his throat. "I don't know when I'm going to be back in town, but…"

To his surprise, she put a finger to his lips, hushing him.

"Right now is all that matters," she said, throwing his words back at him. "Remember? I'm not worried about later."

He frowned again. "But…"

She snuggled against him and he was thrown off. "Just make love to me again," she said. "It'll be enough."

He held her, feeling her heart beat against his chest.

It's not going to be enough for me, he thought. But he was leaving the next morning and he didn't know when he was going to be back. It wasn't fair to ask her to wait for him, was it?

He didn't know what to do. So he did as she said—he focused on the present, making love to her as if it was all they were going to have. Because for all he knew, it was.

EMILY FELT BLEARY-EYED and exhausted. She hadn't gotten any sleep the night before, and it wasn't because of her activities with Colin—although they'd both done their best to make the night memorable. When he had fallen asleep, she'd found herself staring at his face…the way his long eyelashes rested on his cheeks, the way his hair tousled itself against her pillowcase.

She was falling in love with him. She wasn't sure how or why, but it was a fact. Just like the fact that he was on a plane, headed for Europe, and she wasn't sure when or if she would see him again.

She swallowed. She had a few too many facts to deal with.

Emily wandered down to the front desk, thinking that the hotel itself might provide her with a respite from her wayward feelings. A few hours dealing with the day-in-day-out running of the inn ought to be a comfort. But when she got there, she noticed that the front lobby was way more crowded than normal—and that most of the people were definitely not guests.

She recognized Evelyn Albee and her stomach twisted into a knot. "May I help you?" she asked, forcing her voice to remain casual.

Evelyn had been chatting with two other women with her, and they all huddled conspiratorially around Emily. "We were talking this morning, and it struck us how long it's been since you've visited the salon," Evelyn said, in a peaches-and-cream voice that was at odds with the almost predatory gleam in her eye.

"It's been ages!" one of the other women, Shirley Hayworth, agreed heartily.

"So we decided to treat you to a full day of pampering." This from Evelyn's second in charge, Madge Tyler. Madge handed Emily a gift certificate, hand-lettered.

"Thank you," Emily said. A full day of pampering would have sounded nice if she didn't know Evelyn's motive. People tended to find the salon comforting, almost therapeutic—and therefore turned the beauty technicians and fellow customers into a sort of "spa therapy" group. As a result, the salon was a hotbed of gossip and a place for solicited and unsolicited advice from the women of Tall Pines. "I'll see when I can fit it into my schedule."

"Oh, but the roads are cleared," Evelyn said smoothly, smiling at Sue, who was manning the desk and looking apologetically at Emily. "Most of your guests have gone, and Sue was just saying the holiday rush was over for a few weeks at least. So…"

Emily bit back a sigh. "The guests might be gone, but business still keeps grinding along." She tried to keep the annoyance out of her voice. "I've got inventory to do, ladies, but I appreciate the gift certificate. Thanks so—"

"Is Colin still here?" Madge's comment shot out like a bullet.

"Madge!" Evelyn looked incensed. She might be there trolling for gossip, but she wasn't about to be *that* obvious, apparently.

"Well, you said they were making out at the Holiday Ball!" Madge was fiftyish and recently divorced. For her, gossip was more than a hobby, it was a lifeline. "Is it true? Are you and Colin Reese…you know?"

"I don't know what you mean," Emily said, her voice cool.

Evelyn sneered. "I *told* you not to say anything directly!"

"In all fairness, Evelyn, I wouldn't have told you anything at the salon, either," Emily said. "Sorry, Madge."

"It's not fair," Madge grumped. "Colin's like a celebrity. After all those big, crazy buildings he designed, he's been in big magazines. *Newsweek. Time.* Even *InStyle.*" Madge gave a beatific grin; as far as she was concerned, getting your picture in *InStyle* was tantamount to being royalty. "You've heard Ava talking about the women he normally goes with. Models, actresses, flashy businesswomen…"

Emily blanched. Women not like her, in other words.

Of course, now he's got plenty of opportunity to get back to his "type."

"He also has a reputation for leaving them," Shirley said, her voice more quiet than the other two. "How are you holding up, sweetie?"

Emily should have been surprised, but Shirley was about sixty or so and considered herself a sort of universal den mother. Although it wasn't the older woman's business, she accepted Shirley's pat on the shoulder with a wan smile. "I'm hanging in there," she found herself saying.

"Oh, Emily," Madge said, and there was real outrage in her voice. "You, too? All men are *dogs,* honey. Just *dogs.*"

"Well, you knew his reputation," Evelyn admonished, and in that second Emily could have smacked her.

"Excuse me, Emily?"

Emily turned, wondering who was going to be grilling her about her love life now. To her surprise—and relief—it was Joy.

"I don't mean to interrupt," Joy said, "but Emily and I have a business meeting right now."

Evelyn's eyes narrowed. "Aren't you the woman that Colin took to the Holiday Ball last night?"

Emily wished that the earth would swallow her up. "Joy is a friend and a guest. And also in the hotel industry. We were going to discuss, er, some ways to improve the hotel."

"But the hotel's perfect, sweetie, just the way it is," Shirley assured her. "You run the place like a top."

"If you'll excuse me?" Emily said, feeling an edge of desperation to her words.

"Fine, fine." Evelyn was obviously unsatisfied. "But don't forget about that gift certificate, all right?"

"You deserve it," Madge added. "*Dogs.* The lot of them."

Emily watched the retreating figures of the three ladies, then dropped the gift certificate on the desk like a hand grenade.

"Wow. That was like something out of Stars Hollow."

"Excuse me?" Emily rubbed at the back of her neck. She should've stayed in bed—except her sheets smelled like Colin's cologne, and she couldn't face a whole day surrounded by reminders of him. Of *them.* "Stars what?"

"It's the small town in that TV show *Gilmore Girls,*" Joy explained. "Very cute, if a little overbearing."

"That's one way of putting it," Emily said ruefully.

"Do you have time? For a meeting, I mean."

Emily started to say no but then saw another wave of townspeople heading toward the lobby—with obviously no intention of renting rooms. "Certainly. Why don't you come with me to my office."

She led Joy to the room she'd converted for office use. Joy whistled. "This is gorgeous," she said, looking at the dark maple furniture. "I've worked in multibillion-dollar hotel chains that didn't look half as good. You've done something special here, Emily."

"I try," Emily said, sitting at at a small occasional table and gesturing to Joy to sit next to her. She poured them both a cup of coffee from the coffeemaker on her credenza. "I didn't know how much went into running a hotel, but I've always been a quick study."

"And you're amazingly good at it," Joy said, taking her own seat. "But, you know, with a few strategic improvements, you could make this place even bigger."

Emily smiled tiredly. "Yeah, if I had a billion dollars and a cast of thousands at my beck and call…"

But Joy's expression was serious. "I hope you don't think this is out of line," she said hesitantly, "but I drew up some numbers and some strategy ideas." She slid a piece of paper over the surface of the table.

Emily looked at it. The strategy was clear, precise, in Joy's neat handwriting. Then she looked at the income expectations. The number took her breath away. She closed her eyes, rubbing them, then read the number again.

It was still the same. She had thought that fatigue was making her hallucinate.

"You wouldn't necessarily see those profits first year," Joy said easily, as if they were simply swapping recipes instead of discussing a huge change in Emily's business. "But with the right combination of management, marketing and some key overhauls, you could quadruple your profits in under five years, easy. With that much money, you could start hiring that cast of thousands to help you."

With that much money, she might not want to keep working, period, Emily realized. "This is more than I could have sold the house for by itself."

"Tall Pines is going places," Joy said and her voice lit with excitement. "It could be the next big bedroom community for larger cities, and it's getting a good reputation as a tourist attraction. If you really pursued it, you could help put Tall Pines on the map."

Emily's head swam. In her sleep-deprived state, it was too much to contemplate.

"I know you think I've been patronizing, gushing about this place," Joy said. "But this isn't a joke, Emily. If I know one thing, it's how to make a hotel a success."

"But…this is my home," Emily said, feeling dumbfounded. "The changes you're suggesting…"

"I know," Joy said, and her voice was rich with sympathy and what sounded strangely like envy. "It's a lot to think about. But do you really want to keep struggling at this level for the rest of your life?"

Emily thought about it. She wasn't hand-to-mouth anymore, granted, but it was hard, managing the hotel. More money would make her life easier. Wouldn't it?

At the same time—did she *want* to manage a hotel for the rest of her life? She'd only taken it on so she wouldn't lose the house. On the other hand, giving up the hotel would effectively take the Stanfield house out of her family for good…an idea her father had vehemently disagreed with.

Realizing Joy was still there, waiting for a response, Emily bit her lip. "Sorry. This is all so sudden."

"I'm staying through the end of the month," Joy said. "I know how emotional the whole thing is for you. Think it over, take your time. If you decide to move ahead, I'd be happy to help you plan, get financing, whatever."

With that, Joy started to get up and leave the office. Before she could stop herself, Emily blurted out, "Why did you go to the Holiday Ball with Colin?"

Joy turned. "I was bored," she said easily. "Trust me, if I'd known, I wouldn't have gone anywhere near him."

"Known what?"

Joy's eyebrow quirked up. "That you two were involved."

"We're not." Emily felt the burn of the lie on the tip of her tongue. "Not exactly," she amended.

"If I knew the two of you were *anything,* I would've stayed away from him," Joy said. "He's gorgeous, but this is business. And I'm all business."

With that, Joy winked and left the room.

Emily held up the paper with its imposing financial figures on it.

The hotel had been her life for years. The house had been her father's legacy. The town was already up in arms about outside business coming in and changing things too rapidly. It would cause enormous upheaval and disappoint a lot of people.

She folded the paper, unable to bring herself to throw it away. *What would I do if I didn't have this place*? she asked herself.

To her surprise, her mind changed one word in the sentence. *What* could *I do if I didn't have this place?*

She'd never thought about that before.

Sue popped her head in. "Everything all right?" she asked.

"Yeah. Everything's fine." Emily tucked the paper into her desk drawer. "Let's do inventory. It's sort of early, but I'd rather stay away from the public today."

Besides, counting towels and bed linens would keep her mind occupied enough to stop thinking of losing Colin—and now possibly leaving the inn.

COLIN WAS SITTING at Heathrow Airport in London, feeling more disoriented than usual. He tried to chalk it up to jet lag, but he'd had jet lag before. It was different than this over-whelming sensation of displacement—that no matter where he was, it was the wrong place.

He'd only been gone for a day and a half, and as he'd feared, thoughts of Emily crowded his brain incessantly.

He'd stopped himself from dialing the inn's number a dozen times in the past twenty-four hours, mostly because he had no idea what he would say. If he had no intention of having a re-lationship with her, it seemed unnecessarily cruel to both of them to keep intruding on her. Better to simply move on to his new life and let her move on with hers.

He pictured Mayor Tim and gritted his teeth.

She deserves to move on to something better than that, though.

He credited Emily with more common sense than to enter a loveless marriage with a guy who was looking for a "practi-cal" wife. But then, most people probably would have credited Emily with more common sense than to take up with a com-mitmentphobic drifter like himself, too.

Instead he jotted down more notes on the office he'd be opening. He'd already done a ton of work on the plane while his fellow passengers had been napping. Now he was buzzing on a caffeine high and lack of sleep.

He'd get to Paris, buckle down and bury himself in blue-prints for a while. His work was one thing he'd always loved, and he'd gotten so caught up in the holidays and Tall Pines that he'd practically pretended it didn't exist.

Face it—you got tangled up in Emily. And you still are.

His cell phone was in his hand, and he found himself tracing her number one more time.

Only this time, as if it had a mind of its own, his thumb hit *Send.*

He heard the ringing and considered hanging up—but she'd know he called. By now his number was probably showing up on caller ID. He winced, trying to think of what he'd say.

"Hello?"

Emily's voice sounded rough with sleep. Suddenly he remembered he didn't know what time it was in London, much less Connecticut.

"Oh God, I'm sorry. It's late, isn't it?"

There was a pause. "Early, actually," Emily said, sounding much more alert. "How are you?"

He paused, too, trying to frame a reply. "Tired," he answered honestly.

"Me, too." He heard the smile in her voice. "Although I'm glad you called."

"Maybe I should call back," he said, wincing. "I didn't mean to…"

"Why are you calling?"

That one caught him flat-footed. "Honestly? I don't know." He ran his hand through his hair in a gesture of frustration. "Yes, I *do* know. I miss you. That's nuts, isn't it?"

She laughed. "No. It's nice." The warmth in her voice was clear as crystal even over an intercontinental cell phone line. "I miss you, too."

"So what are we going to do about this?" His voice was almost demanding, and he toned it down. "I've never felt like this. It's confusing and uncomfortable, and damned if I know what to do next."

"Well," she said slowly, "it probably would've been better to have this conversation when we were, say, two feet away from each other instead of several thousand miles."

He chuckled. "I know. That is, I know that *now.*"

"So I don't know what to tell you," she continued. "You're there. I'm here. That makes a lasting relationship hard."

"But not impossible, right?" He blinked. Had he really asked that?

She seemed surprised, as well. "Is that what you want?"

"I think…yes." He sighed. The loudspeaker was announcing that his connecting flight to Paris was boarding. "I have really lousy timing."

"Sort of," she admitted. "I really care about you, Colin."

"I care about you, too," he confessed, feeling his heart expand in his chest. "I meant to tell you when I was there, but I chickened out. And I didn't know where it would lead, anyway. Where it *could* lead."

"I still don't know that it can lead anywhere." Emily spoke softly. "The bottom line is, we had some wonderful nights together.…"

"You can say that again," Colin said, his body going taut at the mere memory.

"But we only spent less than two weeks together. That's hardly enough to say one way or another how we feel."

"I know how I feel." *I'm falling in love with you.* Sudden or not, he was certain of that.

"Well, no matter how you feel, the bottom line is you didn't feel strongly enough to stay here and discuss it with me face-to-face."

He grimaced. She did have a point there.

The announcer broadcast his flight again. He'd have to hurry if he was going to make it. "Listen, I have to catch this plane. Can I call you back at a more decent hour?"

"If you want," Emily replied noncommittally. "But…Colin, think about what you really want with me before you do. Because I…I wasn't expecting to feel the way I feel about you. And, to be honest, it's starting to hurt."

He felt guilt crash on him like a wrecking ball. "I never meant to hurt you."

"I know," she assured him. "I know you didn't."

But if he was only going to string her along, he'd be hurting her anyway. Colin heard what she wasn't saying as clearly as what she was.

"Listen, I should've said all this back in Tall Pines. I know that now."

"You've got to catch a plane," Emily said. "Call me when you get to Paris and…I don't know, Colin. I can't promise anything."

"Okay," he said weakly. *Tell her! Tell her you love her!* "We'll talk soon."

"All right," she agreed. "Good night, Colin."

"'Night." He hung up the phone, then stared at it.

Minutes later, the announcer was calling out his name. "Is there a Colin Reese? Colin Reese. We're looking for passenger Colin Reese. Your flight is awaiting departure."

Colin rushed up to the desk. "I'm Colin Reese."

The flight attendant smiled thinly. "You're late, Mr. Reese. You're our last passenger. We've been looking for you."

"I'm sorry," Colin said. "But I have to change my plans."

Her eyebrows went up. "Beg pardon?"

"I have to get a flight back to Connecticut. How can I arrange that?"

8

"I'D LIKE A MANICURE and a facial, please. I'm using your gift certificate."

Emily said the words clearly enough to be heard over the chattering of the crowded beauty salon. As she'd expected, the whole place fell silent when they recognized her voice.

"Certainly, certainly." Madge ushered her over to a manicure station. "You sit right here. How are you doing?"

How was she doing? It had been two days since Colin had left, and she couldn't remember feeling quite this way before. Missing him was like a dull ache, countered only by feelings of foolishness and confusion. When he'd called, she had felt excited at hearing his voice and then abruptly depressed by reality. Would that be their relationship from then on? Long-distance phone calls and maybe the occasional transatlantic flight for a weekend of passion? Maybe a whole week if they were lucky? Would that be enough?

Then again, considering the big, bleak romantic desert of her life, was she being too damned picky?

She realized Madge was still waiting patiently for an answer and quickly cleared her throat. "Sorry. I'm fine, really. I've just been sort of out of it lately."

"Oh, no problem," Madge said easily. "Cynthia? Could you do a manicure for Emily here?"

Cynthia was about twenty-three. Emily had babysat for her

in high school. She quickly started to soak Emily's nails. "Man trouble, huh?"

Emily straightened her spine. She'd decided to simply brave the lion's den rather than hide in the inn. "No," she said. "No trouble."

"I don't blame you," Cynthia said sympathetically. "That guy Colin was *seriously* yummy."

Emily cringed. She remembered when Cynthia used to watch *Sesame Street,* for pity's sake. Hearing her call Emily's lover "yummy" was disturbing.

"I'm fine. It's fine."

"So dish." Cynthia's youth and enthusiasm bubbled through her like some high-sugar, high-caffeine soda. "What was he like?"

"Um, I don't think I'm comfortable discussing my love life in graphic detail," Emily said. "He was a dear friend and we…considered having a relationship, but the reality is, he's living in Paris and I'm living in Tall Pines and it simply wasn't feasible, so…"

She let the words trail off. She'd been crafting that careful public announcement for two days. Now she understood why celebrities sent out cautiously worded press releases when they had high-profile breakups. It made things easier all around.

Cynthia made a face. "You sound like a banker. Wasn't the sex any good?"

Emily goggled. She'd expected questions but nothing quite this blunt.

"Good grief, Cyn," Madge said, smacking her lightly on the shoulder.

"What?" Cynthia looked bewildered. "Don't tell me you're not wondering, either. A guy that gorgeous you don't dump unless there's a big problem."

"And the fact that he's living a whole other continent away isn't what you'd consider a big problem?" Emily asked sarcastically.

Cynthia shrugged. "There are planes, aren't there?"

Emily blinked.

"So you dumped him because he's not living here in town?"

Cynthia made a *tch-tch* sound in her throat.

"Who's saying I dumped him?"

"Well, you wouldn't be here acting all mopey if you hadn't."

It was hard to refute the logic of a twenty-three-year-old, Emily thought with a wry smile. After all, they knew everything. She certainly had when she was twenty-three.

"We parted amicably," Emily said, remembering the party line.

"Yes, but was it his idea?" Madge pressed.

Emily realized that, for the moment, she was the center of attention at the salon. Women had even shut off their dryers to hear her commentary. She sighed.

"No. It was my idea."

They collectively gasped at that bit of news.

"Well, what was I supposed to do?" Emily finally broke down. "He lives in *Paris,* for pity's sake. If I'm lucky, I could see him, what, a couple of times a year?" She shook her head. "I don't think that would work."

"I guess you're right. I mean, long-distance relationships have, like, a twenty percent success rate," Cynthia said sagely, buffing Emily's nails. "I read that in *Cosmo.*"

"There's also more of a chance that you'll get cheated on," Madge interjected darkly. "All that temptation, and you're miles away."

That comment hit Emily like a fist in the gut. She focused on the tray of nail polish colors as if her life depended on it, trying not to picture Colin with some other woman—probably some stylish Parisian woman with no body fat and a fabulous wardrobe.

The more she tried not to see it, the more vivid the picture became.

"Well, at least you got back up on the horse," Evelyn said…then promptly burst out laughing.

"Oh my God." Emily tried to cover her face with her hands, but Cynthia had already applied the base coat of polish, and they were still wet. Cynthia giggled.

"I think she meant that more *figuratively,* hon," Madge clarified helpfully. That was the straw that broke the camel's back, apparently, because the entire salon joined in, laughing raucously.

If Emily's face got any hotter, they could toast marshmallows in front of it. Brave the lion's den, huh?

This was such a bad idea.

"Come on, come on," Evelyn said, and she gave Emily a small half hug around her shoulders. "If you can't talk to the girls at the beauty shop, then you can't talk to anyone. Besides, I think a big part of your problem is that you bottle things up, sweetie."

"I didn't know I had a problem," Emily said. *Boy, could this get any worse?*

"Hmm. That's also part of the problem." Evelyn seemed to size her up, then nodded, as if making a decision. "You know what? We ought to get you drunk."

Emily choked. *"Excuse me?"*

Cynthia clapped her hands together. "Ooh! And hire a stripper!"

Madge poured herself another cup of coffee. "Just tell me when and where," she declared, "and I'll be there."

Emily glanced around. Mrs. Rutledge, who had been at the mayor's Christmas dinner and was seventy-four if she were a day, was placidly reading a *People* magazine, her hair covered in foil from her dye job. "Mrs. Rutledge, I'm so sorry," she said. "This is so inappropriate."

Mrs. Rutledge didn't even look up. "That's all right, dear," she responded. "Considering my neighbors are swingers, I suppose I'm harder to shock than most."

Emily's eyes bugged out. *"The Carltons are swingers?"*

"Not those neighbors." She sounded appalled. The Carltons were somewhere in their eighties and pillars of the community. "The Smiths. Good grief, girl, they've been wife swappers for years," Mrs. Rutledge said disdainfully. "Where have you been?"

"This is what happens when you don't make your regular hair appointments," Evelyn added.

Within the next hour Emily went through an eye-opening epiphany. She also became best friends, it seemed, with every woman in Tall Pines. Or at least every one that was a customer at the Magnifique Beauty Salon…which was actually pretty much every woman in Tall Pines. By the time she'd gotten herself talked into a haircut and style *and* a pedicure, she'd divulged her entire brief sexual history and relationship woes.

"After Rick," Emily found herself saying, "I didn't want to hurt like that again. So I figured I'd focus on other things. Running the hotel was hard enough."

"Emotionally, too, I'll bet." Mrs. Rutledge was long done with her hairstyling, but had stayed on for the conversation. "It was a big change turning the mansion into a hotel."

Emily nodded. "I wasn't sure whether or not my father would've approved," she admitted. "I'm still not."

"Now, now," Evelyn said. "You know, as much as we all love your family, sometimes you can be awfully…"

Emily looked at her as she trailed off. "Awfully what?"

"Well, stiff." Evelyn frowned. "Hmm, that's not the right word, either. But sometimes you're a little too proper."

"The whole town didn't like the hotel at first," Emily reminded her.

"Maybe not," Evelyn agreed. "We're sort of stuck in the mud sometimes ourselves. But we always liked *you.*"

Emily grinned. It was that kind of support that made her love

Tall Pines. She suddenly felt better than she had since Colin left. In some ways, better than she had in years.

"So now that Colin's gone," Cynthia said, "I guess you're going to date Mayor Tim, huh?"

The women surveyed her eagerly.

"After everything I've told you," Emily replied, "I don't know. I don't think I can go from someone like Colin to someone like Tim."

There were some mixed comments after that statement.

"There's more to life than passion," Evelyn said sagely. "I love Dale, but let's face it—he's no male model." She grinned wickedly. "Of course, he *does* have his moments."

Hearing about the "moments" Dale Albee had was more than Emily could handle right now. She cleared her throat. "Well, I'm not going out with Tim again. And as for Colin, I can't honestly believe there's a future there. And now that I know what I'm missing, I don't think I want to settle for anything less."

The women around her cheered.

The door opened and everyone turned to welcome the new arrival.

Emily's eyes bugged.

"Hi, Emily," Colin said quietly. "Sorry. Sue said I could find you here. She was expecting you back hours ago."

"You're supposed to be in Paris," she said, feeling dumbstruck. "What are you doing here?"

He stared at her for a second. Then he smiled. "Do you have to ask?"

"Oh." Madge dabbed at her eyes. "This is like something out of a movie."

"Are you done?" The question was a plea as he shifted uncomfortably under the intense scrutiny of the women.

"Have fun, dear," Mrs. Rutledge said with far too suggestive an edge for a septuagenarian.

Emily stood up, going for her wallet.

"It's all on the house, dear." Evelyn shooed her money away. "It's more than worth it. We'll be discussing this for weeks."

Emily put on her coat and walked out with Colin, hearing the explosion of conversation as she shut the door behind her.

He cleared his throat. "Was it bad?" he asked.

"Was what bad?" Missing him was bad. Thinking he was gone for good—that was bad.

"The grilling." He sounded worried. "I'm sure they were terrible."

"They actually weren't that bad," Emily said, smiling. "I'm glad you're back."

She wrapped her arms around him, giving him a long, lingering kiss.

He growled, pulling away from her. "You can't do that in broad daylight," he said, his eyes gleaming. "Not unless you want to shock some of these fine townfolk."

She grinned, remembering the wife-swapping tidbit. "They're harder to shock than you think." Then she frowned. "Wait. That's not why you're back, is it?"

"I couldn't leave you to face the fire alone."

She felt her stomach clench. It wasn't the reason she'd been hoping for. Still, he'd flown all the way back, so that had to say something. And he *did* care for her.

It wasn't going to be clear in one day, she thought resolutely. "Come on," she told him. "Let's go over to the hotel."

As usual, she'd enjoy whatever time she had. However long—or short—that was.

FUNNY, HOW HIS exhaustion seemed to disappear the minute he saw her. And walking into her apartment was more like coming home than walking into any of the residences he'd rented in the past five, ten years, he realized as he hung his coat up on her coatrack. It had been excruciating walking into the beauty salon, surrounded by all the town's busiest bodies but at the same time he'd found that he simply couldn't wait for her another minute.

That tells you something, doesn't it?

They would have to figure this out. He had a job, a life to get to in Paris. He couldn't keep jetting back here to Connecticut just because he couldn't function without her.

She turned to him, cheeks rosy from the cold, eyes sparkling like gems. "I can't believe you came back," she repeated for the tenth time.

"I'm having a little difficulty believing it myself." He took her into his arms. "We need to talk."

She kissed his jawline. "Right this second?"

In a snap, his body went taut as a bowstring. "Well…wait. Yes." He wasn't going to get sidetracked by his body. He'd flown thousands of miles and postponed moving into his new apartment to get back to this woman. They had a few things to straighten out. Namely what the heck they were going to do about this…this *thing* that was going on between them. "We definitely need to talk."

"All right." She played up a pout, looking kittenishly sexy. Then she sat down on the couch, patting the space next to her.

He thought about it. Sitting that close to her would definitely make conversation difficult. "Why don't we stand," he suggested. "In the kitchen." So far, that was the one place that they didn't have any sexual memories. Besides, kitchens reminded him of home, family gatherings—intrinsically nonsexy memories. That ought to be some kind of insurance against getting sidetracked.

She smiled, obviously amused, and walked over to the kitchen. "Mind if I fix myself a snack?" she asked.

"Sure." He paused. "If you don't mind, I'm kind of

hungry—starving, actually. All I've had is some snacks and airplane food in the past forty-eight hours."

"Poor baby," she said, stroking his face, and for a second he felt like saying *to hell with conversation* and dragging her over to the bed. They had plenty of time to talk, didn't they?

He clamped down on the instinct. They had plenty of time for the physical stuff, too…and the talk, at this point, was more important.

"So what did you want to talk about?" she asked over her shoulder, opening her well-stocked fridge.

"This. Us," he clarified. "What's going on with us?"

She leaned against the refrigerator door, looking puzzled. "Honestly, I have no idea. But I am enjoying it."

"So am I," he hastily assured her. "But… hell. I'm moving to Paris. We're going to have an ocean between us."

"That *did* cross my mind," she said, bringing out cheese, meat, croissants and an assortment of fruit. "This okay?"

"Fine," he answered absently, watching as she arranged the food attractively on a platter. He leaned up against the counter. "So if we're going to be thousands of miles away from each other, where does that leave us?"

"I don't have an answer to that," she admitted. She handed him a croissant sandwich, and he wolfed it down. "Maybe we should approach this from a different standpoint. What do you want to happen?"

I love you and I want you to be with me.

Colin frowned. He'd never lived with anyone in his life—his relationships had been far too brief, and he'd never been comfortable sharing that much of his space and his time. And that would mean turning her entire life upside down. Was that what he wanted? And was that something he had the right to ask for after, what, two weeks?

What if she moved to Europe, and hated it? And you?

He winced. No, that wasn't a good solution.

"I'm not sure," he prevaricated. "All I know is I think about you all the time and I love being with you."

There. He was creeping toward the *L* word. Maybe it was hasty, but he wanted to lay the groundwork.

She jumped up, sitting casually on the countertop of her kitchen island, next to the platter of food. She picked out a chocolate-covered strawberry, dipping it in a bowl of whipped cream and taking a slow, thoughtful bite.

His mouth went dry.

She put the stem down on her plate. "I love being with you, too," she said, her voice low and musical. She picked up another, this time licking it slightly before biting it. He wondered if it was deliberate, as his cock hardened just watching the fruit tickling those full lips of hers. "Are you saying you want a relationship?"

"Yes," he said, watching as she licked some stray chocolate from the corner of her mouth. "That's exactly what I'm saying."

She frowned. "Long-distance relationships don't have a really high success factor," she stated, then grinned ruefully. "If *Cosmo* is to be believed, anyway."

"I wouldn't want it to be long-distance." He couldn't help it. He picked up another strawberry, holding it out to her. Emily smiled, then delicately bit into it, some juice dribbling down her chin. She laughed.

That was his breaking point. He leaned forward, licking the stray juice from her. She sighed happily.

"So what would you want?" She looped her arms around his neck, kissing him slowly.

"I want to see you all the time." He nuzzled her neck, and she wrapped her jean-clad legs around his waist. He could feel the heat of her burning him. "I feel like I'm going crazy when I'm not with you."

Her breathing sped up and he kissed her hungrily. "I know," she moaned. "I feel the same way. I've never felt like this before in my life."

"Me, neither." The food was forgotten—they were practically clawing at each other with need.

She reached down, undoing his pants, and he did the same, their mouths never separating. She kicked off her shoes, and he tugged her pants and panties off, leaving her gasping. He barely took the time to pull down his own briefs and roll on a condom before he was entering her, right there in the kitchen.

She threw her head back, panting loudly. "Oh, this feels so *good…*"

He leaned his head on her shoulder. The countertop was the perfect height for them. She wrapped herself around him and he pushed into her, rocking against her. His body fit hers perfectly. He withdrew, leaving her whimpering with desire, then he plunged in, devouring her cry of pleasure.

"Emily," he murmured against her lips as his body increased its tempo. *"Emily."*

"I love the feel of you inside me," she whispered back, her hands digging into his shoulders, pulling him as close as possible to her.

They moved as one, straining against each other. When the climax hit, it hit them both simultaneously—and it hit like a freight train.

When it was over, he leaned against her, holding her as if he were too weak to stand on his own. They were both breathless.

"You know," he panted, "I used to have enormous self-control before I met you."

She giggled. "I never needed self-control before I met you."

They wound up stripping off the rest of their clothes and eating a more substantial meal naked in front of the fire. Colin couldn't remember the last time he'd felt this relaxed and comfortable—and he knew it had nothing to do with the cozy nature of Emily's home but more with the nature of Emily herself. The way she laughed. The way she listened, no matter what he was saying. The things she thought about.

He was fascinated with her.

"I've known you for years—well, known *about* you for years," he ventured, leaning against her couch as she rested her head against his shoulder. "I can't believe we never...you know. Before now."

She nibbled on his earlobe, simultaneously stroking his chest with one warm palm. "It wasn't for want of trying, believe me."

That surprised him. "You wanted me?"

"Are you kidding?" She laughed. "The hot, mysterious, lone-wolf Colin Reese? I wanted you since the moment I was old enough to understand what wanting was."

He felt pride and excitement bubble up from his chest. "Where the hell was I?"

She punched him lightly on the shoulder. "As I recall, having sex with most of the senior-class girls before importing a few from out of town."

He chuckled. "Trust me, my reputation was vastly overrated." He recalled his senior year fondly. "Well, maybe not that vastly—*ow*."

She punched a little harder but grinned. "Anyway, what would you have seen in a nerdy, type-A sophomore?"

He stroked her cheek. "The same thing I see now," he said softly. "Someone thoughtful and sweet and beautiful."

She stared at him, her eyes misting slightly with a sheen of tears. He kissed her tenderly.

"What can we do?" she asked finally.

It took him a second to see that she had looped back to his

initial conversation—the one he had meant to focus on solely before getting sidetracked, as always, by his intense desire for this woman. He stroked the hair away from her face, then kissed her shoulder.

"I think there's only one thing *to* do."

She frowned, puzzled.

He sighed. "I think I need to take you home to meet my parents."

EMILY HAD BEEN TO Ava and Harry's house dozens of times over the years, so in a way it felt ridiculous to feel so nervous now. But then she had been a guest, either for a committee meeting or Ava's Secret Santa party or the book club. Now she was coming as an entirely different entity: their son's girlfriend. Although *girlfriend* felt like a shallow and frivolous word for what she felt for him—and, considering they'd only been together less than a month, it was at the same time a bit of an overstatement.

She was confused enough when it was just the two of them.

"Hi, honey," Ava said, hugging her son before turning to Emily. "He's never brought *anyone* home for dinner, much less somebody that he jumped on a plane from Europe for!"

"Ava," Harry warned, before giving Emily a hug. "Nice to see you, Emily. Hope you like ribs—I've spent the morning making up a whole batch."

"Are you kidding? Your ribs are famous." Emily grinned. She liked Harry. He had a way of making her feel comfortable. "I remember them from the firehouse barbecue last year."

"Well, these are oven-cooked rather than grilled," he said critically, "but they ought to do all right. I guess."

Ava frowned. "I told you—ten degrees is way too cold for you to be grilling, Harry."

Emily laughed, then turned to Colin, who was looking skittish and unnerved. "You okay?" she murmured.

"Just dandy," he replied in a low voice, taking her coat.

She bit her lip. She knew this was going to be a high-pressure event for him. His parents, darling though they were to her, seemed to be a big part of his aversion to Tall Pines. This was probably harder for him than braving the beauty salon had been for her.

"I heard you got a gift certificate for the full-day beauty package over at Evelyn's shop," Ava called from the kitchen before emerging with a tray full of appetizers. "Sounds like you had quite the afternoon."

Emily winced. Suddenly she felt as uncomfortable as Colin looked. She took a shrimp puff from the tray Ava offered. "I got my nails done," she said inanely. "And, er, got a facial. And a cut and style."

"Well, you look great," Ava said, although her eyes glinted mischievously. "And then Colin walking in, looking for you…"

"Need help in there, Dad?" Colin said, then fled the living room, heading for the kitchen. Emily was left with Ava, who gestured to their large sectional sofa.

"Have a seat, dear. Make yourself comfortable."

Emily had sincere doubts that she'd be feeling overly comfortable during this intimate get-together and abruptly wondered why she'd thought it was a good idea when Colin suggested it.

"So, now that the men are out of the way—" Ava put her tray down on the coffee table "—I can't tell you how happy I am that you're together with my Colin!"

Emily looked down at the floor. "I'm happy, too."

"I mean, I love my other two kids, but Colin has always been…troubled." Ava sighed. "I've been wishing and praying for him to find some nice girl to settle down with. I had no idea you two would hit it off so well. And so quickly!"

Emily fought against the blush that threatened. "Neither

did we," she admitted, taking a few more shrimp puffs and a small pig in a blanket. They really hadn't eaten much today. "But…well, here we are."

"So," Ava said, folding her hands in her lap. "When is he moving home?"

Emily choked on a puff. "I'm sorry?"

Ava glanced at the door to the kitchen, then lowered her voice conspiratorially. "I've never seen him like this. And, like I said, he's *never* brought a girl home. You're special. I think he's in love."

Emily felt her chest expand, like a large bubble blowing up inside of her, filled with happiness.

I hope so, she thought, *because I think I'm in love with him.*

"And for him to fly all the way back? Well, that means something," Ava pronounced with authority. "He's serious about you."

"What does that have to do with him moving home?" Emily asked in an equally low voice, hoping that Colin wouldn't hear.

Ava looked surprised at the question. "Well, he can't marry you if he's all the way in Europe, now, can he?"

"Marriage?" Emily put the rest of her appetizers down on the coffee table, her appetite suddenly waning. "We've only been together for a couple of weeks. Don't you think you're jumping the gun there?"

Ava frowned. "He wouldn't have brought you here if he wasn't serious." Her tone said, *At least he'd better not have or he's in serious trouble.*

"I'm not saying he's not serious," Emily backpedaled. "But…we aren't sure how we're going to work all this out yet."

Ava's face smoothed out in relief. "Oh, well, I'm sure you'll figure out a way," she said, leaning over and patting Emily's hand. "You'll get him to see that what he needs is a wife and a family and a home. I hate seeing him so rootless."

"It seems to work for him," Emily pointed out. "He likes seeing different things, doing different things, having adventures."

"Well, sure, that's fine when you're young," Ava said dismissively. "But he's going to be thirty-five this year. Time to start thinking of settling down. He's had enough adventures."

Emily found herself frowning. She was only thirty-two, about to turn thirty-three, but she didn't think she had had enough adventures. Actually, she hadn't had *any* adventures— which was, she realized, a big part of the chain of events that led her to Colin and, consequently, to here.

"What are you two talking about?" Colin asked, bringing Emily a mug of hot spiced cider.

"Oh, nothing," Ava lied breezily, winking at Emily. "Girl stuff."

He looked suspicious—and nervous. *And he's right to,* Emily thought, considering the topic of their conversation.

He sat next to Emily and then took her hand. She felt some of the tension that had been tightening her muscles slowly unravel.

"Oh, there, now don't you two look cute?" Ava gushed, and the tension snapped back into place.

"Ava, where did you put the big platter? I want to get these ribs out on the table," Harry called from the kitchen.

Ava shook her head, smiling at Emily and Colin. "I swear, that man would lose his head if it wasn't attached to his neck. I'll be right back."

When she disappeared into the kitchen, Colin let out a long, beleaguered sigh.

"Why did you think this was a good idea again?" Emily whispered.

"Because you're important to me," he answered, not taking it as the joke it was meant to be. "We're in a relationship. This is something you do when you're in a relationship."

Emily thought about that. *Wouldn't it be more important to decide logistics...like how often you'll fly here or I'll fly there or whether or not one of us is supposed to move?*

"Besides, I wanted to see what this was like," he added.

"This?"

"Bringing you home," he said. Then paused. "Being around my family."

"Oh." And suddenly it did make sense.

He's trying to see if he could live here, this close to his family. In his own way, he was figuring out logistics.

Suddenly the dinner took on an element of pressure that she hadn't even believed was possible.

They sat down to eat, and as usual, Ava did all the talking, chirping happily. Emily tried to steer the conversation to safe topics, something that should have been easy to do since she and Ava actually had a lot in common. The more they discussed Tall Pines community stuff, however, the more Colin seemed to withdraw. Emily felt his discomfort like rippling waves, buffeting her without meaning to.

"And, of course, there's the Easter egg hunt coming up in April," Ava said, pausing only long enough to pass the mashed potatoes and make sure everyone had a second helping of her "world-famous" corn bread. "The little ones are always so cute wandering around the lawns of the square." She winked. "You two might be enjoying that pretty soon, hmm?"

"Mom," Colin said warningly.

Emily quickly turned to Harry. "These really are fantastic ribs."

Ava refused to be deterred. "After all, you're not getting any younger...."

"*Really* good ribs," Emily interjected. "You know, I heard about a rib recipe recently..."

"And Emily here loves kids..."

"It had maple syrup in it, and, er, nutmeg," Emily continued desperately.

"And you know, Colin," Ava said thoughtfully, "I've always known you'd make a wonderful father...."

"And, er, chocolate syrup, as well," Emily blinked. "Wait. That's not right."

"Sounds intriguing, though," Harry said, chuckling. "Ava, you're making our guest white as a sheet. They've only started dating. Would you let them mail out wedding invitations before you throw the baby shower?"

Ava smirked self-consciously. "Maybe I *am* jumping the gun a tiny bit."

"You think?" Colin muttered.

Emily struggled her way through dinner. Ava meant well, she really did—but she was so intent on her picture of a perfect family that she was like a heat-seeking missile, unable to go off course once she'd locked on to a target. Her other children and their families lived in neighboring towns, just twenty minutes or so away. Colin was the one element of her perfect picture that didn't fit...and now she saw a way to get him to finally come back to the fold.

Watching Colin endure his mother's machinations actually made Emily queasy, forcing her to refuse the "world-famous" key lime pie that Ava had prepared.

"So how long are you going to stay in town?" Ava asked as they got ready to leave.

"I'm not sure," Colin said. "That hotel's not going to build itself, so probably not longer than a week."

Emily's heart sank. She'd known it wouldn't be much time, but a week? Would they be able to come up with a conclusion by then?

Especially since it looks like it'll be a cold day in hell before Colin moves back to Tall Pines. No matter how strongly he felt about her, she'd gotten the feeling that he was a wild animal caught in a trap as they'd sat through dinner.

"Well, come back anytime," Ava said expansively, hugging Emily. "I'm so glad, dear. So very, very glad."

Emily smiled wanly, then left with Colin. He let out an explosive breath as they got into the car.

"I thought that would *never* end," he burst out.

She laughed, a weak sound compared to her usual laughter. "Yeah. I love your mom, but she's pretty intense, huh?"

"She was adopted," he said as they drove back. "She's obsessed with family being close by. I love her, too, but…"

He let the sentence trail off and he looked pained.

"But you've got to be you," Emily said.

He stroked her shoulder. "You understand me," he said.

She nodded.

"Emily…"

"Don't," she interrupted. "We've still got a few days to figure something out. But I think I've had enough thinking for one night."

He was silent for a moment, then made a monosyllabic noise of assent. "Yeah, I understand that one." Then he grinned. "So what shall we do with the rest of our evening?"

She pulled the car into the driveway, looking at him beneath lowered eyelashes.

"Surprise me," she said huskily.

They'd worry about the future tomorrow. Right now, the confident and relieved smile on his face was all she could ask for—and the most she could handle.

9

COLIN HID HIS wince of discomfort as he and Emily walked through the door of Halloran's, a family-style diner that represented some of the only nightlife the town of Tall Pines had to offer. It was, as usual, packed to the rafters full of regulars. Everybody who was ambulatory, it seemed, hung out at Halloran's, either eating dinner, having monster ice cream sundaes or enjoying whatever sporting event was playing on the big-screen TV over the bar. It was loud, boisterous and crowded, just as he remembered.

He had to be crazy to take Emily here, of all places. But there was at least a method to his madness this time around.

"Are you sure about this?" Emily asked, pressing close to him, her breath brushing against his ear as she struggled to make herself heard over the strains of the jukebox. He reveled in the feel of her compact body molding itself against his for a second, then nodded.

"If we're going to do this," he said, his lips tickling her earlobe, "then we might as well dive in."

There was more to it than that, though. He knew exactly what was going to happen. They would be seated, then everyone in town would take the time to greet them, interrupting their dinner to not only ask about whether or not they were a couple but probably to weigh in on their relationship. Emily would then be forced to see just how problematic living in Tall Pines could be if they were going to be together. She knew it logically; she'd mentioned it when they first got together, after all. But he thought that a real-life demonstration of the small-town fishbowl that would be their dating atmosphere might be a more effective argument. He'd also see just how much he could take.

He wasn't betting on much. After one night, he figured he would remember exactly why he couldn't move back to Tall Pines…as if his entire visit hadn't been reminder enough.

And after tonight, when she was frustrated and distracted, he'd ask her if maybe she wouldn't mind visiting him in Paris for a few days. Maybe a long weekend. From there he'd show her the vast contrast between her life in Tall Pines and the glory of living out in the world. He'd show her adventure. New sights, new sounds, new people, all the things he loved about his job. He felt confident that she'd be won over.

Then he'd work, slowly but surely, on convincing her to stay with him and leave Tall Pines behind.

"Emily!" Mr. Halloran yelled from behind the bar. "And…good grief, is that Colin Reese?"

Just like that, the whole restaurant miraculously went quiet, except for the belting lyrics of "What'd I Say?" by Ray Charles. Colin watched as Emily blanched.

"Long time no see," Colin said easily, watching as Mr. Halloran came out from behind the bar to give Emily a big hug. To his surprise, he gave Colin a burly hug, as well.

"What, you get too accustomed to ritzy food that you can't come back to Halloran's?" he asked Colin, giving him a punch on the shoulder that actually stung a little. Not as much as the guilt, Colin realized. Mr. Halloran managed to make him feel about twelve years old. He half expected the large older man to put him in a headlock and give him a noogie, rubbing his knuckles across Colin's skull, for staying away so long.

"Whatever, it's nice to see you—both of you," Mr. Halloran declared expansively. "Hey, Janie! Look who's here!"

Janie, his wife, smiled broadly, hugging them both, as well. "I can't believe it," she gushed, as conversations started again around them.

"I do leave the inn occasionally," Emily said, blushing. "I mean, I love the burgers here...."

"No, no, not that," Janie said, ushering them through the crowd. "I can't believe you two came *here*. You just started dating, right? I would've expected you to want a little more privacy." She wiggled her eyebrows. "If you know what I mean."

Now Emily's blush was scarlet. Colin coughed. "Uh, we thought we'd come up for air and sustenance," he joked. This was working out better than he'd thought.

Janie laughed raucously. "Here's the best table in the house for you two love birds." She gave them a booth far from the music and the bar. It was relatively quiet and secluded.

"Thanks," Emily said, her voice ringing with appreciation. She took the seat that didn't face the room. Colin automatically sat across from her. "Maybe this wasn't such a good idea," she added when Janie walked away after leaving them with menus.

"If we're going to be a couple, we might as well get used to being seen together, right?" Colin asked mildly, looking over the menu. It hadn't changed one bit since he'd left. "Are the fries still as good as I remember? And the milk shakes?"

Emily nodded, distracted. "About being a couple..." she started, her voice tentative.

He gripped the menu a little tighter, but kept his voice steady. "Yup?"

Before she could continue, Evelyn Albee and her husband, Dale, came up to the side of their table. "How cute are you two!" Evelyn gushed, clasping her hands together. "Aren't they cute, Dale?"

"Adorable," Dale said, rolling his eyes. "How should I know?"

"Honey, honestly, you can be such a man sometimes," she said with a dismissive *tsk* noise. "Colin, all the ladies are still going on about you coming all the way back from Paris."

Colin shifted in the vinyl booth. This was exactly what he'd wanted to happen, but that didn't make it any more comfortable. "Emily's worth it," he said. And meant it.

"*Awwww*." Evelyn's eyes misted. "That is so precious."

"Evelyn." Dale nudged her. "You promised, remember?"

"Hmm? Oh, yes," she replied, straightening. "Anyway, we girls at the salon were talking…"

Colin braced himself.

"And we came to the decision that we really need to let you alone for a while."

It was like running off the edge of an escalator. Colin felt off balance. "What?"

Emily smiled gratefully. "Thanks, Evelyn. That's very kind."

"It can't be easy to start a relationship in this town," Evelyn said, shrugging. "Sure, watching people fall in love is something of a spectator sport here, but that doesn't mean that we can't respect some boundaries."

Colin blinked. This was not what he had been expecting.

"We figured that Colin hasn't been here in a while and he's probably having some trouble adjusting," she continued, speaking directly to Emily. "Madge said that you don't want to scare him off. After all, he's never really felt comfortable here anyway."

"Uh, hello, I'm sitting right here." Colin waved, nonplussed.

"Colin, you never *have* felt comfortable here, have you?" she repeated, turning to him with eagle-eye scrutiny.

He didn't know how to answer that. His mouth worked wordlessly, like a fish flopping on the deck of a boat. She laughed.

"Don't worry," Evelyn reassured him, laughing. "We'll make it nice and easy for you. It might take a little work, but I bet you'll be surprised at how quickly this place grows on you. Especially now that you're not a rebellious teenager. You've lived around the world and gotten a lot of that stuff out of you. Now maybe you can appreciate what you had growing up."

Colin stared at her, aghast at her observation. Was that what she thought? Was that what *everybody* thought? That it wasn't them—it was *him* that was the problem?

"Anyway, you kids have a nice dinner," Evelyn said, leaning over and hugging Emily, then patting Colin on the shoulder. "How long are you in town for, anyway?"

Colin was still stunned, so Emily answered. "We're not sure. He's going to have to go to Paris pretty soon. Maybe a week?"

"A lot can happen in a week." She winked at Colin, who gaped at her. "Have fun." With that, she linked her arm in Dale's and the two walked away. Colin noticed that everyone else in the restaurant was studiously avoiding looking over at him and Emily. Evelyn wound up talking to almost everyone before finally taking a seat at a table with Dale.

"Wow," Emily breathed with a deep exhalation. "How about that?"

"How about that," Colin echoed weakly.

"Are you all right?" she asked. "You look sort of nauseous."

"Huh? No. I'm fine."

But he wasn't fine. His mind was suddenly racing, turning over Evelyn Albee's words in his mind, testing them for validity. Feeling completely and foolishly unsure.

Emily didn't seem to notice his reticence as they ordered Halloran's Famous Patty Melts, French fries and milk shakes. "See them?" she said, nodding at a young couple holding hands at their dinner table. "That's Bobby Rothchild. His dad's younger brother was my boyfriend in college. Everybody was shocked when Billy started dating Molly Rutledge...."

He listened as Emily pointed out various people in the restaurant, marveling at the fact that he knew most of them or at least their families. Instead of being bored, he found himself laughing as Emily painted the portraits of what had happened to each, illustrating the history of the town since he'd moved away to college. He'd tuned his mother out so often he didn't realize how much he'd been missing...or how much he would actually enjoy catching up. The food was even better than he remembered, and he was surprised to discover that instead of putting up with his surroundings, he was slowly and inexorably being charmed by them.

It's because of Emily, he thought. With Emily, everything was brighter, sweeter. Better.

The jukebox started playing a slow tune, something bluesy and yet still romantic. Colin stood up, holding out his hand. "Want to give 'em something to talk about?" he asked, wiggling his eyebrows.

"Why, Colin," she said, batting her lashes outrageously. "Are you asking me to dance?"

"That's not all, if you're lucky."

Her eyes widened. "Here at Halloran's?" she whispered, sounding scandalized.

He laughed out loud, noticing several people turn at the sound, eyes wide. Was he that taciturn that people were shocked by his laughter? He shook his head. "I meant later at the inn," he clarified. "Dance first."

She smiled, putting her hand in his, and they headed to the postage-stamp-size dance floor. Merging with the crush of people, Colin put his arms around Emily's waist, smiling to himself as she rested her head on his shoulder. He breathed in her vanilla scent, nuzzling the crown of her hair.

"This is nice," she murmured against his chest.

They swayed easily, back and forth, while the other dancers cleared a path for them, keeping a respectful distance. He noticed people smiling warmly at him, and for the first time in his memory he felt like a part of the small town. Embraced by them. He held Emily tighter, enveloping her in his arms.

"I could get used to this," she added.

He leaned down, nudging her chin up with his fingertips. Without another word, he kissed her, long and slow and thoroughly.

They must've been that way a long time, because he slowly surfaced when the sound of whistling, applause and good-natured catcalls drowned out the music. He pulled away, blinking.

"Good one, man!" the teenager, Bobby, said, whistling loud enough to hail a cab. His date was applauding wildly. Evelyn and Dale were also clapping. Others joined in. Mr. and Mrs. Halloran were looking on proudly, beaming as though they were new parents.

"Wow," Emily said. "Maybe we should move to the 'later' portion of the program." She waved, then put her arm around Colin's waist, leading him toward the door.

He put his arm around her shoulder in response, marveling at the smiling faces surrounding them.

He'd been so convinced that it was horrible living here. Now, as he walked outside into the pristine winter night with Emily, he started to wonder if he'd been wrong, if it had just been teenage perception that had colored his view of the town and its inhabitants.

If that's the case, he wondered silently, *how am I going to convince her to leave with me?*

He closed his eyes as an even more disturbing thought pierced his mind.

And what if that's not the best solution?

"THANKS FOR COMING to this staff meeting," Emily said, sitting in the cramped office at the inn the next afternoon.

"No problem," Sue said, leaning back in her chair. "What's going on? I figured you'd be too busy, er, entertaining guests to get bogged down in inn details," she added with a mischievous grin.

Phillip made a sour face. "I don't think that's necessarily appropriate," he said sternly to Sue. Then he looked at Emily hesitantly. "Besides, her…uh, *guest,* is going to be leaving soon, anyway. Isn't that right? Which means we'll be getting back to business as usual." He looked smug at this observation.

Emily looked at the ceiling for a moment. She loved Sue, and Phillip had been a good employee for the few years that the inn had been open. But the fact that they were so close did make it difficult to discuss business without personal stuff getting mixed into it.

Which was going to make this discussion that much harder.

"Let's focus here," she urged instead. "Financially, according to the bookkeeper, we're doing okay, keeping afloat. A few more years like this fall, and we'll be doing well enough to make some improvements. Maybe even get a raise or two, add some staff."

Sue cheered at this. Phillip preened.

"The hotel has had some rough years, and we've all tightened our belts," she continued slowly. "But we've always had lots of potential, and I think that we're not the only ones to see it."

Now Sue and Phillip looked confused. "You're losing me," Sue said. "What's this about?"

Emily took a deep breath. "I've been…kicking around some options. About the future of the inn." She paused. "About my future."

Sue's eyes widened. "You're talking about Colin, aren't

you?" Before she could continue, Phillip broke in, his voice irate.

"You're talking about getting rid of the inn and leaving, is what you mean," he said sharply. "Putting us out of jobs, no less!"

Now Sue looked concerned. "Really, Em?" she asked, her eyes troubled. "We'd lose our jobs?"

"I didn't say that," Emily quickly reassured them, cursing Phillip mentally. "But I am thinking of selling the hotel. In a general, vague sort of way."

She didn't cushion the blow as well as she'd hoped. Sue looked at her as if Emily had run over her cat. Phillip, on the other hand, looked as though Emily had run over *him*.

"You can't do this to us," Phillip pleaded, his voice more impassioned than she'd ever heard him. "You can't do this to Tall Pines!"

"How would you even start going about doing something like that?" Sue sounded bewildered. "I mean, it's not like you can just put it for sale on eBay or something."

Emily leaned back in her chair. "Like I said, it's tentative," she said, keeping her voice strong. Then she slumped a little. "But, er…I was thinking of asking J.P.—I mean, Joy. She's run hotels for years."

Sue turned white. Phillip turned purple.

"You've already looked into it?" Phillip shouted with outrage.

"Okay, you need to calm down, Phillip," Emily told him sternly. "We're friends, but I'm still your boss, and it's my inn besides. Quit yelling at me!"

He crossed his arms, his expression sullen, but he did fall silent. Sue looked near tears, so Emily focused on her next.

"I'm not making any decisions on short notice. You know me, Sue. I wouldn't do anything without giving it a lot of thought."

"You've been thinking about it for a while," Sue accused. "You weren't sure you wanted to turn the place into a hotel in the first place, but you were afraid to get rid of it. Afraid of letting down your dad."

Emily's mouth snapped shut as Sue's words stung her heart. "I love this hotel," she said, tears forming at the corners of her eyes. "And I told you that in confidence. *As my best friend.*"

Phillip pounced. "If you sold the hotel, they'd change the name. You could say goodbye to the Stanfield Arms forever."

Another pang, one she hadn't expected. Emily bit her lip hard, blinking to keep the tears from falling. "I said I haven't made any definitive…"

"They'd bring in new people," Sue said, anguished. "You know they would. I don't have any experience in the hotel business. They wouldn't want me to be a manager!"

"You've got five years of hotel experience," Emily said, exasperated.

"No, I don't!" Sue wailed.

"You've got the experience *here,* you goof! Remember? Worked here for five years?"

"Oh." Sue sat back, momentarily put off stride.

Emily felt the muscles in her back and neck tense into knots. This was going much, much worse than she'd expected.

"But they'll have better people," Phillip pointed out, making matters worse. "They'll want people who have outside experience. They'll probably bring in their own staff."

"Phillip, would you stop that?" Emily snapped. "Honestly. It's like you're yelling 'Fire!' in a theater. You're just trying to get Sue riled up, and I don't appreciate it."

If he weren't a grown man, Emily would've sworn the guy was pouting. No, she was right. He *was* pouting.

"Nothing would happen overnight," she promised, enunciating clearly and tapping her finger on the tabletop with each syllable. "And I still haven't made any firm decisions. Can we repeat that together? I'm not going anywhere."

"Not yet," Phillip muttered.

She glared at him and he shut up.

"Okay, that wraps it up for our staff meeting," Emily said, standing up. "Phil, you'd better go work the front desk." She waited until he left, then turned to Sue. "Are you okay? I thought you'd be surprised, but I didn't expect you to get so unhinged."

"I'm sorry." Sue sniffed. "It's not your fault. It's just...I think I'm pregnant."

Emily's eyes widened, then she rushed over to her friend, giving her a hug. "That's great news!"

"Thanks," Sue said, hugging her back. "But it's made me crazy emotional. I never know how I'm going to react to anything. Besides, I hate the thought of you going away."

"How many times do I have to say this? I haven't—"

"—Made any firm decision," Sue repeated with a watery grin. "Yeah, yeah, you said. But you're thinking about it. And you've got a six-foot, gorgeous reason to leave waiting upstairs in your apartment."

Emily felt the heat of a blush on her cheeks. "This doesn't have to do with him."

Sue stared at Emily in utter disbelief.

"Okay. It doesn't have to do with him *completely*," Emily amended, embarrassed even further.

"I'm glad you're getting back into the dating pool," Sue said seriously, clasping her hands together. "And I don't want you to think I'm a lousy friend. I want what's best for you."

"Thanks." Emily relaxed, feeling relief for the first time since she'd called the staff meeting.

"But I'm not sure that Colin and Paris and selling the inn is really what's best for you," Sue continued slowly. "You're small-town, Emily. You love this place. And I know you. Could you really forgive yourself if you gave up your father's house?"

Emily winced. That cut to the heart of it pretty much.

"I've got a lot to think about," Emily said slowly.

"Yeah, you do," Sue agreed. "There's a lot of excitement and passion in an affair, Emily, but it's not a marriage."

She stiffened. "What do you mean?"

"I mean, did it ever occur to you," Sue said slowly, "that Tall Pines is your longest relationship? You're married to this town. You're married to this life."

"I wouldn't say that," Emily said, completely disconcerted.

"You wouldn't say that?" Sue laughed ruefully. "You, the woman who's been on almost every town committee since she was fourteen years old? The girl voted most likely to have a statue erected to her in high school? Are you kidding me?"

"There's more to me than that," Emily protested.

"That's not the point," Sue countered. "The point is it's a big part of you. Too big a part for you to just walk away from."

With that, Sue walked out, leaving Emily alone and confused in her office. She unconsciously headed back upstairs to her apartment, her body numb, her mind churning.

Is that all people see of me? Is that what they think?

It disturbed her. Sue was her best friend, but apparently even she couldn't see Emily moving out of the small town. They saw it as a betrayal.

Is it such a bad thing to want to grow?

Colin was sitting on her couch watching TV when she walked in. She sat next to him on shaking legs.

He quickly shut off the TV. "Are you okay?" he asked, his voice rich with concern.

She tried to nod, but wound up tilting her head to hold back the tears instead. "Do you think that I'm small-town?"

His eyes widened. "It depends on how you define *small-town*. Do you mean unsophisticated, closed-minded, a hick?" He shook his head emphatically. "In that case, absolutely not.

But if you mean warm, open, friendly and compassionate, then yes, you have some definite small-town elements."

She hugged him, feeling comforted by his heat, his strength. "Do you think that I'll never leave Tall Pines?"

She felt him go quiet, every muscle freezing in place beneath her hands. "No," he said, his voice sounding oddly strained. "I don't think that."

"Really?"

"Really." He kissed her temple, his hands starting to stroke down her back in delicious, lazy glides. "I think that you might have lived in Tall Pines all your life, but you've got the soul of an adventurer. And given the opportunity, I think that you'd leap at the chance to try something new."

She grinned at him. He always knew just what to say. She leaned up, kissing him softly at first, then with growing passion.

"Speaking of trying something new," she said, feeling a streak of mischievousness shoot through her, "I was thinking…have you ever had chocolate-covered strawberries?"

He shrugged. "Sure."

She tugged him toward the kitchen, shedding clothes as she did. "Not like this, you haven't."

COLIN WALKED INTO the town hall with Emily on his arm and lovemaking on his mind. The woman was right—he'd never had chocolate-covered strawberries presented in quite so exotic a fashion. She'd melted some dark chocolate, warm and liquid in a glass bowl, with cut strawberries presented on a plate…and herself naked on the dining room table. He'd never had so enticing a platter to eat from before. He'd painted her nipples with the chocolate, licking them off with a slow thoroughness, then placed a strawberry between her thighs, amusing himself by nibbling it out, then lapping up the sweet strawberry juices that had drizzled into the soft folds of her labia. She'd licked chocolate off his cock, taking him in deep, circling the flesh of his blunt head with her curious tongue. Sticky, coated with fruit juice and chocolate, they'd taken a shower and then made love standing up under the pounding water, so turned on they could barely stand it.

He could never get enough of Emily, he knew that. If he was willing to put up with a Tall Pines town meeting, it had to be love.

"Colin?" his mother said, astounded. "What in the world are you doing here? Oh, you're with Emily. Of course! Why don't you two sit here by us?"

Colin looked at Emily, who smirked at him. Apparently Evelyn Albee's Mafia-style assurances that the town had agreed to leave them alone did not apply to his parents. He wasn't really surprised, but he *was* disappointed. Emily sat next to him on one of the uncomfortable wooden folding chairs.

"I'm sure it'll be a short meeting," she reassured him, her eyes glowing. She took his hand, lacing her fingers in his. Her smile reminded him of the dining room table and their "dessert."

He swallowed, leaning over. "Don't suppose you want to take a quick tour of the boiler room?" he croaked.

She laughed, but for a second her expression turned devilish. She'd considered it, he felt quite sure.

He grinned back. The town meeting always had an intermission after an hour. He could always change her mind then.

"All right, all right," Mayor Tim said, pounding his gavel against the hardwood podium, looking serious. Colin had largely overcome his jealousy for the man now that things had worked out. Mayor Tim might want a passionless marriage of convenience with Emily, but Colin knew firsthand that there was no way Emily could live without that flash and burn of desire. He stroked the delicate skin on the inside of her wrist, his eyes never leaving the front of the room. He heard her gasp softly and smiled secretly to himself. That was a pleasure point for her, he'd discovered—much like the soft bend of her inner elbow and the dimple just under the curve of her buttocks. It was like charting unexplored territory, each new spot a treasure trove of pleasure and suspense.

She was one of the best adventures he'd ever pursued.

"We've got a lot to cover. Can't we start, for once, on time?" With that grouse, Tim managed to get a lot of the chattering citizens of Tall Pines to quiet down. "We've got a short agenda, and it might be nice to leave after two hours. So let's move briskly. First item—the upcoming Valentine's dance at the Otter Lodge—"

"Wait a second," a man's voice yelled from the back of the room. "I thought that you needed to ask if there was any new business first! That's always the first item!"

Colin noticed that Emily stiffened, whipping her head around to look at the loudmouth. He glanced back.

It was Phillip, the manager at the inn. The pain in the ass who always gave Colin a dirty look.

"Who's running the inn?" Colin asked, surprised.

"Sue, I guess," Emily said, sounding puzzled...and nervous. "But she's not supposed to be. Phillip's never been interested in town politics before. He lives for the inn."

Her palm turned moist in his hand, and Colin realized she was sweating. "What's wrong?" he whispered.

Before she could answer, Tim cleared his throat. "Well, yes, but I thought we'd skip it tonight. I don't think anybody has any new business. At least nobody mentioned anything to me this week..."

"Well, *I* have new business," Phillip continued imperiously. "Business that affects this whole town."

"And you are?" Tim asked, amusement clear in his voice.

Phillip gave him a withering stare. "You *know* who I am, Tim. I lived down the street from you for eight years!"

"Let me rephrase that," Tim said easily. "What exactly has happened to *you* that is so earth-shattering we've got to introduce it as new business and dedicate God knows how long to dealing with your problem?"

Colin smothered a grin. Now that he wasn't in competition with the guy, Tim seemed pretty cool.

Phillip's expression was one of supreme distaste. "Well, I thought that it might concern the town that one of their leading landmarks would be sold to outside interests," he proclaimed, his voice ringing through the auditorium like a Shakespearean actor's. "But I guess it's *far* more important for you to discuss the Valentine's dance."

"Sell a landmark?" This from Mrs. Rutledge, who sounded outraged. She got to her feet, frail but still an imposing presence. "Who's selling what to whom?"

Tim's frown was deep. "I have no idea what you're talking about, Phillip," he said, impatient. "Want to cut the theatrics and explain yourself?"

"Maybe you should ask *Emily*."

Emily went pale. Colin clutched her hand. What was going on here?

"Emily," Tim prompted. "Do you know what he's talking about?"

She stood up, and the auditorium went silent as a tomb. All eyes were on her. Colin still held her hand, feeling her tremble slightly beneath his fingers.

"What he's talking about," she retorted, her voice betraying only the slightest tremor of nerves, "is not of any concern to the town. It was a *private* conversation, an *internal* conversation, and it was just in passing besides."

Everyone looked confused by this, and Colin watched as Emily turned a poisonous glare at Phillip. Phillip stood his ground.

"I don't think it's private or internal," he countered, "if

you're thinking of selling a building that's been in this town for over three generations."

Colin heard everyone in the meeting gasp collectively and he winced. *Oh crap. Here we go.*

Emily wilted under the scrutiny, slumping slightly. He squeezed her hand, trying to give her some comfort.

"Is this true, Em?" Tim asked, sounding scandalized. "You're going to sell the inn?"

"I hadn't made any decision about it," she said. "I was just thinking about it and I discussed it with Sue and Phillip. I didn't think it was anything that the town needed to know about yet."

"Well, it affects all of us, missy," Mrs. Rutledge replied sharply. "You can't throw around an idea like that and not expect it to ruffle some feathers!"

Sell the inn? Colin was gobsmacked…and heartened. If she was willing to entertain the idea, then she was already thinking of leaving the town. Hopefully to be with him.

He smiled to himself, cheered immensely by the thought.

"Like I said," Emily repeated, "I'm not sure…"

"You couldn't possibly sell the Stanfield house," Ava Reese interrupted, looking distraught. "It's been in your family for so long. Your father would be heartbroken!"

"Mom," Colin whispered fiercely, seeing Emily's stricken expression. "For God's sake."

"What? It's true!"

"You're upsetting her," he said a little louder than he'd intended.

"What do you have to do with this anyway, Colin?" This came from old Mr. Carlton, a well-respected member of the community. "You're not even a part of this town! Haven't been for years!"

Colin turned, surprised at the vehemence in the man's voice. "Emily's my concern."

"Obviously you're her concern, too," Phillip said snidely, "since she never considered selling the place before you showed up and *moved into her apartment.*"

Colin's jaw clenched, and the muscles in his arms bunched. That was hitting below the belt. He suspected that Phillip had a thing for Emily, and now that Emily was connected with Colin, Phillip was lashing out in the only way he knew how.

Unfortunately, his verbal assault was doing its damage. Emily looked sick, and she held on to the back of her chair for support.

"That's none of your business," Colin barked. "And it is *not* fodder for the town meeting."

"Colin," Emily said, shaking her head.

"What?" he asked, confused. "It isn't. We're adults. And our relationship has nothing to do with anything in Tall Pines."

"She's talking about selling the Stanfield house," Tim said, his voice mild even though his expression was dismayed. "It's one of the oldest houses in the town, on one of the biggest parcels of land. Which she got rezoned for commercial." He sighed heavily. "I hate to say it, but it *does* affect the town. If she sells—or if she's even considering selling—it's a matter of public debate."

"She said she wasn't sure," Colin prevaricated. He looked at Emily. "You're not sure, are you?"

She looked pained. "No."

"There you have it," he said. "Now leave her alone...."

"This is all your fault!" Phillip shouted, undeterred. "You never gave a damn about what happened to this town. You just wanted to get out as soon as you could. This place could burn to the ground for all you cared! So don't pretend that you've got any say in what she does or doesn't do. You don't belong here. *You never did.*"

"Will you *shut up?*" Colin growled.

He glanced around at the faces staring at him. He saw it

then—the sentiment that Phillip had shouted so crazily echoed in their expressions.

He didn't belong here. He was jeopardizing the town by affecting one of its leading citizens and convincing her to not only leave but to possibly destroy one of their most famous homes. He was changing things.

He might be grown-up, but he was still Hell-Raiser Reese, the troublemaker. The kid that didn't fit in.

He grimaced. "Come on, Emily," he said, pain and alienation slamming through him like a freight train. "I don't think I'm wanted here."

"I'll be there in a moment," she replied, looking at him imploringly. "I'll meet you back at the hotel."

He stared at her, then nodded curtly. He turned on his heel, stalking out of the auditorium, feeling every pair of eyes watching his exit.

In that moment he'd never felt more like a stranger. And without Emily, he'd never felt more alone.

10

EMILY'S BLOOD WAS pounding in her temples as she watched Colin walk out of the auditorium, surrounded by the judgmental gazes of the townspeople that she'd considered her friends for so long.

She had been quiet, the model citizen, for her entire life. But in one moment something inside her had snapped.

"How dare you?" she demanded, addressing the group at large. "What gives *any* of you the right to discuss my private life this way or to talk to Colin Reese that way?"

"Now, Em," Tim said, trying to get control of the situation. "We're just—"

"No, Tim," she said, walking up to the podium. She felt as if electricity were sizzling through her skin as she grabbed the microphone, tugging it down to her chin. "You ask me if I'm going to sell the hotel. Say that it's something I'd need to discuss with the town. Well, the thing is, if I had decided to sell, I would have told each and every one of you. I would have brought it up at the town meeting and at Evelyn's salon and at the post office, the grocery store and every committee meeting. You all know me and you *know* I don't do anything lightly."

There was a general murmur of assent. "Which is what makes this all the more disappointing, dear," Mrs. Carlton said, sounding confused.

"Yes, it *is* disappointing, Mrs. Carlton," Emily retorted.

"Disappointing that because of one...one *loudmouthed butt-head,* you all decided that I somehow have impaired judgment and believed that I'd hurt the town. You believe that not only do I have a responsibility to disclose every detail of my private life, you actually think that *you've got a right to interfere with it*. And, finally, you believe that because I'm sleeping with Colin Reese that somehow *he's* the one to blame!"

Tim had the grace to look shamefaced. Ava and Harry Reese simply looked shocked. Phillip still looked angry but also a little nervous. Not as nervous as he should be, Emily thought acidly, but it was a start.

"Well, you know what? I'm *tired* of being the town's golden girl." She slammed her palm down on the podium, punctuating her statement with all the passion of an evangelical preacher. "I've loved living here, so I've put up with the interference and the gossip and the meddling. But I am not going to watch you righteously stomp all over me and hurt Colin simply because you feel like I'm not doing what's best for the town."

"What are you saying?" Mrs. Rutledge said, sounding aghast.

"I'm saying that the hotel is mine," Emily replied. "Selling it is not a matter of public debate. You can gossip about it, you can be disappointed with it, but none of you has a say in what I decide."

"And I suppose *Colin* has a say?"

She looked at Phillip, noting the undisguised hatred in his eyes, the fury in his voice. "It's my decision," she shot back. "Just like this one—Phillip, you can consider yourself fired."

Phillip finally looked stunned.

"Now, Em." Tim stepped in. "Let's all calm down here. Things are getting out of hand. You're acting too emotionally and you're going to say and do things that you'll regret later...."

"That's the thing, Tim," Emily said, her voice clear and

even. "I'm not. I've thought about selling the place a million times since I inherited it, but I never said anything. I worried about what my father would think or what you would think or what would happen to the town. But now I know that you all think that what happens to the town is more important than what happens to me. And I don't agree with that."

"Come on, Emily." The mayor crossed his arms. "That's not fair."

"No, it isn't," she agreed. "Mrs. Carlton, did you once think that it might be hard for me to run the hotel by myself? That some months I've had trouble making ends meet? That I can't afford staff and I did a lot of the work myself, starting out?"

"Well, no," Mrs. Carlton said.

"And Mrs. Reese, you say that my father would be heartbroken if I sold the place. Wouldn't you think that he loved me enough to want me to be happy?"

Ava didn't say anything. She just looked away, embarrassed.

"None of you know me," Emily said. "Not the way I'd hoped you would. The fact that you think it's okay to jump into my life like this…well, let's just say *I'm* disappointed in *you*."

With that, she stepped away from the podium, heading down the aisle and walking toward the door.

Phillip stepped in front of her. "You don't mean that," he said. "I know it was wrong of me to say all of this in front of everybody, but I just wanted to shock a little common sense into you, that's all."

"Well, surprise," she said, trying to sidestep him. "You betrayed me and made an ass of yourself. Oh, and lost your job. Congratulations on that."

"I only did it because I care about you," he protested, sounding desperate. He put his hands on her arms. She tried to shrug them off, but his grip was tight. "I've been in love with you since I started working at the inn. Longer. You just never saw me!"

She should've suspected—there were plenty of clues. The way he always volunteered to work late. How he'd sometimes deliver dinner to her apartment, staring as if he were waiting to be invited in. It had made her a little uncomfortable, but he'd been such a good manager, and she'd needed the help…maybe she just hadn't wanted to see. She shook her head.

"I don't feel that way about you," she relented. "And I'm sorry. But you had no right to do what you did tonight."

"You're making a big mistake with Colin," he said, sullen as a child. "I've stood by you, just like this town has. He doesn't have any loyalty. He's just in it for himself."

She stiffened. "And you're the prime example of loyalty in Tall Pines?" she asked. "Get your hands off me."

"Emily…"

"Now."

He released her. She walked out the door.

There was a light snow flurry, fat flakes dancing out of the dark blue sky. She walked carefully toward the inn, letting the cold air clear her head.

Emily felt heartsick at what had just happened. How could it have gotten so out of control so quickly? She knew how much the inn meant to the town, but she had no idea that they thought they could actually dictate to her what she should and shouldn't do. She wasn't a child. And as much as she loved the town, it wasn't her family.

She wasn't going to keep worrying about what people would think. She was making this decision on her own.

She walked into the hotel. Sue was at the front desk, looking concerned. "You all right?" she asked.

"No," Emily answered. "I need you to work some extra shifts."

"Uh, okay," Sue said uneasily. "For how long?"

"Until I can find a replacement for Phillip."

"You *fired* Phillip?"

"Yes. I'll tell you the whole thing later," Emily said, cutting off Sue's barrage of questions. "Right now I've got some things I need to do."

She left Sue wide-eyed and shocked. Instead of going up to her apartment, she headed to Joy Webster's room.

Joy answered her knock. "Hey, there," she said. "What's up?"

"When we talked before, you mentioned financing," Emily said. "Do you know people who might buy a hotel?"

Joy looked surprised. "Well…yes. But are you sure you want to sell?"

Emily took a deep breath. "I'm not positive. But I do want to get the ball rolling."

Joy nodded. "It's such a lovely place. I haven't had this relaxing a vacation in I don't know how long. I am in love with this town."

I'm not, Emily thought but bit back on the urge to share her current bitterness. "It's got its moments," she said instead. "But I've lived here all my life and I'd like to explore some new options."

"My father buys hotels." Joy rubbed her chin slowly. "He'd snap up this place in a heartbeat. But… I don't know that I can recommend that."

"Who else might buy?"

"I'm not sure," Joy answered. "I could look, but it'd take some time."

"But your father would buy it in a hurry," Emily echoed.

Joy nodded, looking unhappy.

"I know it's a big favor, but would you contact him?" Emily paused, her expression pleading. "I'll even give you a finder's fee."

"I'll do it for free," Joy said. "But…are you *sure?*"

Emily closed her eyes.

"Yeah," she said. "Yeah, I'm sure."

"All right, then. I'll get the ball rolling."

Emily suddenly felt dizzy. "I appreciate it."

"I was going to pack up and leave tomorrow," Joy added, "but I guess I'll hang out for a while longer. See how this deal goes. I don't have anything pressing and I enjoy it here, anyway."

Emily nodded, barely hearing what Joy was saying. "I have to go," she said finally. "I will call you." She left in a rush, heading upstairs to her apartment. She opened the door to find Colin pacing in the living room in front of the fireplace. His face was like a storm cloud.

"What happened?" he asked. "Are you all right?"

She smiled. He was angry, and rightfully so—but not because of how they'd treated him. He was angry because he was worried about her.

He always put her first.

She threw her arms around him, kissing him fiercely. After a moment's surprise, he kissed her back with the consuming passion she'd grown accustomed to. When they parted, she rested her forehead against his broad chest.

"I'm selling the inn," she murmured. "At least I think I am."

"You don't have to make any decision tonight," he reassured her, stroking her back.

"Can you get me out of here?" she said, curling into his arms like a cat, enjoying the comfort of his touch. "I just…I want to get out of town for a while. I want to feel better."

He smiled at her. "Sure, sweetheart," he murmured. "I think I've got just the place."

"COLIN, THANK YOU," Emily breathed. "It's so beautiful. I had no idea."

Colin looped an arm over her shoulders, breathing in the crisp winter air as they walked together. They were crossing one of Paris's many gardens, the Tuileries, and had spent the morning in the Louvre after having a breakfast of coffee and pastries in an open-air café. They'd wandered through the city for the past two days. Emily wanted to go everywhere, see everything. More importantly, Colin wanted to show her.

She'd asked him to take her out of town, so he'd taken her on a long weekend…to France. With any luck, it would be a short jump from convincing her to take a vacation, to convincing her to stay.

"What else do you want to see?" Colin asked, feeling like a conquering hero. "Anything. The city's your oyster."

"Actually…I'm getting tired," Emily said, looking embarrassed. "Would it be all right if we went back to your apartment for a bit?"

"Sure, sure," Colin said quickly, feeling badly. "Jet lag?"

She made a noncommittal noise. "I don't know. Haven't flown this far before."

He was so used to flying around the world, he'd forgotten how tough it could be for other people. She hadn't gotten her clock adjusted to European time.

He brought her back to his apartment, just off Saint-Germain-des-Prés. It was three stories up, an older building with an irregular circular staircase and a great view of the street. She stood at the window, wrapping her sweater around herself while he made them espresso.

"I made these strong," he said, handing her a small cup and saucer, "but if you'd rather nap, maybe…"

"No, no," she said, taking the coffee. "I need to get used to Paris time."

She sipped at the drink, still staring out the window.

He sighed to himself. She wasn't content—and it had nothing to do with Paris. She was still feeling guilty about the hotel and the sale. She'd already spoken with Joy Webster several times since they'd arrived in Europe. She wasn't backing down, but she obviously wasn't happy.

He wasn't sure how to feel. On the one hand, he loved the idea of her being free to move as she liked, especially since he wouldn't mind having her stay with him for a while to see where things would lead. But on the other hand, she was obviously having seller's remorse. She had been hurt by Phillip's accusations and the small town's knee-jerk response to any sort of drastic change. He didn't know if she wanted to keep the hotel, but he knew that deep down she didn't want to sell it like this.

He rubbed her shoulders. They were like slabs of ice, cold and stiff. She moaned softly as he worked out the knots of tension.

"That feels wonderful." She sighed, leaning back against him.

"I offer full massage services," he murmured against her ear. "You'd have to get naked, of course."

"Well, if that's the only way," she teased, then put her cup down and followed him to the bedroom.

Emily stretched out on the bed, pulling off her sweater, then unbuttoning her prim white blouse. She tossed both to the floor. Then she undid her jeans, sliding them off her legs, taking off her socks with them. She was left in matching underwear, a black bra and French-cut panties. "Completely naked?" she asked innocently with a gleam in her eyes.

He rubbed his hands together. "'Fraid so."

She chuckled low in her throat, then reached back and unhooked her bra, tossing it by her sweater. Then she inched the panties down, slipping them over the long length of her legs before kicking them also to the floor. "Ooh, it's chilly," she said, tugging back his covers and crawling under. "Turn the heater on."

"All right," he said, doing as she asked, "but trust me—in a minute you won't need the heater."

She pulled the covers up to her chin. "Why, what do you mean?"

He took off his clothes, then dived into bed with her. She laughed as they tussled briefly beneath the covers. "This isn't a massage!" she cried, shrieking with laughter.

"It's better," he huffed, playfully wrestling with her. "Hey, you want to get relaxed or not?"

The two of them collapsed in a heap, laughing madly. Then he settled himself on top of her, his naked skin covering hers, and all humor ended. He kissed her slowly and tenderly, his lips nipping at hers. He captured her full lower lip between his teeth, sucking softly, and she gasped, her nipples turning into hard pebbles, raking against his bare chest. His cock went hard, pressing against her stomach, and the kiss turned more serious.

"Emily," he murmured, his breath hot against her skin. He sucked at her neck with gentle pressure, and she gasped, arching against him. The edges of her nails clawed down his back gently, and she scooted up so his erection was nestled between her thighs, cradled against her moist heat. "Wait a second. Let me get a condom.…"

"No, wait," she said, twisting under the covers. She reached down, taking his cock into her soft, smooth hands. Then she angled herself downward, moving him from her palms to the wet heat of her mouth. When she started to suck, he groaned, moving on his own toward the juncture of her thighs. With all the concentration he could muster, he parted the auburn curls at her opening, pressing his fingers into her slowly, his penetration eased by her growing dampness. She moaned around his penis, the sound stroking him as softly as her tongue. Colin leaned forward, exchanging fingers for his mouth. He caressed her softly, first with his teeth, then by flicking his tongue and tasting her honeyed wetness. She gasped and bucked against him in surprise, then her thighs eagerly parted to give him better access. He continued tracing her clit with his tongue as his finger moved in and out slowly, pressing inside her, searching for the elusive spot of her pleasure.

She hummed, increasing her speed slightly, taking him deeply into her mouth, her hands cupping his balls and tracing them with featherlight delicacy. He almost came then and there but fought his way back from the edge, moving his mouth and fingers in careful orchestration. She was moving more frantically now, and he struggled for self-control.

She pulled away, her breath coming in short, panting gasps. "I want to feel your cock inside me," she said.

She didn't need to ask twice. He grabbed the condom, rolling it on hastily with shaking hands. She pressed him against the mattress, tossing the covers aside, then lowered herself inch by inch onto his hard, eager erection. He groaned softly as she enveloped him in her wet softness. "That feels so good," he muttered through gritted teeth. She lifted herself up, then slid back down even more slowly, her thighs clenching together, her body tightening around him. He lifted his hips, burying himself deeper inside her. She swiveled slightly, and his world went gray around the edges.

"Emily," he murmured, clutching her hips, grinding her against him. She twined her legs with his, her breathing turning shallow and quick as she moved with force, sliding her clit along his cock, rubbing it where the shaft met his body. She made soft little cries of pleasure every time their bodies met, when he was buried in her fully.

"Oh, right there," she purred, sliding with purpose against him.

He was close to the edge. "I want you to come, baby," he murmured. "I'm close. I want you there."

"Yes," she breathed. "Oh, *yes*…"

She moaned as he lunged inside her. He clutched at her hips, holding her flush against him, burying himself fully, and she covered his hands with her own, urging him to hold her tighter, grip her harder, go even deeper. The feeling was intoxicating. He found himself moving to the ever-changing rhythm she set.

"*Yes!*" she screamed, and he felt the force of her orgasm spasming around his cock like a vise.

Just like that, he was forced over the edge. He thrust into her over and over, emptying himself inside her. She met his every movement, impaling herself on his hardness, making tiny mewling cries of ecstasy that matched his groans of release. Afterward, she collapsed on top of him, both of them breathing hard.

When they recovered, Colin cleaned himself up, then went back to bed next to her. He kissed her softly. "Now I need a nap," he said, yawning.

She shook her head, smiling. "I do feel more relaxed," she admitted, propping herself up with one arm. "So I guess you did your job."

He studied her face. Unfortunately, the smile didn't reach her eyes.

His heart fell. If their lovemaking couldn't cheer her up, what could? "You're still upset," he noted, his voice low.

Her eyes widened. "No, I'm not."

"You think I can't tell?"

Emily looked as if she was going to argue the point, then she let out a long exhalation. "No," she said. "I won't bother. I am still upset."

"Does staying there mean that much to you?" He steeled himself for the answer.

"No," she replied, and he let out a breath he didn't know he was holding. "I've daydreamed about leaving tons of times.

Long vacations, sabbaticals. Early on, when I was having so much money trouble, I used to dream about the place burning down," she said, looking sheepish. "That was just stress, though. But I still love the place. And the town." She twirled an auburn lock of hair around her fingers, nibbling at the end. "Guess I want to have my cake and eat it, too, huh?"

Some of his guilt subsided. "If you're just selling it for me," he declared, "then don't."

She looked as if he'd pinched her. "What?"

"I mean it," he said slowly with more bravery than he was feeling. "Because if you move here and live with me, I want it to be because you genuinely want to…because you're excited to be with me and you're thrilled with the adventure of it all. Not because I railroaded you into it. Certainly not because the people of Tall Pines pissed you off." He sat up, cupping her face in his hands. "If you move here for any other reason, then it'll always hang between us, and I don't think that's a good way for a relationship to start."

She stared at him silently. He stroked her cheek, then put his hands down by his sides. He wondered if he'd said too much. Had he scared her off? Been too aggressive? Too brutally honest?

When she still hadn't said anything a full minute later, worry turned into paranoia. "You're killing me here," he finally muttered. "What are you thinking?"

She closed her eyes. When she opened them, they were rimmed with unshed tears.

"Oh, jeez," he said, appalled. "I didn't mean…"

"You're asking me to live with you?"

He blinked. "Well, yeah. I thought that was obvious."

"You thought it was obvious," she echoed, shaking her head and laughing. "We may want to work on our communication a bit."

Then she kissed him, a slow, lingering kiss that only had the slightest hint of sadness to it. When she pulled away, she looked at him with wonder.

"You want to try that again?" she said with a small grin.

"Huh? Oh." He cleared his throat. "If you're going to sell the hotel anyway…"

She frowned.

He started over. "No matter what, I want you to move to Paris. I want you to live with me. I want you to enjoy a whole new life. I want to share my adventure here with you."

"Very nice," she said, snuggling against him.

"So what's the answer?"

"I don't know," she said.

"You don't know?" he yelped. "But…"

He looked down at her face and he could see her confusion…and pain.

He closed his eyes, counted to ten. Then opened his eyes. "All right. You take your time."

She kissed him sweetly, lingeringly. "I love you," she whispered.

He felt a zing through his system like a power surge. "I love you, too," he murmured. Then Colin held her tight and hoped against hope that everything would work out for the best.

"ARE YOU SURE YOU can't stay longer?" Colin called from the kitchen.

"I'm stretching my vacation as it is," Emily said ruefully, stepping out of the bedroom. It was Wednesday, and she'd only meant to stay till Tuesday at the latest. "I have to be back by the end of the week. Sue is probably frantic without Phillip there. It's not fair to her."

"You're right." He sighed, putting a plate of pastries out on the table. She'd gained five pounds in the few days she'd been here, easily. Or at least she would have if they weren't walking for miles every day.

"You've got to have stuff to do," she said, wondering again if she was preventing him from focusing on his work.

"I'm meeting with the building crew next week as well as the owner. So I guess I will be pretty busy." He sat down next to her, rubbing her shoulder. "But I'm going to miss you every second you're gone. You know that, right?"

She warmed under his attention like a flower facing the sun. No one else had made her feel this cherished, this incredibly special before.

"At least stay till Sunday," he murmured, nuzzling her neck.

"Colin," she protested weakly.

He made doe eyes at her, trying hard to look harmless. She laughed at the attempt.

"Let me call the hotel," she relented. "If Sue's swamped, there's no way I can stay."

He grinned like a little boy on Christmas morning. She laughed again, then picked up the phone. With effort, she dialed the international code and the phone number of the inn.

Sue picked up on the fourth ring. "Stanfield Arms," she said, sounding frazzled.

Emily immediately felt guilty. "Hey, Sue," she greeted her. "How are you holding up?"

"Oh, hey, Emily," Sue replied, some of the stress vanishing from her voice. "I'm hanging in there, but I gotta tell you, I am going to be *so* happy when you're here where you belong. When's your vacation over again? Tomorrow?" She sounded hopeful.

"Er, I was thinking maybe Sunday," Emily said tentatively.

"Oh, hell." Sue let out a long breath.

"But I can come back sooner," Emily quickly added. "Friday okay?"

"That'd be great," Sue said gratefully.

Emily bit her lip. "I shouldn't have fired Phillip before ;aving," she said, then amended her statement. "I mean, I *should* ave fired Phillip. I should not have left immediately after."

"Phillip wouldn't have helped, I don't think. You know ow much he depended on you. He would have freaked out vhen he had to make all the decisions." Sue paused. Honestly, I didn't know how much *I* relied on you being here ɔ run the place."

"I'm sure you're doing a great job," Emily reassured her. It's good that I left, I think. Now you know you can handle hings without me, and it'll be that much easier next time."

"Next time?" Sue repeated, aghast. "You've leaving *again?*"

Emily's heart fell. "Not immediately," she said. "But I was oping…"

"We really need to talk when you get back," Sue interrupted.

"What about?"

"About finding a replacement for me as well as for Phillip," he said with a hiccupy little sob.

"Oh, Sue." Emily cradled the phone. "Are you all right?"

"I can't do this all by myself," Sue said. "I never realized how much you handle until you left, and if you're going to be eaving a lot…well, with being pregnant and everything, it's more than I think I should deal with right now."

Emily nodded even though Sue couldn't see her. "I thought you needed the job, though."

"When Vernon found out about the baby, he took that higher-paying job in Hartford," Sue informed her with evident pride. "He said he wanted me to stay home once the baby's born. So you'll definitely have to replace me, no matter what."

Emily felt flabbergasted.

"But you're going to sell the place anyway," Sue continued,

"so I figured it wouldn't matter. You can find someone tempo rary to fill in for Phillip, and I'm sure I can ride it out until th sale goes through."

"There's that," Emily agreed, nibbling at her thumbnail.

"So it's all working out," Sue said. "There's a stack of paper work that Joy left for you. Whoever she lined up to buy th place is apparently really, really hot to close the deal."

Emily felt as though she was in freefall. In one short wee she'd gone from staid local innkeeper to European jet-sette who was about to sell her childhood home and unload he business in one fell swoop. It was all a bit dizzying.

"Want me to fax it over?" Sue asked, interrupting he mental ramblings.

"Uh, no," Emily replied. "I'll be back soon enough. I'll dea with it then."

"By the way, Tim's been calling every day," Sue said. "He' frantic, but he won't say why. Do you mind if I give him Colin': number in Paris? He's saying it's an emergency."

Emily squinted, thinking hard. What could possibly be ar emergency that Tim would want to discuss with her? Hopefully it wasn't anything personal, like the fact that his "potentially perfect political wife" Emily was slipping away. "I suppose it': all right," she finally answered slowly.

"Great. Thanks, Em. Oops, customers. I'll see you on Friday!' Sue hung up the phone.

Colin walked in the room, then stopped. "You okay?"

"I'm not sure," Emily said, recounting the conversation with Sue.

"Well, then, it's all working out," Colin said, sounding sat isfied. "I'm sorry you can't stay longer now, but the sooner you sell the hotel, the sooner you can come here and live with me." He made it sound simple, like ordering a latte.

Emily shivered. "It's all happening faster than I imagined."

Colin sat down next to her, rubbing her shoulders. "Seller's remorse?" he asked seriously.

She closed her eyes. "A little." Then she opened them, looking deeply into his. "But it's not that bad. I'm sure whoever buys the hotel will take care of it, probably better than I can. They'll be able to modernize it and make adjustments that I haven't been able to afford. Maybe even hire a few more people from the town." She smiled. "Who knows? It's probably going to be the best thing that ever happened to Tall Pines."

"More importantly," he declared, taking her thumbnail away from her mouth, "it's probably going to be one of the best things that's ever happened to you."

She grimaced, embarrassed. "I haven't bitten my nails in years."

"You're nervous," he said comfortingly. "It's a big change."

He could say that again. There was so much to deal with. Selling the hotel. Moving in with Colin. Moving to Paris. She didn't even speak French, at least not beyond rudimentary high school classes.

Her stomach clenched nervously.

On the other hand, her visit had been beautiful. She'd quickly and irrevocably fallen in love with the city and despite the jet lag, she'd also fallen in love with the idea of being Emily the adventurer. She knew that the only thing marring her good experience was residual guilt over her last angry words to the town at the meeting. She'd been too harsh. She'd fix that when she got back, as well. She'd make sure that the new owners got fully acquainted with all the locals and would do anything she could to make the transition as painless as possible. She'd also visit a lot, Emily thought with a smile.

She felt the knot of tension in her stomach release inch by inch and she reached for a chocolate cream puff, sighing with pleasure as the sweet cream filling overwhelmed her taste bud: like a vanilla cloud.

Oh, I could get used to this.

"Now that's more like it," Colin said, leaning forward and kissing her. "You're not leaving until Friday, right?"

She nodded, licking her lips to get any stray wisps of cream

"Well, then," he said, reaching for her and tugging her out of the chair, "we'd better not waste any time...."

Before he could continue, the phone rang.

"Saved by the bell." Colin wiggled his eyebrows at her and she laughed. He picked up the phone. *"Bonjour."*

Emily watched as his eyes widened with surprise, then narrowed with suspicion. "This is unexpected," he said in a cold voice. "I see. Hold on a second."

He turned, then held the phone out to her. "It's Mayor Tim for you."

"Oh, sorry," Emily whispered. "I forgot to tell you—Sue said it was an emergency, so I let her give him this number."

Colin crossed his arms. "This better be good," he said, not leaving the room. "After everything that happened at the town meeting, the guy's got a lot of nerve calling you while you're on vacation."

Emily felt the same, and the briskness of her voice reflected it. "Hello, Tim," she said. "What do you want?"

"I've been trying to reach you for two days," he complained. "Em, I know that after the meeting fiasco you're probably still ticked with Tall Pines in general, but I don't think that you actually hate us. Not enough to go through with this."

"This is your emergency?" she asked with disbelief. "You're calling me from three thousand miles away to let me know that you think I'm making a mistake in selling the hotel?"

"Hang up," Colin suggested, his expression stormy.

"Don't hang up," Tim pleaded, obviously hearing. "I don't

care if you want to sell the hotel, Em. I don't care if you want to move away from Tall Pines and never hear from us again. I don't care if you want to marry Colin, have twenty kids and live in a frickin' shoe on the outskirts of Amsterdam, for pity's sake!"

Emily smiled reluctantly. "Now, there's an image."

"The point is, you don't know who you're selling to," he said. "Have you done any research at all on the group who's interested in buying the inn?"

Emily felt the first skitterings of uneasiness. "Not yet," she hedged. "But they're recommended by Joy, and I trust her judgment. She's taught me a lot about being a hotel owner and she comes from a family of hotel magnates."

"That's the thing. It's *her* family," Tim continued, his tone ominous. "They're rich, powerful and bloodthirsty. Anywhere they can make a profit, they *will* make a profit."

Emily chuckled nervously. "Come on, Tim," she said. "It's a small hotel in the middle of a small town. It's not like they're going to be making a killing by running what's basically a glorified bed-and-breakfast."

"You're right there," Tim said. "That's why they're going to tear the place down."

"What?" she practically yelled.

"They're already inquiring about demolition contracts, building codes, parking and traffic," Tim informed her. "They're judging how best to use the land."

"But...you could stop them, couldn't you?" Emily asked. "I mean, can't you turn them down when they try to get it rezoned?"

"You already got the place zoned for commercial," Tim pointed out. "I could give them the runaround as far as building permits, but they've got money and lawyers, and if nothing else, they'd have the land. They're looking to gut the Stanfield Arms."

Emily felt sick. This wasn't what she'd had in mind at all.

"You're not going through with it, are you?"

Emily swallowed. "I'll be back as soon as I can," she promised, then hung up.

Colin looked at her. "What happened? What did he want?"

"The buyers just want to buy the inn to level it," she replied.

Colin nodded thoughtfully. "That doesn't surprise me."

His answer surprised *her*. "You knew that would happen?"

"I'm an architect," he said. "I know buildings and land. Big businesses have been trying to get into Tall Pines for years. If I were buying the inn I'd probably turn it into condos or a corporate-housing hotel. Something bigger and more modern."

"That's my home," she said, anguished. "And the town would never be the same!"

Colin sighed. "I'm sorry, sweetie. I thought you knew."

"I have to go. I have to fix this."

The only problem was, she had no idea *how*.

11

"IT'LL BE ALL RIGHT," Colin said to Emily as he drove her to the airport.

She stared out the window disconsolately, not responding.

He felt terrible about how everything had worked out. He knew that he'd set off the chain of events that had led her here to this painful dilemma. He wasn't sorry that he'd asked her to live with him, but he was sorry that she was going through all of this in order to do so.

"I wish I could go with you," he added.

"Me, too," Emily said softly, not turning from the window.

"But I've put off starting this building project long enough," he continued, feeling like a heel regardless.

She finally turned to him, her blue eyes full of understanding. "I know, Colin," she reassured him with a smile. "I don't want to take you away from your work any more than I already have. You've got enough on your plate."

"Like you don't?" He let out a frustrated huff as he negotiated the Paris traffic. "I want to make things easier for you, but I don't know how."

"It's all right, really," she said, and he knew she was trying to comfort him. That made him feel even worse. "I've managed on my own this long."

"That's the thing," he said. "You shouldn't have to figure all this out by yourself. You had to turn your home into an inn so you wouldn't lose it and disappoint your father. Then you decided to sell the inn so you could be with me. Then everybody you trusted turned on you and said you were being some kind of traitor because you didn't put their needs first!"

"Then the people I decided to sell to turned out to be greedy corporate land pirates," she added. "I knew the whole recap, but, hey, when you put it that way, I *have* had a hell of a holiday season, huh?"

Colin let out a short laugh. "You're amazing."

"I'm practical," she corrected. "I still want to be with you. But I'm not going to ruin the town to do it."

He nodded. "I wouldn't expect anything less." He might not care if the town got a big new shopping mall, but he knew that Emily loved Tall Pines too much and was far too loyal to allow anything like that to happen. And *he* loved that about her—that fierce loyalty.

"I figure they're not the only buyers in the world," she said. "I'm sure I can find someone interested in buying and keeping the Stanfield Arms the way it is."

Colin was less confident, but he didn't say anything.

"It might take a bit longer," she admitted, "but I'll do what it takes."

He felt his heart drop. It might take years, he thought with an edge of disappointment.

She glanced at him. "Would you wait for me?"

He thought about it. They'd only been together for a few weeks. But in that time frame he'd asked her to change her whole life. He'd agreed to change *his* life by moving in with her. Would he wait for her?

"Yes," he answered, his voice clear and strong. "Absolutely. But I am going to be selfish enough to hope the whole thing happens quickly. I'll miss you too much."

"You can always come and visit," she said, stroking his leg.

He smiled as heat curled through his system. "Every chance I get," he agreed huskily, then shook his head. "Unfortunately, I don't know how many chances I'm going to get in the next year. The owner is under a tight deadline."

Emily went silent and her expression was thoughtful. He distrusted the undercurrent of sadness he was sensing. They arrived at the airport, and Colin slowly made his way through the concrete multilevel parking garage, heading for the top level to avoid any hassles fighting for a spot.

"What are you thinking?" he finally asked.

"This is real life intruding," she replied, her voice rueful, almost resigned. "It was different when it was a holiday fling. Now we've got lives to deal with and businesses to run." She took a deep breath. "Do you think we can make it, Colin?"

He pulled into a spot on the isolated floor, then leaned over and kissed her, hard and passionately.

"I *know* we can make it," he whispered against her lips. "If we want to make it work, then we'll find a way."

"Oh, Colin," she breathed, hugging him tightly and kissing him back wholeheartedly.

He held her close, his mouth moving over hers, his tongue tickling hers slightly. His body was aflame for her, but it was more than that—it was always so much more than that.

After long moments, he pulled away, breathing heavily. "Unless you want me to take you here, in a very tiny car in a public parking lot," he warned, "we'd better stop."

He expected her to kiss him, then get out of the car. He was in for the shock of his life when her eyes gleamed.

"There's no one around," she said in a low voice, her hand rubbing over the fly of his slacks.

His jaw dropped. *"Emily!"*

"Don't tell me you've never made love in a car," she teased, her rubbing increasing in pressure, slowly caressing his semi-erect cock to full hardness.

"Not at the airport," he said in a strangled voice. "And certainly not in a car this size."

"It'll be a challenge." Her voice was rough with desire.

He glanced at her, suspicion running through him. "I wondered why you were wearing a skirt for a flight. Seemed impractical."

"Like I said, I'm very practical," she replied, laughter hidden in her voice. "You just need to know what I'm going after. Can that seat scoot back a bit?"

He glanced around, making sure that there really wasn't anyone there. It felt illicit...exciting. Even as Colin knew it was foolish, he wanted her too much to protest overtly. The fact that it was her idea only made it that much more appealing.

He pushed the seat all the way back, reclining it. She slid her panties down her legs, then unzipped his fly, nudging his pants down enough for his cock to spring free. She pulled a condom out of her purse, smiling as she opened it, then placed it on the tip of his cock.

Then she leaned over, rolling it over his engorged flesh with her mouth.

He groaned, his head lolling back against the seat's headrest. The feeling of her moist, tight mouth circling him was incredible.

She sat up, smiling, then clambered over clumsily, covering him with her skirt. He felt his penis nudge the opening of her, wet and slick already with arousal. "You're soaked," he marveled. Then all talking ceased as she slid down over him, her body covering him like a snug, warm glove. She let out a long, satisfied sigh, her thighs tightening on either side of his hips. "You feel unbelievable."

"We have to hurry," she said, but her body worked at odds with her words, slowly gyrating against him, stroking his penis with leisurely, graceful movements. She bit her lip, her eyes closed.

He reached up, cupping her breasts through her thin shirt. He was sorry that she wasn't naked, but as he looked at their surroundings, the fact that they were both clothed added even more of a thrill to it. He held her hips, jerking her down to him, and she gasped at the roughness before smiling with wicked abandon.

"That's it," she murmured, moving faster.

The pressure building was incredible. He buried his face in her breasts, his arms wrapped around her as she increased both speed and pressure, bucking against him with a steady rocking motion. She started to pant, her fingers clawing down his back as he thrust up against her. His knee hit the steering wheel, but he ignored the pain in the face of the mind-blowing pleasure that was pumping through his system. He leaned up, kissing her, and her tongue plunged into his mouth, mating with his in a rough frenzy.

He angled his hips, aiming his cock so his shaft rubbed against her clit and the head targeted the elusive spot of pleasure, high and forward in her pussy. She threw her head back in a shriek of ecstasy, and he knew he'd found what he was looking for. He drove up inside her as much as the small confines of the car would allow, and she gripped the back of the seat and his shoulder, riding him like a bronco, her thighs gripping him like a vise.

"*Colin!*" Her voice rippled with the sound of her orgasm, and his name was an explosive shout of release.

He felt the strong contractions rocking through her, milking him, and he gave in to the sensations battering him. His answering orgasm shuddered through him, and he clung to her, jerking against her as she ran her fingers through the hair at the nape of his neck and rocked her hips to meet his every thrust.

When it was over, he caressed her, whispering unintelligible murmurs of love and longing against her thundering heartbeat. She stroked his shoulders, not speaking, simply pressing kisses wherever her mouth could reach.

"We'd better get going," he said with regret. "Somebody might come."

They laughed as they clumsily maneuvered their way out of the car, making sure they were fully and respectably dressed before exiting.

"How do I look?" she asked, smoothing down her skirt and then twirling for him.

He did a quick visual survey. Her eyes were bright, her hair slightly mussed, her lips full and bruised-looking.

"You look like you just had sex," he said hungrily, which earned him a playful swat. "Damn, I'm going to miss you."

He grabbed her bag out of the trunk, rolling it for her. "Get things handled as soon as you can," he ordered, putting an arm around her waist. "Then come back to me."

She leaned into him, resting her head against his shoulder. "Find a break in your work schedule," she ordered back, "and visit when you can."

With those commands, they kissed one last time. Then he handed her the bag and watched her walk through the glass doors of Charles de Gaulle Airport and out of his life.

Not for long, he comforted himself. But some sinking premonition told him it would be longer than either of them wanted.

EMILY TOOK THE sheaf of escrow papers from the top of her desk, handing them to Joy, who was seated across from her. "I'm sorry for wasting your time, Joy. I'm not going to sell."

Joy nodded, folding up the papers and putting them back in her briefcase. "Doesn't surprise me," she said. "When you asked me if I knew of a buyer, I thought of my family, but I wasn't sure if that's the route you wanted to go."

"Why didn't you warn me?" Emily asked, feeling shaken.

"I tried to, but you were in such a hurry," Joy answered, shrugging. "I figured once you had a little time to clear your head, you'd change your mind—and if that didn't do it, then you'd definitely back out once you did some due diligence and found out what the plans were for the inn."

"I feel like such a fool," Emily groaned, leaning back in her chair and rubbing at her eyes with the heels of her palms. "I've created this tempest in a teapot, and all for nothing."

Joy made a sympathetic sound. "It's not that bad," she said. "No harm, no foul."

"Actually, I fired one of my managers, and the other one's quitting," Emily said ruefully.

"Ooh." Joy wrinkled her nose. "I'm sure you can find people to replace them."

"Not here in Tall Pines. Remember when I first started taking your course? I had just hired the two of them. I can't afford someone from out of town. And, frankly, nobody *in* town has the experience I need."

"But I thought the inn was doing well," Joy interjected.

"It is," Emily said. "But it's going to need some overhauls, and I put all my money into keeping this place afloat. Now I won't have the money to make any changes or improvements. I'll barely have money for the necessary stuff, especially if I have to shell out for an increased salary or two to replace Sue and Phillip." She sent Joy an apologetic expression. "I'm sorry again, Joy. This isn't your problem. I don't know why I'm dumping on you this way…especially after you stayed, hoping for a finder's fee."

"I stayed because I'm sort of at a crossroads right now," Joy said, her voice earnest. "I've been teaching hotel management, true, but they're online courses. I can teach them anywhere. I haven't run a hotel in about a year and a half. My family's been pressuring me to rejoin their business, but, frankly, it hasn't been appealing."

"Why not?" Emily asked, thinking that their high-priced, fast-paced lifestyle was probably right up Joy's alley.

"I don't approve of how they do business," Joy said primly. Then she sighed. "And, to be honest, I'm burned out."

Emily stared at her. "I never would have guessed," she said. "You look so…together."

Joy's smile was bright, but now that she was looking, Emily could see the tightness in her expression. "I've been hiding it for a while. It's not hard to keep up a front if you practice."

Emily thought about her years in Tall Pines, being the perfect Stanfield. "I hear you," she said with feeling.

"So what's next?" Joy asked, and Emily got the feeling she was changing the subject.

"I'm going to look for another buyer. I can't keep doing this by myself. I'm burning out, too."

Joy looked shrewd. "And there's the little matter of a gorgeous guy waiting for you in Paris, huh?"

Emily laughed uncomfortably. "Been listening to the gossip, huh?"

"I got my hair done at the salon." Joy chuckled. "It was better than watching a rerun of *Desperate Housewives*."

"I would like to get back to Colin," Emily said. "But I have to handle all this first."

"Have you ever thought—"

Sue knocked on the door, one quick rap, before opening it up. "Emily?" she said, looking excited. "Tim's here. Sorry to interrupt, but he said it was important."

Emily looked at Joy, who stood up. "No problem. I'm staying through the end of the week anyway, if that's okay."

"We love having you," Emily said, and she meant it. She might have spent less than a month with the woman face-to-face, but she'd known her for years online. Besides, it was nice to have someone she could talk shop with, someone who understood the ins and outs of the hotel business. "If you're not busy, maybe we could grab dinner at Halloran's."

"Sounds great." Joy bumped into Tim as he burst into Emily's office. "Excuse me."

"Sorry," Tim muttered, giving Joy a quick, nervous once-over…then a double take. Joy was dressed to kill, her usual getup, and apparently Tim appreciated it. Then he must've remembered who she was—and who she represented. "Hope I'm not interrupting any important business," he said with a slightly disapproving tone.

Joy grinned brightly at him. "Just girl talk," she replied with a flirtatious wink that obviously threw the mayor off. "See you at dinner, Emily."

Emily shook her head. The woman might say she was burned out, but she certainly put on a good act.

Tim waited until Sue shut the door behind Joy, then he sat down in the chair she had just vacated. "You can't sell the inn," he said bluntly.

Emily gritted her teeth. Admittedly, she'd come to the same conclusion, but the hackles on the back of her neck still rose at the town's dictatorial stance. "Tim, you can't just tell me what to do."

"After what I told you about them bulldozing the Stanfield Arms to the ground and bringing in a huge chain supermarket or building cookie-cutter condos or whatever, you're still up for entertaining the offer?" He sounded shocked and appalled.

"I didn't say that," she replied. "I'm just saying…Tim, you're a good guy, and Tall Pines is a good town. But the whole reason I pursued selling the inn in the first place was because you all got too pushy."

Tim's handsome face went pink. "We were a little heavy-handed," he admitted in a low voice. "The whole town meeting got absurdly out of control, and I apologize for that."

Emily leaned back in her chair, feeling mollified. "To answer your question, I am not going to sell to the Webster Collective," she said—and she saw Tim slump in his chair with relief. However, there was something in his expression that made her uneasy.

"Thank God," he said, making a gesture of wiping off his forehead. "That's a bullet dodged, huh?"

Emily closed her eyes briefly, thinking of her issues with the hotel…and the fact that Colin was three thousand miles away. "I'm still going to look into selling," she told him earnestly. "I know it's a disappointment to you and to the town, but it's what I want."

Now Tim looked really uncomfortable. "But won't you miss it all?" he asked, a note of pleading in his voice. "You love this town. You love this house. Can you really just sell it and move away for good?"

Emily felt a pang. "I will miss it. I still love Tall Pines. And, yeah, I love the hotel. But it's getting to be too much for me to handle, Tim. I can't keep slogging away by myself."

Tim shifted in his chair, his expression pained. "I'm sure you can hire some more people…."

"With what money, Tim?" She shook her head. "No. I'll try to find someone who will keep the inn the way it is, hopefully someone who has enough money to turn it into the showplace I know it can be. And I'll come back to visit. Heck, I'll probably even stay here for old times' sake," she said, with a slow grin. "But I'm going to sell the inn, Tim. There's no question about that."

He looked dejected. "Actually…er, there is some question about that."

She looked at him, not comprehending. "What are you talking about?"

"The Stanfield house has been here for four generations," he explained, his pale gray eyes begging her for understanding. "It's one of the oldest buildings in the town. It belonged to one of the founding fathers of Tall Pines. It's mentioned in the town charter and any number of documents in the town records. It's even in old letters that we have in the historical section of the main library."

"I still don't understand," Emily said. "I already know how much the house means to the town. But you know my reasoning."

"Em," he said, "we were really worried that you were going to sell the place to a monster land developer, somebody who would crush the spirit of the town that we've been working hard to preserve."

"Well, I'm not," she pointed out, irritated. "Damn it, Tim, what's going on?"

"While you were gone," he said slowly, "we had an emergency town meeting."

Emily felt a cold chill ball in her stomach. "Somehow I'm not shocked." It was probably the hottest gossip they'd had in years. "Other than discussing how terrible I was for three hours, what conclusions did you come to?"

"We don't think you're terrible," Tim said quickly. "We thought you were…upset. And that Colin—"

"Don't even bring Colin into this," Emily snapped. "Not unless you want me to kick you out right now."

"Okay. No Colin," he agreed.

"Just get to the point, Tim."

He took a deep breath, and his face was hangdog ashamed. "You can't sell the inn, Emily."

Emily growled. "I know you don't want me to, all right? I got that. And if that's all you came here to—"

"No, you don't understand," Tim clarified. "You *can't* sell the inn. Not without the town's written permission."

Emily stood up. "What?"

"We had the Stanfield house turned into a historic landmark while you were in Paris," he said in a low voice. "We made it so you can't sell the inn to anyone."

Emily stared at him, agog. "You won't let me look for buyers."

"That's about it." At least he sounded apologetic, and he stood up, reaching for her to give her a hug.

"Get away from me," she said, her voice cold.

Tim sent her one last sad look, then left.

She sank back down in her chair, her head in her hands. She had no help, no money to make improvements and now she couldn't even look for sympathetic buyers. The town had found a way to keep their golden girl there, possibly forever. She wouldn't be able to take a vacation to Paris in the next few years, much less move there.

Tall Pines. Her childhood home. For many years her favorite place on Earth.

She felt the tears start to crawl down her cheeks.

And now I'm trapped here.

THE PHONE RANG IN Colin's apartment. He looked up from the blueprint he was going over on his drafting table, answering it automatically. *"Bonjour?"*

"Hey, Colin."

"Emily," he said, smiling and relaxing for the first time in days. "I was just thinking of you. Haven't stopped, as a matter of fact."

"That's nice," she said. "I haven't stopped thinking of you, either."

That's when he heard it—the little catch in her voice, the tiniest tremor. She was upset. "What's wrong?" he asked quickly, bracing himself.

"I can't sell the hotel."

"Well, not to those people," Colin said, confused. "There's a big world of investors out there, though, and I'm sure you—"

"You don't understand," she interrupted. "I didn't at first, either. The town declared the inn a historical landmark while I was gone. Now it's political. I can't sell the hotel without the approval of the town."

Colin felt his blood run hot with fury. "They *what?*"

"They declared the Stanfield house a historical landmark," Emily said, her voice drowning in fatigue. "I couldn't believe they could move so fast, but I guess when they all really, really want something…"

"So what does that mean?" Colin asked, trying not to let his anger get out of control.

"It means I need to get permission from the town council and the mayor's office to put the house up for sale. They need to approve anybody who buys it, making sure that they uphold the usage and preserve the monument for future generations."

"It's a nice inn, but a monument?" Colin said, flabbergasted.

"Yeah, I know," Emily answered. "I doubt they'd think of it as a monument if they knew what I know about the plumbing in room five. Not to mention the attic."

He clutched the phone until his knuckles turned white, the only thing that prevented him from throwing it in a fit of anger. "I can't believe it," he said slowly. "No. I *can* believe it. Those bastards."

"Wait a minute," Emily said slowly. "I felt upset at first, too, but I'm trying to stay positive about all this."

"Positive?" Colin yelped. "They're just looking out for themselves and their interests and making sure that not a damned thing changes in their perfect little Americana world."

"Come on. Don't you think that's a little harsh?"

"Are you actually defending them?" he replied. "You're the one they're screwing over. They've taken away your right to determine what you do with your own business and your own house. They've basically *chained* you there." He realized he was close to yelling and clamped down on his wayward emotions, forcing his voice to level out. "After all that, you're just going to let them get away with it? You're going to try to convince me that it's okay?"

"It's not okay," she said sharply. "But I know why they did it. Now nobody can tear the place down and build some corporate megalith here."

"And you can't leave," Colin added.

"I'm sure that wasn't the point." But Emily didn't sound sure at all.

Colin ground his teeth together, hard enough for them to rasp. He growled in frustration. "What about us, Emily?"

There was a long pause. "I don't know." She sounded lost.

"Damn it!" He knew he shouldn't be losing it this way, but he'd been thinking of her almost every moment since he'd dropped her off at the airport. Especially after their stunning goodbye in his car. He couldn't drive it without thinking of her, a precarious development. "I'm sorry, Emily. I just…"

"I know," she said, and her voice was ragged. "Believe me— nobody's more disappointed than I am by this turn of events."

"I think I could debate you on that," he said. "There's got to be some loophole. Some way to get out of it."

"I'm still looking into it. But with Sue quitting on me, I'm swamped with stuff that needs to be done in the hotel. By the time I get a minute to research the details of the landmark decree, I'm usually blurry-eyed and exhausted."

Colin thought about it. "You could just abandon it," he suggested.

"Sorry?" she said. "Did you say…abandon the hotel?"

"They're the ones that put you in the position." He had a sinking feeling. "It would serve them right to deal with what you've had to deal with all this time."

"I know that what they did wasn't right," she said in a placating tone. "But screwing them over just because they screwed *me* over doesn't feel right."

He exhaled loudly, trying to relieve some of the tension skittering through his system. "I knew you were going to look at it that way," he groused. "So, again…where does that leave us, Emily? What are we going to do?"

She laughed weakly. "I don't suppose you've got a vacation coming up? I've got a bed waiting here at the inn for you."

His stomach turned. "I can't go back to that town knowing what they did to you. What they're doing to *us*. It's pure selfishness and small-mindedness, and as far as I'm concerned, they can rot in their cozy little houses, for all I care."

"You don't mean that."

"I can't begin to tell you how much I mean that," Colin said, his voice curt. "Emily, I know you're a good person, and I admire you for turning the other cheek. But you got *reamed*. You can't just sit there and take it."

"It's my decision." She exhaled sharply. "You're not the one who's trapped, I am. And I'll deal with it my own way."

"Fine," he said. "But you can't expect me to go there and put on a good face for all those people. I won't do it, Emily."

"Are you kidding me?" she yelped. "Like I don't have enough problems, now you're refusing to visit me?"

"As long as you're going to roll over and play dead while they stomp on you, yes!"

Another long pause. "I don't need this," she said softly.

"If you're choosing to submit to them without even a token fight," he replied, "I can't go along with it. You have to see my point."

"It's official. I have snapped. I have completely *had* it with all of you," Emily yelled.

"So do something about it," Colin said, warming up.

"I am." Emily took a deep breath. "It's been real, but we've had our run."

He blinked. "Wait a minute. You're breaking up with me over this?"

"I've had enough ultimatums in the past week to last me a frickin' lifetime," she said. "I don't know what I can do about the town, but you were supposed to know me, and love me. You of all people, were supposed to back me up."

"I can't help you if you won't help yourself," he countered, feeling uneasy.

"I am doing the best I can," she stated.

"Well, when you come up with an answer…"

"I thought I meant more to you than your animosity for Tall Pines."

That took him aback. "You do."

"Not that I've noticed." Her words were bitter, acidic. "You're so interested in punishing them and showing that you're a bigger moral force that you're willing to let the woman you supposedly love just twist in the wind all by herself. Just so you can be right."

"Emily," he said, stricken.

"No. I'm done." She was crying. He could hear it in her voice. "Have a good time in Paris—or Borneo or wherever your damned buildings take you. I'll still be here in Tall Pines."

With that, she hung up. He heard the buzzing European dial tone and slammed the phone into its cradle.

"Damn it!" he repeated, punching the air ineffectually. How could one small town make him so crazy? Why couldn't they let Emily sell the hotel and move on with her life?

Why couldn't she see why he was right—that they were blackmailing her and she couldn't give in to them?

Colin closed his eyes. He'd made a mistake, obviously. She was too set in her ways, too small-town. She'd rather put up

ith them than stand up to them once and for all. Well, at least
e'd found out now rather than when she'd moved all the way
Paris to be with him.

He swallowed hard, feeling emotion choking his throat.

I love her, he thought. *I miss her. I want to be with her.*

He closed his eyes. So this was what real heartbreak felt like.
t sucked something awful.

He turned back to his plans. He'd focus on his work and not
hink about Emily or Tall Pines or any of it.

12

"SO ARE WE ALL agreed?" Ava Reese said, rapping her water glass on the Formica tabletop. "Instead of the usual red and pink hearts and streamers for the Valentine's dance at the Otter Lodge, we're going to go with silver, black and gold balloons and confetti, tealight candles on mirrors for centerpieces and the big black-and-white movie posters of romantic couples? I think it'll be striking—and not so cliché."

There was a general murmur of assent from all the ladies present, and she cheerfully checked it off her list.

Emily sat in the living room at Janet Cunningham's house surrounded by the twelve members of the dance committee. Valentine's Day was only two weeks away. They were behind on the planning, and all the women were scurrying around, gossiping lightly, complaining about how they were still recovering from the holidays.

Emily was still recovering from other things. Sue was hanging on, trying to help even though her stomach now showed the beginnings of a bump. In the meantime, Emily was interviewing candidates, running through numbers and doing whatever she could to ignore the fact that it had been two very long, very painful weeks since she had heard from Colin.

"Can we take a break?" Mrs. Rutledge asked. "We've been here for an hour, and I'm starving. I brought some fresh-baked banana bread."

"All right." Ava was clearly reluctant to give up the floor.

"Come on into the kitchen," Janet invited. "I've got plenty of food, tea, coffee. Help yourselves."

Everyone but Emily and Ava stood up. Emily noticed that most of the women either avoided looking at her completely or sent her the occasional look of confused apology mixed with disappointment. Emily didn't react to either the sentiment or the avoidance. She didn't react to anything anymore, it seemed.

Mrs. Rutledge came back to the couch, a piece of banana bread on a small paper plate in one hand, an earthenware mug of coffee in the other. She put the mug on the coffee table, then turned to Emily with determination. "I understand you've recently gotten back from Paris," she said, her tone casual. As if she'd never said anything at the town meeting, much less accused Emily of betraying the town's trust. "How was your trip?"

Emily stared at her for a second. She hadn't let go of the situation, not entirely. But Mrs. Rutledge was old, and it wasn't going to change Emily's situation at all to be bitchy to a woman she'd known all her life. She decided to take the high road. "Paris was nice," she offered.

It was a small olive branch, but Mrs. Rutledge grabbed it. "Paris is so lovely," she enthused. "Even in the winter."

Emily nodded. "It was one of the most beautiful cities I've ever seen."

There. Easy, comfortable conversation.

Then Mrs. Rutledge studied her with scrutiny. "Will you be visiting again anytime soon?"

Emily stiffened. She wasn't asking about vacation plans. She was asking about Colin.

"Not in the foreseeable future," Emily said, her voice frosty. "I'm far too busy with the inn."

"Ah," Mrs. Rutledge said, sipping her coffee. "I don't suppose you're expecting any visitors, then?"

Mrs. Rutledge was subtle, at least—or tried to be. Emily had to give her that.

"No, no visitors," Emily answered. It was as if they were speaking in code. "Joy may drop by—it seems she's fallen in love with the town. But otherwise I'm not expecting anyone."

"I see." Mrs. Rutledge nibbled at her cake, obviously weighing her next words. "I know you're busy, dear, but you shouldn't let your correspondence fall behind. It's a nice thing to keep in touch with the people you love, especially the ones who are so far away."

Emily didn't know what to say to that, so she didn't say anything.

"And do send letters," she added. "E-mails are so terse and common. Letters, on the other hand, are a lost art."

"When I think of what to say, perhaps," Emily hedged.

Mrs. Rutledge smiled knowingly. "Perhaps."

Ava stared at Emily throughout the whole exchange. "You know, I have something for you out in the car," she said, getting to her feet and nudging Emily. "Walk with me?"

Emily started, feeling dread. She hadn't been alone with Colin's family since before she'd left for Paris. She couldn't think of any reason to say no, however, so she got up, accompanying Ava. They stepped out Janet's front door into the chilly air. "I should have brought my jacket," Emily said inanely, wrapping her arms around herself. "If you…"

"I'm so sorry, dear."

The statement brought Emily up short. "For what?"

"The town meeting. The landmark decision. Colin." Ava looked miserable. "Everything."

"It wasn't your fault," Emily demurred, feeling off balance. Then her eyes narrowed. "What exactly about Colin are you apologizing for?"

"I thought it would be wonderful for him to fall in love with a girl from Tall Pines," Ava said. "He'd finally understand what it means to settle down and…oh, I'll admit it, I was selfish. I'm adopted, did I ever tell you?"

Emily blinked. "I seem to remember something…."

"I was raised by my aunt and uncle, the Stewarts. They were wonderful to bring me in, but…" Ava frowned delicately. "They weren't really children people, if you understand."

"Oh," Emily said, feeling uncomfortable. What could you say to a statement like that?

"At any rate, I've always had this vision," Ava shared wistfully, "of having all my kids around me, a big, happy family." She went quiet for a minute. "When Colin went off to school and then made it clear that he wasn't coming back, my heart broke. I knew my son—when he sets his mind to something, he does it."

Now, *that* Emily could relate to. She patted Ava's shoulder awkwardly, trying to comfort her.

"When he brought you home to dinner, I was beyond thrilled," Ava finally said. "It never occurred to me…"

The sentence petered off, and Emily prompted her, "Never occurred to you that what?"

"That he'd break your heart, too."

Emily felt tears sting at her eyes, completely without warning. She turned away, keeping her eyes wide to keep them from spilling over.

"He cares about you," Ava said, and now she was the one offering comfort. "I think he may really love you. But he's never coming home to Tall Pines, dear. I've finally accepted that."

The cold felt insubstantial now. Emily had lost all feeling in her body, and it had nothing to do with the weather. "You think he's staying away because he hates the town?"

Ava looked startled. "He's hated Tall Pines since high school. He wouldn't change his opinion of it for his family, so I thought…"

"He's not coming back because of what the town did to me," Emily said with a slightly hysterical laugh.

Now Ava looked shocked. "I know that the decision to make the hotel a historical landmark was a disappointment, but I didn't think it would bother you that much," she said, sounding puzzled. "You love it here. Besides, it was in the best interest of the town."

"I know." Emily wiped at tears with the backs of her hands. "But the town didn't care what it did to me. I was expected to fall into line, no questions. When I tried to do something for myself, you all called me a traitor."

"Now, now, that was just in the heat of the moment," Ava said quickly. "You know how Martha Rutledge is during a town meeting. She's incorrigible."

"I don't care." Emily raised her voice. "All I know is I'm drowning under the obligations of the inn. I've been able to keep it afloat and I'm not hurting for money, but at the same time, I can't rest. When the inn was all I had, I didn't care. But now I've found someone I love and a life I want to pursue…and I *can't*. Because of Tall Pines." She sniffled loudly, cursing herself for losing it.

Ava looked stricken. "I didn't know," she murmured. "None of us knew. Why didn't you say you were in trouble?"

"Because I don't see it as being in trouble," Emily said. "Or at least I didn't. I don't want to complain and I'm not expecting anybody to save me. But when I tried to take care of myself, all I got were accusations, and then you went behind my back and forced me to do what you wanted. Did it ever occur to any of you that I'd never betray this town?"

Ava shook her head.

"Why didn't you trust me?" Emily's throat hurt. "Why didn't you…oh, why am I bothering? It doesn't matter."

"And Colin…?" Ava said slowly before Emily could walk away.

"Colin is sick of all of you." Ava winced at the comment. "He can't believe I'll still defend you and that I'll stay here after how Tall Pines treated me. So instead of helping me or comforting me, we wound up breaking up because I can't do what he wants, either."

Ava looked green.

Emily closed her eyes. All the emotions she thought she'd successfully walled off were now bubbling out of her like lava from a volcano. "I have to go," she said, going back into the house.

Janet stared at her. "Why, Em, honey, what's wrong?"

Emily didn't say a word. She grabbed her jacket and her purse, ignoring the other women's words of concern, and left the house. She stumbled through the snow blindly, heading for the inn.

"Emily?" Sue asked, bewildered, when she stumbled past her in the lobby.

Emily kept walking, heading straight for her apartment. When she locked the door behind her, she sank onto her couch, feeling the floodgates of emotion start to break.

It'll get better. It'll get better. She chanted it in her head. But she kept on crying.

"HI, EMILY," Joy said a few days later, standing in Emily's apartment doorway. "What did you want to talk to me about?"

"Come on in," she said, gesturing to her couch.

Joy came in, sitting down, then studying Emily's face carefully. "You okay?"

"I am now," Emily answered with determination. "I see you're going to be leaving tomorrow."

"It's been a long vacation," Joy answered. "Longest I've taken in my life. I was hoping to get a few things figured out."

"And did you?"

Joy nodded thoughtfully. "I know I don't want to go back to my family's business. That's for sure."

"Uh-huh." Emily poured them both a cup of coffee.

"At the same time, I don't want to go back to teaching," she said, sipping from her cup. Joy shrugged. "Anyway, I'm sure I'll figure out something. I'm just glad I stayed here. It's been wonderful."

"We're happy to have you. And I can't thank you enough for pitching in."

Joy smiled. "Don't worry. That wasn't work—that was fun. So how about you? Have you figured out what you're going to do?"

Emily's responding smile faltered. "I think so," she murmured. "But it depends on a few things." She took a depp breath. "I've been looking at that piece of paper you gave me. The ideas. for building up the inn's business."

Joy looked embarrassed. "Oh, that was before, you know, everything happened," she said. "I wouldn't expect you to do all that by yourself. Especially not now."

"I think you're right," Emily agreed. "I think it could work."

"It would mean added money," Joy protested. "And more managers."

"I know," Emily said. "But I've got an idea…"

THE WALK ALONG THE left bank of the Seine River was like something out of a movie: the sky gently overcast, the water rippling with the gusts of wind, the ancient stones beneath his feet all picturesque. In fact, it was like living in a black-and-white French film, complete with lovers kissing under bridges and monuments like Notre Dame popping into the frame every time you turned around. Ordinarily Colin liked Paris. He'd chosen this project with his fondness for the city in mind, hadn't he? The place he was going to spend the next two years? He loved the food, the architecture, the style, the flair.

But now he seemed to walk endlessly, restlessly. And, yes, he wasn't stupid enough to pretend he didn't know why.

I miss Emily.

He headed over to the temporary office that was right across from the future building site. He'd spent more time there than in his home, it seemed. Despite her brief stay, the apartment was now inextricably linked to Emily. In a fit of despair one night, he'd even considered moving in an effort to get away from the memories each stick of furniture seemed to evoke.

"*Bonjour,* Colin," Francois, the owner, said, adding, in lightly accented English, "You're here early, yet again."

Colin was glad that Francois's grasp of English was nearly flawless.

"You're here, period," Colin responded, grinning slightly.

"*Oui,* but then I am going to Germany, then Monte Carlo," Francois countered. "Besides, I love when buildings are just starting. So much potential!"

Colin shrugged. "We're off to a good start, but we've got a long way to go."

"*C'est bon,*" Francois said easily, clapping him on the shoulder. "It is beyond good, in fact, my friend. Your reputation is well deserved. In fact, everything I heard about you was true and more…except for this rumor of your constant partying." He laughed. "I expected to see you cavorting with some scantily clad women, dashing in front of the Moulin Rouge with a topless dancer. But, no, you come here early, you stay late and otherwise you wander around the streets with an expression like this." Francois demonstrated an exaggerated dour face.

Colin smiled. "Maybe I'm a brooding poet."

"Ha," Francois scoffed. "You're a man in love."

"Really?" Colin tried to sound amused. "How can you tell?"

"I'm French."

Colin waited, but Francois seemed to think that was all the answer required, so he let it drop.

"Who is she?"

Colin winced. "I like you, Francois," he said hesitantly. "I mean, you're a great guy. But you're also my client, and…well, this is sort of personal…."

"Of course it is," Francois said. "Which is why I asked now, before any of your crew got here."

"No, I mean it doesn't have to do with business." Colin wondered if maybe there was a language problem after all.

"I know what you meant," Francois said with a dismissive wave of the hand. "But I beg to differ. You are working far too hard, my friend. I know how you Americans are. You're driven by the clock, shall we say?"

Colin shrugged. "I thought that was why you hired me."

Francois grinned. "*Oui,* there is something to be said for someone who believes in pushing to get things accomplished. Not to disparage my countrymen," he added hastily. "But while I appreciate your dedication, this is not mere work ethic. This is mania." His forehead furrowed. "I am concerned, Colin."

Colin fidgeted with his watchband. "Don't worry," he said. "I won't let it affect work."

"It affects *you,* Colin. It affects everything."

Francois was a nice guy, affable, charming in the way that only Europeans seemed to pull off. But he was also a tank. Colin got the feeling that Francois would not budge on the issue until he had an answer.

"Yes, there is a woman," he muttered, feeling foolish. He felt even more foolish when Francois nodded sagely.

"As I knew," he said, rubbing his beard. "Where is she? What happened to make you so unhappy?"

"She…" He was about to say, *She left me,* but saying it would hurt too damned much. He opted for a classic instead. "We agreed that the relationship was not going to work, so we broke up."

Francois looked puzzled. "Why wouldn't it work? You love her, don't you?"

"Yes."

"She doesn't love you, then?"

"She does love me," Colin protested reflexively.

Francois nodded sympathetically. "She's married, then?"

Colin choked. "No!"

Francois frowned. "So what is the problem?"

"She lives in the United States," Colin said heavily.

"Ah." Francois said the word with exquisite delicacy. His frown deepened and he gestured with his hands. "And…?"

Colin rubbed his face. "It's complicated."

"I would assume." Francois paused. "Certainly we don't know each other well enough to share confidences, but you must know me enough to realize I am going to give you advice whether you want me to or not."

Colin let out a short, surprised bark of laughter. "Shoot."

"Would you really rather have this job than the love of this woman?"

"Are you firing me?" Colin asked. The French were romantics and all, but this seemed excessive.

"*Non, non,* of course not. I did not mean to give you that impression," Francois said hastily. "Your work is very much appreciated. But it's obvious to me that if you're willing to let an obstacle like an ocean get in the way of your love for this woman, then perhaps she was right to break up with you."

"I didn't say she broke up with me!"

Francois' smile was condescending. "Colin, please."

"Right. You're French," he said, fighting not to roll his eyes. "It's not that easy, though."

"It's not that hard, either," Francois countered. "At least it doesn't need to be."

"She's living in a tiny town in Connecticut—the town I grew up in—and she won't do what it takes to leave and be with me," Colin said. "If she's not willing to make the effort to defend herself or fight for us, then I can't stand by and watch her get hurt."

Francois' expression turned sad. "It's better, then, to let her suffer her hurt all alone?"

Colin fell silent, stunned as if Francois had hit him with a brick.

"Perhaps she needs your love and your understanding. If she is in a difficult situation, you might want to give her time."

"What are you, France's answer to Dr. Phil?"

Francois frowned. "Who is this Dr. Phil?"

"Nothing. Bad joke. Never mind." He rubbed at his temples with his fingertips. "Aren't you a little tall to play cupid?"

"Aren't you a little old to be so obstinate?"

Colin grimaced. "Point taken."

"You've been moping around here for two weeks, working like a demon, and I was beginning to wonder when you would burn out," Francois said briskly. "I thought I would find out what was happening. Love is a specialty of mine, incidentally. This is my city, after all."

"Huh?"

"Paris. The city of love, *oui?*"

"I thought that was just for the travel brochures."

"We do get a good number of tourists," Francois admitted. "Listen now. I would not say this to anyone else. I hired you because I knew that you were the best. I am selfish enough to want to keep you that way rather than lose you to overwork and stress halfway through the project. If this woman makes you happy, then we must do what we can to keep you happy. You see?" He grinned mischievously. "It's completely practical."

Colin shook his head. "I don't know how to fix things."

"Don't you have the saying 'Love will find a way'?" Francois grinned broadly, leaning back in his chair. "So. We find a way."

He grimaced. He was still angry with the town of Tall Pines for how it had treated her—how it had treated him. "I swore I'd never go back there," he found himself saying.

"What, to the town this woman lives in? Why?"

"Because they don't accept me."

"Does she accept you?"

Colin thought about it. "Completely."

"Then who gives a damn?" Francois shook his head. "If this is all that's been keeping you from this woman, I will be very disappointed in you, my friend. Old ladies and nosy neighbors are no reason to break up a perfectly good love affair."

Put that way, Colin felt like an ass. "The commute's a bitch," he said.

"Computers, phone and fax. Come into the office as often as you can, but you're in charge of this project," Francois pointed out. "You can be here or not, as you like. I trust you."

Colin tapped his fingertips together, something he normally did only when working on a particularly difficult design.

"It'll take some planning," he muttered, reaching for a piece of paper. "The logistics…"

"There you are," Francois said, his tone imminently satisfied. "You see? Love finds a way when you let it."

"And when I stop being a butthead," Colin muttered, glancing at his calendar.

"Yes," Francois agreed, stepping out the door. "That, also."

"SETTLE DOWN, SETTLE down," Mayor Tim said plaintively at the next town meeting. "Do we *really* have to do this every single time? Really?"

The crowd reluctantly hushed, slowly coming to order, with pockets of rebellious chatter here and there. Emily didn't sit in her usual seat but, rather, sat hunched in the back. She didn't want to be there in the first place, but Sue had cajoled her.

"Don't give 'em the satisfaction," Sue had said, and after everything, Emily realized she was right. She was tired of being a wounded duck about all of this. If they were going to box her into a corner, then she was still going to come out swinging.

It was going to be a town meeting to remember, that was for sure.

"So," Mayor Tim said, straightening his tie. "Any new business before I go through the agenda?"

Emily stood up. "I have some new business."

There was an expectant rustle through the crowd, which fell silent far more quickly than when Tim pounded his gavel. All eyes turned toward her.

"We're here to listen," Tim said. "What's on your mind, Emily?"

"While I was away on vacation, the town council saw fit to declare my building a historical landmark. Without consulting me. They somehow thought they had the right to dictate what I did with my family property."

Tim reddened. "Now, Em…"

"I love this town," Emily said, her voice throaty with emotion. "But I have to say I was very disappointed by the lack of trust that action showed."

There was a rumble of throat clearing and embarrassed coughing, but otherwise the room remained silent.

"I still love this town," Emily continued. "But it's not fair for you to dictate what I'm supposed to do with my building without giving me any funds to take care of it."

Tim's eyes bulged. "Give you…funds?" He looked at the council sitting in the front row. "We don't have the budget.…"

"Barring that," she said, "I do not need the town's approval to get investors. I have other interests and I no longer wish to be sole owner of the Stanfield Arms. I may need your permission to sell the place outright, but you can't dictate my choice in partners."

"No, we can't," Tim agreed.

"So I'm taking on as a partner…" She gestured, and Joy stood up. "Joy Webster."

There was a low outcry. "You're partnering with the group that would've flattened your house?" Evelyn Albee said, sounding scandalized.

"No, she's partnering with me," Joy said, and her smile was like sunshine. "I'm not working with my family on this one."

"Joy is going to be a hands-on partner from now on," Emily explained. "She'll be taking over the management duties for a while, then we'll be hiring more people as we get some more cash inflow." She crossed her arms. "And when we finally get enough money…I am leaving."

"No," Mrs. Rutledge said, her voice sad.

"I've stayed here long enough," Emily continued. "I love you all, but…it's…" She choked up and pressed her hand to her lips.

"It's time for you to move on," Ava Reese said, surprising her. "Try new things. Have an adventure or two."

Emily nodded, smiling a little even though tears threatened at the corners of her eyes. "Exactly."

"How much money would you need?"

Emily blinked. "Uh…I'm still working the numbers."

Ava looked around. "She's right, you know. Our behavior was terrible. She's been one of our best and brightest for years, and we yelled at her, accused her and then put her under house arrest."

"You're just saying that because she's hot for your son," a heckler yelled.

Ava stood regally, her stare withering. "Scott McPhee, do you really want me upset with you?"

Scott slumped in his chair. "Uh, no, Ava. Sorry."

Ava nodded. Emily would've laughed if she wasn't so blindsided by the events taking place.

"It seems to me like the least we could do is help her out,"

Ava continued. "I've got some money put aside. And I've been looking for an investment opportunity."

"Whoa, wait a minute," Emily protested. "I didn't mean…"

"We owe you," Ava said, waving away her hesitation. "You've done so much for our community. We can all pitch in to help out one of our own, can't we?"

"Count me in," Mrs. Rutledge said, smiling. "I've felt terrible, dear. And I've got gobs of money. It'll be fun."

"Uh…" Emily quickly saw their helpfulness spiraling out of control. It was bad enough that they had dictated what she could do when she wasn't there. What would they do when they were *investors?*

Ava seemed to read her mind. "Not to worry, dear. We'll help out if you need us to, but we won't expect to run the inn. That's still up to you. And your new partner there," she said, smiling at Joy. "We'll just be silent partners. You know, the type that gives money." She winked. "Although if you want to give us a break and let us host a few things in your ballroom, I wouldn't say no."

Emily felt the anger and resentment that had been brewing inside her dissipate like steam in front of a fan. When she looked around the room, she saw the love and support she remembered—the reason she'd always loved Tall Pines.

"I'd love your help," she said and the crowd cheered.

"I'll get it all set up," Ava said briskly in her businesslike way. "We'll be the Tall Pines Investors' Club. Ooh! Fun!"

Emily shook her head. The woman was unstoppable.

"Now, once you have the money," Ava continued, "I imagine you're going to have some plans."

Emily felt her cheeks heat with a blush. "I was considering moving," she said slowly.

"Moving?" Tim repeated. "What, to Paris?"

"Paris?" Scott McPhee piped up. "Why so far?"

"Because of Colin, idiot." Madge rolled her eyes. "Don't you know anything? He went there because he had some big building thing to take care of and now she's going to move in with him."

Emily blinked. "Are you guys bugging my apartment or something? You're worse than the FBI."

"I like to think of it as being well-informed," Madge said. "Besides, I did Ava's hair last week, and she said so."

Ava made a quick *ahem* noise, and Madge fell silent. Emily grinned. If Emily was the princess of Tall Pines, then Ava was definitely the queen.

Ava turned to address the crowd. "I've been more interested in preserving our town's history and traditions and its homelike feel than pretty much anyone else here," Ava declared. "But I've recently become aware that we can't have everything picture-perfect no matter how we try to control things. Sometimes we have to take some risks and let things change."

The crowd let out a muted wave of confusion and dissent.

"I didn't like it, either," Ava added with a small, self-mocking grin. "But there we are. So, if we really love Emily— and I love her like she was my own," she said, smiling at her warmly, "then we have to let her go. It's the right thing to do. It's the only thing to do."

The crowd slowly quieted down, still murmuring.

"And anybody who has a problem with Emily's decision," Ava finished firmly, "can discuss it with me."

The crowd went silent at last. Nobody in his right mind crossed Ava Reese if he could help it.

"Well, then," Mayor Tim said slowly. "I guess congratulations are in order." His tone turned gentle and he sent Emily a lopsided grin. "I'm sorry about everything, Em. We might have been heavy-handed and short-sighted, but I hope you know we've always cared about you."

Emily felt tears hovering and smiled back.

"Good luck in Paris," Tim finished. "We're going to miss you."

With that, there was a slow eruption of applause, gradually growing into a thunderous echo in the meeting hall. Emily was shocked—and touched. Joy handed her a tissue, and Emily realized she'd started to cry.

Ava hustled up to her, hugging her. "You take care of that son of mine," she said, her voice thick with emotion.

"I'm not going to Paris for your son," Emily said under cover of the applause.

"Sure you're not," Ava agreed, her voice turning business-like. "If you're going to move to Paris, you'll have a million things to do. What do you need help with? Moving? Packing? A ride to the airport?"

People heard Ava's comment, and there was an outbreak of helpful offers. It was a whole kind of new business—something they could really help with.

"Dale would be happy to crate up any breakables," Evelyn said. "I can pack up your china myself."

"I'm an expert at packing clothes," Madge said proudly.

"I'll help out with the paperwork," Mayor Tim volunteered. "I owe you big-time. Might as well make some use of my bureaucratic position, huh?"

"Well, I don't like your leaving," Mrs. Rutledge conceded. "But if you're going to go, I do hope you write me some letters." She sniffled. "Why is it the wife swappers stay when the good people leave?"

"You leave the Smiths out of this," Ava reprimanded, and Emily coughed.

"Man," Joy marveled, "I am going to love living here."

"I did," Emily said, her voice rich with emotion.

But she got the feeling she'd love living in Paris just as much...if she could just solve the Colin problem.

13

COLIN WAS EXHAUSTED. It had taken a few flights and a lot of strings, but here he finally was—at the Stanfield Arms, on Emily's doorstep. Armed with a laptop and all the accoutrements necessary for telecommuting, he planned on staying for at least two weeks this go-round—which ought to be enough to fix things with Emily and figure out how they were going to negotiate the rest of the year.

Not to mention, hopefully, the rest of their lives.

He wasn't looking forward to doing this much traveling indefinitely, he thought as he tromped up the steps of the hotel and headed for the front desk. But he had high hopes that, by the end of a year or two at the most, they'd come to a more workable solution. The important part, at this point, was seeing Emily.

He couldn't wait.

He lugged his baggage to the front desk. Joy smiled at him broadly. "Hello, and welcome to the Stanfield Arms. How can I help you?"

He blinked. "You're working here?"

"Working, nothing," she said. "I'm part owner."

"Owner?" Obviously a lot of stuff had happened while he'd been away.

"I'm here to see Emily," Colin said, wondering what else he might have missed. He'd felt fortunate to not run into any townsfolk when he got in, but now he wished he'd caught up on the gossip. "Could you tell her I'm here?"

Joy smiled, revealing deep dimples. "Actually, I can't."

He leaned forward, his voice beseeching. "I imagine you're being loyal. She probably told you about our fight, and you probably think you're doing the right thing by blowing me off," Colin said slowly, trying to remain reasonable despite his exhaustion. "But let me put it this way—I have just been on three connecting flights after being up all night packing. I've put off I don't know how many meetings and run up all kinds of air-phone charges, all so I could be here, with the woman I love. If that doesn't earn me some kind of brownie points, I don't know what will. In short, I don't know and don't care what the hell your problem with me is. Now, please, *go get Emily.*" Colin's voice meant business.

"Colin, what are you doing?" Emily's friend Sue rushed up, and Colin sheepishly turned from the amused-looking Joy.

"He wants me to go get Emily," Joy said, her voice almost rippling with humor.

"She won't tell Emily I'm here," he said.

"No, Colin," Sue clarified, looking more flustered than amused. "I meant what are you doing *here?*"

"I'm here to—"

Before Colin could finish, a gaggle of women trooped into the lobby of the inn bearing a large number of cardboard boxes, tape and twine. His mother was heading the group, he noticed.

"Colin!" she said, eyes wide. "What are you doing here?"

"Why is everyone asking me that?" he snapped, lack of sleep and frustration at not seeing Emily making him doubly irritable. "Could somebody *please* go get Emily?"

"Well, no, actually," his mother said. "We can't."

Colin stared at her. "*Why not?*"

"Because she's not here, dear," his mother answered, chuckling. "You know, this is like that story *Gift of the Magi.* Do you remember that one?"

"Mom, I love you, but right now I'm at the end of my rope," Colin pleaded as the other women laughed amongst themselves, chattering away. "Would somebody please tell me what the heck is going on here?"

"Emily's gone," Sue said.

"Gone?" He stared at her blankly. "Gone where?"

Now everyone laughed. Colin was beginning to feel furious.

"Paris," his mother finally answered.

"Paris?" he echoed.

"She wanted to surprise you for Valentine's Day—which is tomorrow, I might remind you," his mother said, grinning.

"I know," he said. "That's why I came here. To surprise her."

"That *is* ironic," Joy said.

Colin gave her a warning glance. She merely smiled back at him cheekily.

"Well," he said, sighing, "I'm glad that she's forgiven me. And hopefully she won't have to travel so far to visit me from now on. At least not for a few weeks out of the month."

"What do you mean, dear?"

Colin took a deep breath. "I mean I'm moving back to Tall Pines. Sort of."

"What?"

"I'm going to be telecommuting," he said. "I'll still have to be in Paris a lot, and it means a lot of traveling, but…well, I was stupid for a while, but slowly I figured out that I don't want to live without Emily, no matter what. So I'm doing what I have to to stay with her."

"Oh," his mother said, putting her hand on her chest and smiling wistfully.

"That's the most romantic thing I've ever heard," Evelyn

Albee added. "Almost as moving as Emily's speech at the town meeting before we all became investors."

"What?" Colin felt distinctly at a loss with this whole conversation. To make matters worse, he really didn't have time to straighten it out. He needed to get on a flight and see if he could catch Emily before she got to an empty apartment....

Suddenly the boxes and the women's grins pierced his thoughts. "Wait a second," he said, suspicious. "What are all of you doing here?"

"We're packing Emily up," Evelyn said, her voice smug. "She's moving."

Colin rubbed at his temples. He was really not up to this conversation. "Moving where?"

"*Paris,*" Evelyn said. "Where have you been? We just told you she wanted to surprise you."

He stared at them, the whole thing seeming too surreal to be believed. Then he put down his bags and leaned against the counter. "Okay. From the top. Mom, could you explain to me what exactly is going on here?"

His mother smiled. "Emily decided that she's had enough and that she wants to be with you. So she sold most of the Stanfield Arms and she's moving to Paris." She cleared her throat. "Of course, I think she was planning on visiting and then telling us when we should ship things—and where," she added, staring at him meaningfully, "but in the meantime, the whole town's volunteered to help her move."

"Apparently she loves Paris so much she's going to move there whether you want her to or not," Sue said, with a gimlet smirk.

Colin felt as though he'd been hit by a train. "Why didn't she call me?"

His mother crossed her arms. "Why didn't you call her," she asked logically, "before you decided on your grand plan to telecommute?"

Colin could've sworn he was blushing. "I feel like an idiot," he admitted.

"Well, it's touching that you two care enough about each other to make such big sacrifices," his mother said, stroking his cheek. "I only have one request. I know you love Europe and all, but will you at least come home—I mean *here*—for the holidays?"

He hugged her. "Fair enough."

All the women went *awwww* and Colin shooed them away. "Now I just have to make sure I beat Emily to Paris," he fretted.

Joy sprang into action. "I've got her complete itinerary in the office." She rushed to get it.

"We'll get you to the airport," Evelyn said.

"I'll see if there's some way to contact her," Ava volunteered.

Colin smiled, touched. For the first time in a long time he felt as if he was a part of the whole Tall Pines dynamic. In a way, he'd miss it. He wouldn't even mind coming back for the holidays.

But the most important thing right now was that he wanted to give Emily a Valentine's Day she never forgot.

EMILY LANDED AT Charles de Gaulle airport feeling excited, nervous and jet-lagged. She staggered through the throngs of people, tugging her roller bag behind her.

I should have called. It was a bit late now for that sentiment.

She never should have listened to Ava Reese. "Whatever problems you two have had, it's not going to get solved if you don't get face-to-face and talk about it," she'd said authoritatively.

"I don't know," Emily had protested nervously. "We had a really, really bad fight."

"Honey, there were times when I wanted to brain Colin's dad with my Mixmaster," Ava said with a broad grin. "But we always talked it out."

Privately Emily suspected Ava had simply talked the poor

man into submission. She, too, had found herself getting carried along by Ava's voice and sheer enthusiasm. Before she knew it, Ava had raised a very substantial sum, Tim had started the paperwork for the investors' fund and they'd gotten her a ticket for Paris on Valentine's Day. Business class. She was in the air before she was even fully cognizant of what she was doing.

Surprising Colin for Valentine's Day had seemed like such a great idea back at Tall Pines. They did need to talk, after all, and she loved him. The thought of seeing him had been even more compelling than all of Ava's arguments put together.

But leaving had been her idea—and they hadn't really communicated clearly since.

How did I imagine this was going to work out? she thought, wrung out with fatigue, suddenly hoping that he wasn't upset or angry. Or worse, hoping that he hadn't moved on to some model-skinny Parisian woman named Monique.

She was so intent on her nervous thoughts that she walked right past the limo driver holding up a sign: Emily Stanfield.

Wait. Was that my name?

She backed up, staring. Well, it wasn't as if Emily Stanfield was all that uncommon a name. Still…

"*Mademoiselle?*" the limo driver said, tipping his hat. "Are you Emily Stanfield?"

She nodded. "Well, that's my name," she admitted. "But I didn't…"

"You're coming from…" He rattled off her flight number.

The odds of two women named Emily Stanfield on the same plane were pretty slim. "Yes, that's me," Emily said, feeling mystified. "But…"

"Come with me, please." The driver started to grab her bag.

"Whoa! Wait a minute," she said, tugging the bag from him. "I didn't get a limo. Who sent you?"

He smiled. "This is your Valentine's Day surprise," the limo driver explained. "From a Monsieur Colin Reese."

Colin. Feeling floaty and disoriented, she allowed the limo driver to take her bags and she followed him to the waiting car.

Somehow it wasn't a surprise. Colin knew she was coming—even knew what flight she was on. How had he managed that? Obviously he'd called the hotel and someone had told him. Probably Sue, Emily thought with a smile. It would be like her.

It took almost an hour, but the driver took her from the airport to the city, cruising through the picturesque streets. She felt a growing bubble of excitement.

This is going to be my home, she thought. *With Colin.*

After a long time, they finally wound their way up a hill. "*Voilà.* Here we are, *mademoiselle,*" the limo driver said with a flourish.

"Where is here?" she asked, getting out of the car and stretching slightly.

"*Montmartre,*" the limo driver answered. "Home of artists, poets…lovers. Enjoy!"

She wandered to a set of stairs where people were sitting enjoying the sprawling view of all of Paris below. It was breathtaking. Emily hugged herself.

Suddenly another pair of arms covered her own, hugging her to him. "Hey, you," Colin's voice whispered in her ear.

She turned—and saw a completely bedraggled, disheveled Colin. He had about two days' growth of beard, and his eyes were bloodshot.

"What happened to you?" she asked, concerned.

He laughed. "You would not believe what my last forty-eight hours have been like," he said. "By the way—we need to talk."

She stiffened. "About what?"

"No, I mean we need to talk more than we do," he said, kissing her with a chuckle. "Do you know how many people are swarming all over the Stanfield Arms as we speak? It's like a packing convention over there."

"I know," she agreed ruefully. "I hadn't even decided yet when I was going to move or where, and next thing I knew I…" Slowly his statement sank in. "Wait a minute. You *saw* them?"

"I just got back from Connecticut," he said, kissing her again. "I've been on more planes than I care to think about and I had to pay outrageously to beat you here. I just landed, my-self."

She burst out laughing, hugging him. "We're idiots."

"Yeah," he agreed. "But we're in love. That's got to count for something."

She felt warmth bubble through her. "I got some investors."

"I heard." He hugged her tighter.

"Joy's running the place—better than I ever could," she said, her words tumbling out in a rush. "I'm still an owner, but I don't have to be there anymore. The place stays in my name, and I still can go back whenever I like, but Joy has my apartment. I'm moving here to Paris." She bit her lip. "I was hoping I could live with you. That we could work things out."

"That's the funny thing," he said. "I'd just set up a telecommuting arrangement so I could be with you."

The warmth expanded, enveloping her in its comforting glow. "You would've done that for me?"

"I would have done more." He stroked her hair. "I'm so sorry I wasn't more supportive. I was so intent on all my old hang-ups with Tall Pines that I didn't see you were having trouble keeping your head above water. I was so focused on what *I* would've done," he said, kissing her softly, "that I didn't pay attention to what you needed."

Emily smiled. "It took a while, but I finally figured out that was hiding in my past," she confided. "I was trying to please everyone. The only important thing was making sure that I was doing what I really wanted to do. And as much as I love Tall Pines, I need to grow. I need to try new things." She nuzzled his chest. "I need *you*."

They kissed deeply. Then they turned to look at the city laid out like a present before them.

"Welcome to your new life, Emily Stanfield," Colin said.

She turned to him, eyes glowing.

"I can't wait."

Epilogue

One Christmas later

"JOY'S REALLY DONE wonders with the place, hasn't she?" Emily surveyed their room. It was redecorated in shades of brick-red, deep forest-green and copper and looked like a sumptuous autumn landscape.

"Yeah. The whole town couldn't stop talking about it at the Secret Santa party tonight," Colin said, slipping out of his clothes and climbing on the bed. "Seems like since almost everybody kicked in money for the Investors' Club, they all feel like they're owners now."

Emily felt her heart warm with pride. "I love Paris," she said expansively, "but I have to say, I'm glad to be back."

Colin wore a crooked, bemused smile. "You know," he said with wonder, "so am I."

She grinned. "What did you get tonight, anyway?"

"A six-foot-tall set of footie pajamas," he said, laughing, and she joined him. "I think I've been regifted."

"You won't believe what I got," she began.

"You can tell me in the morning," Colin interrupted, and she noticed that his cock had gone hard and dark. "I've got plans for you tonight, Ms. Stanfield."

Her heart thrilled, and she felt the familiar stirrings in her body. After a year together, they still couldn't get enough of each other. "You'll like this," she said with a mysterious smile. "Just wait there a second."

She went to the bathroom, pulling the odd gift out of its bag and changing into it with lightning speed. She grinned at her reflection in the mirror as she pulled on the matching hat.

"Em, honey, I don't care if somebody got you the Hope diamond on a chain," he called, "I can't wait to…"

His words died on his lips when she stepped into the room.

"What do you think?" she said, doing a little turn in her high heels.

"*Sexy Mrs. Santa?*" He looked torn between laughter and desire.

"Just like the outfit you decked out my poor great-grandfather's statue in—can you believe it?"

"It looks better on you," he said with admiration, his green eyes alight.

She did a little strut, the short fur-trimmed skirt bouncing high enough to show off the bright red thong. She wore white lace-trimmed thigh-high stockings, and the corset-style top propped up her breasts to their best advantage. "What do *you* want for Christmas?" she asked with a sly wink.

"Come here." He reached for her, and she laughed as they tumbled on the bed.

She was still chuckling when he kissed her, but when he tugged down the top of her dress and started sucking on each breast in turn, she turned serious, focusing on the pleasure he was giving her. She shivered as he pushed aside the thin strap of material covering her pussy, stroking her clit with knowing fingers. "Colin," she breathed, leaning her head back until it hung over the side of the bed. Her hat fell to the floor unnoticed.

He pressed his fingers inside, spreading her wider. "You're

all I want for Christmas," he said and he replaced his fingers with his long, hard cock. "You're all I want forever."

"Oh, Colin." She felt his hard length slide inside her slowly, filling her. She wrapped her legs around his waist as he entered her with measured thrusts, cupping her breasts so he could tease her nipples with his thumbs as he rocked his hips against her.

She arched her back, squeezing him with her thighs, tensing her muscles so her pussy clenched around him snugly. He groaned. "I love it when you do that," he said through gritted teeth.

"I do, too," she murmured.

Their lovemaking was graceful, easy...incredible. After all this time, each time was just as exciting as the first—and at the same time amazingly cozy.

She felt the pressure begin to build, and her breathing went shallow, speeding up. He took the cue, his thrusts becoming harder, deeper. She gripped his hips, meeting his every plunging motion as his cock hit her special spot. She let out a rippling cry as the orgasm rolled over her. Moments later, he shuddered against her, whispering her name as he trembled.

"This is the best Christmas ever," he gasped, when he could finally speak, and Emily laughed.

"So where are we going to go next year, when the Paris project's over?" she asked, curling against him as they righted themselves on the bed.

"There's a project in Tokyo that they're offering me," he said thoughtfully. "Or Sydney. What would you prefer?"

She thought about it. "I'd love to see either city," she said. "As long as we can still visit here once in a while. What do you think?"

He smiled at her, and she felt warmth bubble up through her chest.

"I think," he said, his eyes full of tenderness and love, "that whenever I'm with you, I'm home…wherever we are."

She opened her arms. "Then welcome home, Colin," Emily said and kissed him.

* * * * *

Turn the page for a sneak preview
of the first book in the new miniseries
DIAMONDS DOWN UNDER
from Silhouette Desire®,
VOWS & A VENGEFUL GROOM
by Bronwyn Jameson

Available January 2008
(SD #1843)

Silhouette Desire®
Always Powerful, Passionate and Provocative

Kimberley Blackstone didn't notice the waiting horde of media until it was too late. Flashbulbs exploded around her like a New Year's light show. She skidded to a halt, so abruptly her trailing suitcase all but overtook her.

This had to be a case of mistaken identity. Surely. Kimberley hadn't been on the paparazzi hit list for close to a decade, not since she'd estranged herself from her billionaire father and his headline-hungry diamond business.

But no, it was *her* name they called. *Her* face was the focus of a swarm of lenses that circled her like avid hornets. Her heart started to pound with fear-fueled adrenaline.

What did they want?

What was going on?

With a rising sense of bewilderment she scanned the crowd for a clue, and her gaze fastened on a tall, leonine figure forcing his way to the front. A tall, familiar figure. Her head came up

in stunned recognition, and their gazes collided across the se
of heads before the cameras erupted with another barrage c
flashes, this time right in her exposed face.

Blinded by the flashbulbs—and by the shock of that mo
mentary eye-meet—Kimberley didn't realize his intent unti
he'd forged his way to her side, possibly by the sheer strengt:
of his personality. She felt his arm wrap around her shoulde:
pulling her into the protective shelter of his body, allowing he
no time to object. No chance to lift her hands to ward him off

In the space of a hastily drawn breath, she found hersel
plastered knee-to-nose against six feet two inches of hard
bodied male.

Ric Perrini.

Her lover for ten torrid weeks, her husband for ten tumul-
tuous days.

Her ex for ten tranquil years.

After all this time, he should not have felt so familiar but
oh dear, he did. She knew the scent of that body and its lean.
muscular strength. She knew its heat and its slick power and
every response it could draw from hers.

She also recognized the ease with which he'd taken control
of the moment and the decisiveness of his deep voice when it
rumbled close to her ear. "I have a car waiting outside. Is this
your only luggage?"

Kimberley nodded. "I assume you will tell me," she said
tightly, "what this welcome party is all about."

"Not while the welcome party is within earshot. No."

Barking a request for the cameramen to stand aside, Perrini
took her hand and pulled her into step with his ground-eating
stride. Kimberley let him, because he was right, damn his
arrogant, Italian-suited hide. Despite the speed with which he
whisked her across the airport terminal, she could almost feel
the hot breath of the pursuing media on her back.

This was neither the time nor the place for explanations. Inside his car, however, she would get answers.

Now that the initial shock had been blown away—by the haste of their retreat, by the heat of her gathering indignation, by the rush of adrenaline fired by Perrini's presence and the looming verbal battle—her brain was starting to tick over. This had to be her father's doing. And if it was a Howard Blackstone publicity ploy, then it had to be about Blackstone Diamonds, the company that ruled his life.

The knowledge made her chest tighten with a familiar ache of disillusionment.

She'd known her father would be flying in from Sydney for today's opening of the newest in his chain of exclusive, high-end jewelry boutiques. The opulent shop front sat adjacent to the rival business where Kimberley worked. No coincidence, she thought bitterly, just as it was no coincidence that Ric Perrini was here in Auckland ushering her to his car.

Perrini was Howard Blackstone's right-hand man, second in command at Blackstone Diamonds, a legacy of his short-lived marriage to the boss's daughter. No doubt her father had sent him to fetch her; the question was *why?*

* * * * *

Get swept away down under with the glitz
and glamour of the Blackstone empire as
Kimberley tries to determine the real reason
behind her "reunion" with Ric….

Look for
VOWS & A VENGEFUL GROOM
by Bronwyn Jameson,
in stores January 2008.

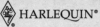

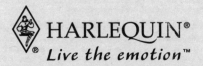

REQUEST YOUR FREE BOOKS!

2 FREE NOVELS PLUS 2 FREE GIFTS!

♦ HARLEQUIN®

Blaze®

Red-hot reads!

YES! Please send me 2 FREE Harlequin® Blaze® novels and my 2 FREE gifts. After receiving them, if I don't wish to receive any more books, I can return the shipping statement marked "cancel." If I don't cancel, I will receive 6 brand-new novels every month and be billed just $3.99 per book in the U.S., or $4.47 per book in Canada, plus 25¢ shipping and handling per book and applicable taxes, if any*. That's a savings of at least 15% off the cover price! I understand that accepting the 2 free books and gifts places me under no obligation to buy anything. I can always return a shipment and cancel at any time. Even if I never buy another book from Harlequin, the two free books and gifts are mine to keep forever.

151 HDN EF3W   351 HDN EF3X

Name	(PLEASE PRINT)	
Address		Apt.
City	State/Prov.	Zip/Postal Code

Signature (if under 18, a parent or guardian must sign)

Mail to the **Harlequin Reader Service**®:

IN U.S.A.: P.O. Box 1867, Buffalo, NY 14240-1867
IN CANADA: P.O. Box 609, Fort Erie, Ontario L2A 5X3

Not valid to current Harlequin Blaze subscribers.

Want to try two free books from another line?
Call 1-800-873-8635 or visit www.morefreebooks.com.

* Terms and prices subject to change without notice. NY residents add applicable sales tax. Canadian residents will be charged applicable provincial taxes and GST. This offer is limited to one order per household. All orders subject to approval. Credit or debit balances in a customer's account(s) may be offset by any other outstanding balance owed by or to the customer. Please allow 4 to 6 weeks for delivery.

Your Privacy: Harlequin is committed to protecting your privacy. Our Privacy Policy is available online at www.eHarlequin.com or upon request from the Reader Service. From time to time we make our lists of customers available to reputable firms who may have a product or service of interest to you. If you would prefer we not share your name and address, please check here. ☐

HB07

Silhouette®

nocturne™

Jachin Black always knew he was an outcast.
Not only was he a vampire, he was a vampire
banished from the Sanguinas society. Jachin, forced
to survive among mortals, is determined to buy
his way back into the clan one day.

Ariel Swanson, debut author of a vampire novel, could
be the ticket he needs to get revenge and take his
rightful place among the Sanguinas again. However,
the unsuspecting mortal woman has no idea of the
dark and sensual path she will be forced to travel.

Look for

RESURRECTION: THE BEGINNING

by

PATRICE MICHELLE

Available January 2008 wherever you buy books.

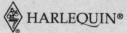

HARLEQUIN®

Blaze™

COMING NEXT MONTH

#369 ONE WILD WEDDING NIGHT Leslie Kelly
Blaze Encounters—One blazing book, five sizzling stories
Girls just want to have fun.... And for five bridesmaids, their friend's wedding night is the perfect time for the rest of them to let loose. After all, love is in the air. And so, they soon discover, is great sex...

#370 MY GUILTY PLEASURE Jamie Denton
The Martini Dares, Bk. 3
The trial is supposed to come first for the legal-eagle duo of Josephine Winfield and Sebastian Stanhope. But the long hours—and sizzling attraction—are taking their toll. Is it a simple case of lust in the first degree? Or dare she think there's more?

#371 BARE NECESSITIES Marie Donovan
A sexy striptease ignites an intense affair between longtime friends Adam Hale, a play-by-the-rules financial trader, and Bridget Weiss, a break-all-the-rules lingerie designer. But what will happen to their friendship now that their secret lust for each other is no longer a secret?

#372 DOES SHE DARE? Tawny Weber
Blush
When no-nonsense Isabel Santos decides to make a "man plan," she never dreams she'll have a chance to try it out with the guy who inspired it—her high school crush, hottie Dante Luciano. He's still everything she's ever wanted. And she'll make sure she's everything he'll *never* forget....

#373 AT YOUR COMMAND Julie Miller
Marry in haste? Eighteen months ago Captain Zachariah Clark loved, married, then left Becky Clark. Now Zach's back home, and he's suddenly realized he knows nothing about his wife except her erogenous zones. Then again, great sex isn't such a bad place to start....

#374 THE TAO OF SEX Jade Lee
Extreme
Landlord Tracy Williams wants to sell her building, almost as much as she wants her tenant, sexy Nathan Gao. But when Nathan puts a sale at risk by giving Tantric classes, Tracy has to bring a stop to them. That is, until he offers her some private *hands-on* instruction...

HBCNM1207